the international

GLENN PATTERSON

the international

BLACKSTAFF
PRESS
BELFAST

1006691188

First published in 1999
by Anchor

This edition first published in 2008 by
Blackstaff Press
4c Heron Wharf, Sydenham Business Park
Belfast BT3 9LE
with the assistance of
The Arts Council of Northern Ireland

Reprinted 2011

Typeset by CJWT Solutions, St Helens, England

Printed in Great Britain by the MPG Books Group

A CIP catalogue record for this book is available
from the British Library

ISBN 978-0-85640-812-0

www.blackstaffpress.com

For Ali

ACKNOWLEDGEMENTS

Thanks to John McCabe for walking me around his memories of the place. If I have gone astray it is through no fault of his.

This novel was begun while I was writer in residence at Queen's University, Belfast. I am grateful to the university and to the Arts Council of Northern Ireland for their financial assistance.

1

If I had known history was to be written that Sunday in the International Hotel I might have made an effort to get out of bed before teatime. I might have put on my white shirt and bow tie, taken my duffel coat from under the stairs, and been at the bus stop on the green in good time for the 5.05 to the city centre, instead of sending my mother down to the phone box at the end of the road to call me in sick. But then if history was so easy to predict it might never have a chance to happen at all for the crowds of people wanting to have their photographs taken to say, 'I was there'. In any case I had worked a fourteen-hour shift the day before and had fallen in love twice and twice been rebuffed, which seemed pretty momentous to me at the time, and I felt entitled to a little self-indulgence. Besides, it was fucking miserable outside. January had been going on for more or less ever by that stage and the wind around the bedroom windowpanes sounded a bit too biblical and final for my liking. (My knowledge of the Bible may have been even sketchier then than it is now, but I'd read enough to know that bad weather was not to be trifled with.) So I turned my back on the bigger story – for, who knows, with all that's been written about this place since, I might well have merited a footnote somewhere:

Daniel Hamilton, a barman working in the hotel, remembers the mood as being 'dignified and resolute' – turned my back and buried my head beneath the covers, comforting myself with bitter-sweet thoughts of Ingrid and Stanley and the campfire stench of my vest and underpants.

*

The day before the inaugural meeting of the Northern Ireland Civil Rights Association in January 1967, the morning of the day of the Portadown Bun Boycott, a blaze broke out in Belfast city centre. I saw the flames above the rooftops as I got off the bus in Glengall Street and being, as usual, half an hour and more early for work, and flames of that size not then being regular sights in the city, I did what everyone else appeared to be doing that morning (fires after all looking much more like our idea of history in the making) and walked towards their source.

'Brand's Arcade,' I was told by a wreck of a man balancing a cardboard box on his head outside the Classic. He had stood on the same spot, with the same box, all day every day for as long as I could remember, his long weird beard tucked down the front of a greasy gabardine.

'Aren't you going to have a look?' I asked him.

The man pointed at the box. On the wall behind him, Audrey Hepburn looked anguished and lovely in a white habit.

'I'd love to, son, but it'd be more than my life's worth to move.'

Round the corner, two fire tenders were parked nose-to-tail at the bottom of Fountain Street and three more had stopped, every which way, where the bulk of the onlookers were gathered, a hundred yards along, across the mouth of Donegall Place. Running unseen between the two, Brand's Arcade, sure enough, was a tunnel issuing thick brown smoke at either end. I joined the crowd at Robinson & Cleaver's and saw over the shoulders of the people in front firemen in slick waterproofs plunge into the entrance to the arcade, while behind them the enormous eel-grey hoses thrashed and slithered on the glistening road. Half a dozen policemen tried their best to press us back, but the spectacle of the fire exerted a far greater force forward and the policemen soon abandoned their efforts and fell to spectating with us. A mannequin ignited in the window of the first-floor department store. Flames darted from the ruined roof, now the purest yellow, now tinged violet and green; the air seemed liquid and the neighbouring buildings wobbled as though they would at any moment melt away entirely. A few yards to my left, a man was sobbing and it occurred to me that some of those watching were seeing their jobs turn to ashes. A few yards to my right, another man whistled through his fingers. I knew before I picked the owner out that the whistle belonged to Barney Keenan.

'Danny Boy!'

He rubbed his hands as I squeezed through the crowd towards him, then held them out, gloved palms up, to the blaze.

'Toasty warm,' he said.

Barney came from down around the Monaghan border and lodged in the International's staff house in Atholl Street, behind the Ritz cinema. Though it was clean and comfortable, nobody could ever accuse the place of being overheated. Barney, however, suffered more than most. These city winters, he said, with their boggy fogs and mizzles were turning his bones to cold mush. To add to his discomfort there had been an outbreak of flu among staff earlier in the week; the toll was high and rising. Barney's precautions this morning ran to a woolly hat, a scarf and several extra layers of clothes, making him twice the man I had last seen leaving the hotel the night before. He closed his eyes now in rapture: '*Toas*-ty warm.'

Beside him, Cecil, the hotel's night porter, pulled on a matchstick-thin roll-up, his cheeks almost meeting in the middle with the effort. When he exhaled he managed the near-miracle that cold morning of blowing nothing whatever out.

Barney nudged me with his elbow.

'Cecil here saw the whole thing start, near enough. Just as he was coming off work. Didn't you, Cecil?'

'You think it's bad now?' Cecil didn't wait for me to ask. 'You want to have seen it earlier.'

Being a night porter, Cecil lived in constant dread of missing out, having apparently convinced himself that the city turned into a place of riotous pleasure and thrilling calamity while he was dispensing indigestion tablets to overindulgent businessmen. He was obviously going to milk this scoop for all it was worth. He smiled a smile as tight as his cigarette.

'The fire brigade'd to get the woman off the roof.'

Barney was nodding. Just then, as though taking their cue, firemen came sprinting from the mouth of the arcade. A moment later a pane of glass exploded somewhere deep inside. The crowd oohed. Barney was still nodding. There was no avoiding it.

'What woman?'

Cecil's cheeks collapsed and the end of his cigarette glimmered then greyed.

'The caretaker's wife. She was up there on the roof in her nightdress.'

'Her *nightdress!*'

Barney slipped his hands into his armpits and frowned, as though in wonder that, the flames having spared her, the cold hadn't done for the woman altogether.

'I'm telling you,' Cecil said and told me nothing else.

There came the sound of more glass breaking. A fireman sat on the kerb and accepted a cigarette from another bystander. His face beneath the yellow helmet was the colour of slate.

'How's it looking in there?' Cecil called to him in the tone of one who knew about these matters.

'How's it looking?' The fireman gave him a stare over his shoulder. 'Bloody terrible, what do you think?'

'I was only asking,' Cecil said, his voice a small thing, disappearing.

Slow handclapping had broken out on the southern rim of

the crowd, in front of the City Hall. It spread, picking up momentum and volume, climaxing in a raucous cheer. Barney raised himself on his tiptoes.

'UTVs arrived.'

That's quick for them,' I said, and the woman next to me said, 'Maybe they heard it on the BBC.'

Soon everyone around me was on tiptoes too. The more energetic bounced on the spot.

Can you see anything? Are they interviewing people?

The first shoves followed shortly.

That's my foot!

Get your fat arse out of my road!

A candy-pink hat was propelled at waist height through the ruck. Only as it neared me did I realise there was still a head inside. A young woman, in a suit to match the hat, stumbled to a halt before me, rearranged her little decorative veil and pressed on once more.

'Bloody journalists,' a man called after her and when I looked again she was indeed taking photographs of the burning arcade.

The scuffling had now become general.

'We should get going,' I shouted to Barney who alone had kept his balance, head and shoulders above the rest.

'My God, Danny Boy,' he shouted back. 'There's Cecil up there. He's getting himself on the TV.'

*

The International Hotel stood on the south side of Donegall Square, directly behind the City Hall. You were unlikely to miss it. A canopy of frosted glass, supported by slender mosaic pillars, thrust the name, in blue lettering, out into the street; low black-marble walls flanked the approach to the main entrance and shielded the stairs which ran down on either side from the foot-path to the basement bars. It was only stunning.

As Barney and I walked towards the hotel, away from Brand's

Arcade, we could still hear whistles and cat-calling and the blast of water on stone. A faint mist hung in the air and a single charred page rode the current higher up, attracting the attention of a couple of sooty-looking seagulls.

'What have you in today?' I asked, and Barney's shoulders slumped.

'The heap. Three o'clock, four o'clock, four-thirty and five: wall-to-wall weddings.'

At the corner of Adelaide Street and Donegall Square South a couple were conducting a whispered argument on the steps down to Cotter's Kitchen. She turned her back. There were tears in his eyes.

'You'd think,' Barney went on, 'people'd have something better to do with their Saturdays.'

'You'd think,' I said.

Twenty or thirty yards further along a taxi was pulled up at the kerb before the hotel. The driver, a yellow-faced man in a brown car coat, was helping the Vances and Jack, the day porter, load the Vances's cases into the boot. Barney lengthened his stride.

'That yous, then?' he called out.

The Vances turned as one and I observed, not for the first time, how Americans seemed fashioned from a more up-to-date, and better-wearing, version of the stuff that went into the making of the rest of us.

'Afraid so,' Mr Vance said.

'All good things ...' said Mrs Vance.

Barney nodded glumly. The Vances were heavy tippers whose largesse had on more than one occasion in the last six days extended into the kitchens and as far down the pecking order as commis chefs like Barney.

Mrs Vance adjusted the fingers of her emerald green gloves. Ten separate tugs. Jack returned, jingling, to the hotel. The taxi driver waited with one foot in the car and one on the road, glancing up and down the street. Everyone else regarded the interior of the car. The royal-blue leather upholstery was as soft and worn-looking as the jeans Mr Vance had astonished the other residents by wearing one morning at breakfast.

'Well,' Barney said.

'Well,' said Mrs Vance.

'It's been a real pleasure.'

'Yes,' the Vances said together and laughed.

They shook hands with Barney. Mr Vance gripped my elbow.

'Another time,' he said, and Mrs Vance glanced at her watch and then they were in the car and gone. Barney waved to them all the way down Donegall Square and into Howard Street.

'Bye-bye tips.'

He scuffed up the steps ahead of me (personally, the kind of steps they were, I always found it hard to resist clicking my heels at the end of them) and paused before the double glass doors.

'Hello drudgery.'

'Hello, Barney.'

Marian Kennedy was on reception and had come out from behind her desk to see how the fire was going. 'Were you round at Brand's? What's it like now?'

'Desperate.' Barney laid a tender hand on her sleeve. Marian flinched. 'Bodies everywhere.'

One of Marian's legs was shorter than the other and she wore a built-up shoe on her left foot. It was this foot she swung now at Barney's backside, but Barney was already running down the lobby.

'Don't worry, Keenan,' she shouted, 'I'll get you later.'

The phone was ringing. Marian pivoted on her long leg and swung round behind reception to answer it.

'Good morning, the International.'

We blew each other extravagant kisses.

'Friday week? Let's see ... No, Friday week looks fine at the minute. Double or twin?'

A guest I didn't recognise, tall and handsomely built, came out of the lift and crossed the lobby to the lounge, a copy of the *Racing Post* tucked under his arm. Looking in through the doorway I counted reflected in the mirrored back wall another half-dozen guests sitting in the lounge's easy chairs reading their papers. Two children, a boy and a girl, played jacks on the crimson carpet at their mother's feet. The Williamses, Room 211. Mr Williams was rumoured to be bad with his nerves and was rarely seen downstairs apart from at mealtimes.

On the other side of the lobby, in the dining room, breakfast had been cleared away and the tables were already being set for lunch. The Master was standing by a pillar (standing by, not leaning on, the Master never leaned) closely observing Paula, the waitress who had started the previous Monday. Paula was not yet sixteen. She had never been away from home before – she was staying with an aunt somewhere in the south of the city – and gave a whole new meaning to bewildered.

'Side plate,' the Master said. Paula slid the one nearest her an inch to the left. Her uniform was all stiff folds about her and plasters showed salmon-pink beneath the heels of her nylons where her new shoes had been rubbing.

'Perfect,' said the Master, and Paula bent a little at one knee under the weight of his unexpected praise.

I hopped out of sight before he could turn. The Master had an unfailing knack of making even the most innocent feel they had done something wrong – pacing the hotel corridors in much the same way, I imagined, as he had paced between the desks of the school where he had taught before his reincarnation as a hotel manager. Carmel Quinn claimed actually to have wet her pants in the face of one of his silent stares; most people preferred to keep eye contact with him to a minimum.

A short flight of steps led down from the lobby to a corridor, always referred to as the Long Corridor, with the cloak deposit and toilets on the right-hand side, a door into the kitchen further along on the left, and a function room, the Damask Room, at the end. Barney was waiting for me on the bottom step, biting his lip. He had cause to be nervous, Marian didn't make idle threats.

'Is she really raging?'

'Murderous,' I said and turning sharply to my left carried on down the stairs to the sanctuary of the basement. Ahead of me, the Cocktail Bar was still in darkness, but lights shone on my right from the doorway of the Blue Bar.

People I knew who had never been to the International before would ask me sometimes, why the *Blue* Bar? And I would simply say, because it is. And it was. Carpets, upholstery – everything that wasn't glass or metal: all blue. Other people, of course, customers and guests, would want to know why the Cocktail Bar was the Cocktail Bar, even though it was as red as the Blue Bar was blue. But a red bar is like a dog with fur, no more than you would expect. I have never known another blue bar, before or since.

I unbuttoned my coat and walked in to find Hugh trimming his fingernails over an ashtray on the counter. Hugh was the head barman in the Blue Bar and was just entering the jowly stage of middle age. He glanced up and down and gave me his usual greeting.

'Danny Boy. How's the big bad world?'

'Up in flames.'

Hugh grimaced as he attacked a thumb. 'Had it coming all the same.'

I slipped my coat off. Hugh examined his cuticles. 'I don't suppose you heard who just checked in?'

His tone was casual enough for it to be someone pretty famous.

'Who?'

'Ted Connolly.'

'*Ted Connolly!*' I said. 'Who's he?'

Hugh looked at me as though I had to be joking. He saw by my expression that I wasn't.

'You don't know who Ted Connolly is? Ted Connolly, Sunderland and Northern Ireland? The Roker Wonder?' He jabbed his forehead towards me in a way I could only suppose was intended to be helpful. '*Bap* Connolly?'

'Hugh, are we talking about the kick the ball and chase it thing? 'Cause if we are …' I passed a hand six inches over my head.

'I know,' Hugh said, 'but everybody's heard of Ted Connolly – hat-trick against Wales at Windsor Park, all headers?'

It was news to me.

'Anyway,' I said, 'it's Saturday, what's he doing in Belfast?'

Hugh had returned to cutting his nails.

'Septic toe,' he said. 'Out for a fortnight.'

I thought of the guest I had seen just now with the *Racing Post* under his arm and tried to remember if he had been limping. I didn't even want to think how you went about getting yourself a septic toe.

Hugh nodded towards a sheet of paper lying on the bar.

'Word from Next Door.' Next Door in the Blue Bar as often as not meant Len Gray, the hotel's bar manager, who was usually to be found there. 'Another two down with the lurgy. Can you do an extra couple of hours the night?'

'Have I a choice?'

'No.'

'Yes.'

'That's the boy.'

I slung my coat over my shoulder and went back out into the hallway. Directly opposite the Blue Bar was the staff-only door in behind the Cocktail Bar and just inside this a short passage ran left to the main store, where we hung our coats. As ever, on reaching the end of the passage, I snaked a hand into the storeroom and switched on the light before entering. Rodent-phobia. Not that I'd ever seen anything myself, but I'd heard the scare stories and, even suspecting scare stories were all they were, was scared. Rats as big as badgers, as fierce as Alsatians. And *drunk*. Thankfully, I had escaped the fate of most new-starts who usually wound up locked in here by way of welcome. The Master himself, I'd been told, had had to endure an hour's incarceration after an unfortunate mix-up with a waiter working out his notice.

No one was much in the mood for pranks, though, when I arrived at the International.

The light on, I counted to ten to give anything four-legged time to make itself scarce – then to twenty for the elderly and the halt – and pushed open the door. The store was an alcoholic's wet dream. Crate upon inviting crate of bottles, the familiar, the exotic and the downright obscure; kegs with tubes running from them, like intravenous drips. The roof was high and arched, the wall stone-cold stone. No frills, no distractions. No sound. No mistaking the fact that you were fifteen feet beneath the ground. I hooked the hood of my duffel over the nearest peg and beat it back to the Blue Bar.

Jamesie showed up a few minutes later, trailing an unpleasant odour of last night's revelries and yesterday's clothes. He went straight to the sink behind the bar, picking up a tumbler and turning on the cold tap. He needed two full pints before he could make his tongue work.

'Bloody nurses,' he said.

'Forcing the drink down your throat, were they?' Hugh asked him.

Jamesie refilled his glass.

'Keep you drinking half the night thinking you're on a good thing, then turf you out on the street without so much as a feel.'

Jamesie's familiar lament.

'Is it any wonder they won't let you touch them,' Hugh said, pocketing his nail scissors, 'the state of your hands.'

Keep your head clear and your hands clean, Hugh had told me on my first day. *Think about it, everything you handle ends up in someone's mouth.*

Jamesie slagged him off, then as now, *Fuck sake, Hugh, take a Phensic*, but I had heeded Hugh's advice. So far it had served me pretty well.

'Jamesie,' I said, 'did you hear who's in? Te – *Bap* Connolly.'

Jamesie drained a third glass of water, burped.

11

'The Roker Wanker,' he said. 'Don't tell me they finally wised up and dropped him?'

Hugh was not pleased, but then, with Jamesie, Hugh almost never was.

We worked, the three of us, checking stock, reloading the optics, without speaking, the only sound the muffled footfalls in the dining room overhead, and as the hands on the clock moved on to eleven o'clock exactly, I crossed the floor to the door giving on to the outside steps and opened the bar for business.

2

Opening time. How I loved those words. Like public house. Such generosity. The instant I turned the key in the lock I felt myself … expand, is the only word I can think of to describe it – forgetting for the moment that twelve hours previously I had turned the key in the opposite direction and prayed never to clap eyes on another customer so long as I lived. It was always the way. In fact, the worse the night before, the greater, perversely, was the anticipation. I liked to think of the entire building holding its breath; we might have been at the bottom of the pile, architecturally speaking, but to me the International was never truly itself without people in the bars.

Every opening time was a new beginning, but Saturday opening time was something else again. I thank the god who gave it its name for Saturday. The people's day. It didn't matter what sort of a fuck-up you made of the rest of the week, Saturday was your chance to put it right or put it behind you. Saturday was a day, I always felt, when anything might happen.

Not that the rest of that particular week had been without incident. Looking back on it now, indeed, I am willing to accept that I had done rather more than I should have done that week, rather more than might have been considered good for me; which of course is exactly the sort of thing I would have expected someone of the age I have become to say, though even then, young as I was, I was conscious, I am certain, of having gone a bit too far. Whether I admitted it to myself or not, however, I was more than usually hopeful for a good Saturday that particular week.

I wasn't alone. Jamesie, fully recovered now from his earlier ill-humour, had rolled his sleeve and was pressing with his fingertips the back of his wrist.

'Oh yes,' he said as I returned to stand behind the bar with him and Hugh. 'I'm definitely feeling lucky today.'

He gave me his arm.

'Well?'

I touched the flesh and pulled my hand away quickly.

'Wow.'

'Told you,' he said, pushing his sleeve down to stop the luck escaping.

Jamesie's lucky feelings were as familiar as his thwarted gropes. Saturday was also the culmination of the pools' week and Jamesie was a member of several of the International's legion syndicates. (He nearly had me talked into one when I started until I caught myself on.) From Thursday lunchtime when the Vernon's man called, Jamesie and three-quarters of the rest of the staff were mentally packed and ready for the south of France. They had their cars picked out, their houses, for the few weeks of the year when they were actually in Belfast, and carried in their heads lists of the people who they would make sure and not remember when they hit the jackpot. Curiously, given that none of the syndicates had ever won more than tuppence-ha'penny, and that, deep in the mists of time, Saturday night was not a low point. With each defeated coupon that he shredded, it all became more of a lark to Jamesie.

'You still here?' Hugh asked him one afternoon when the results were over. Hugh too had resisted the lure of the triple-perm. Gambling, he said, was for mugs and lambs.

'Sure, didn't you hear?' Jamesie said. 'I bought the place.'

Sunday, not entirely coincidentally, was card-school day in the staff house. The basement bars remained shut and the hotel got by on a skeleton staff. All the big pools' players (for Jamesie had rivals on the upper floors) weighed in to Atholl Street for a few hands when they weren't working. A modest win at three-card brag was all that was needed to set the fantasy in train again. Maybe *next* week would be the week that their lives were changed utterly.

I sat in on these card games now and again, for want of anything better to do. In those days in Belfast the Sabbath was kept wholly. This was the town where swings were chained to their frames on Saturday night and not let down till Monday morning. If I was too hard up to play on my own, I'd go on the whack with Barney, who had a reputation as a master bluffer, by default, getting equally agitated by every hand, good or bad, that he was dealt. We had played together the previous Sunday and had come out exactly seven-and-eight ahead. Next morning Barney announced that he had Big Plans for the week.

'You'll go far on three-and-ten all the same,' I said. Barney was not dented.

'There's more to life than money.'

'Just as well,' I said, and left it at that. He could only mean one other thing, and sex and Barney were not subjects I could easily equate. Country people, it seemed to me, either married when they were twelve or when they were sixty. Barney was twenty-two (I had met his parents, they looked about thirty-five) and though he didn't say as much gave every impression that he was Keeping Himself. I pictured a girl, Barney with boobs basically, waiting patient years for the day when he would give up the city and return to her. I pictured the two of them, grown grey and fleshy before their engagement, seated in front of a peat fire – on top of the fire, practically – while Barney burned off the chill of his Belfast winters.

I heard no more of the Big Plans after Monday, heard little

from Barney at all, in fact, until I met him at the Brand's extravaganza. He had more short-term concerns on his mind, like avoiding the flu. The flu had placed a strain on us all. One way and another, it had been a hard old week.

Still there was always Saturday, there was always opening time.

*

The door is unlocked. The glasses are clean, the floor is swept and the counter polished. We are at our stations behind the bar, ready to go public.

Sometimes still I imagine I see us, the way a customer would have seen us, coming in the door. The Blue barmen. An alternating threesome of Jamesie, Hugh, Alec, Sean, Walter and me. I wonder what sort of impression we made: Jamesie with his black, black eyebrows and grudging smiles, as brusque as Hugh was patient and courteous; anxious Alec, half-bald at twenty, forever raising a hand to his hairline to make sure it hadn't receded further since the last time he checked; Walter, the world's worst mimic (there was a vote, I swear – look it up); Sean, the quiet one, distant behind his thick-lensed glasses; and me ... But perhaps we are not the most reliable judges of ourselves. I would be tempted to use a word like 'open', but I know what Jamesie would have said: *Wee lad, you're a wanker.* Would have said? Did say, time without number.

All right, then, I'll not argue, I was a wanker. And I mean that most sincerely folks (sorry, Stanley, a sore point, I know), as Walter used to mimic, badly.

3

First through the door that Saturday morning was Liam Strong. The clock showed all of three minutes past eleven when Hugh set him up with his dark rum and bottle of Carling. He would order two more of each before lunch, when he would go to collect his wife, Rita, from having her hair set. They would call in together around half past six for another couple of drinks on their way to the cinema. Some nights they had more than a couple and then they would forget to leave until closing time.

Liam and Hugh had been friends over thirty years, since the days when Hugh was an apprentice barman and Liam an apprentice drinker in the Hemisphere down Pottinger's Entry. It was the beginning of an illustrious career for both men on opposite sides of the bar. I'm not saying Liam was a complete dipso. I had never seen him off-his-face drunk, though after three minutes past eleven I had not often seen him entirely sober. He was a stalwart, a *regular*, a highly prized customer in our line of business, and it was not the least advantage of Hugh coming to work in the hotel that he was followed by numerous other regulars from his numerous other ports of call. In this respect at least, the International was unique then in Belfast. People who had never set foot in a hotel in their lives looked upon its bar as their local; their living room, some of them. Liam's own steadfastness to Hugh bordered on the fanatical, his only significant separation from his old friend having been brought on by the war, which Hugh had spent in the Beehive on the Falls Road and Liam in Crumlin Road gaol, interned for an IRA membership he had long since renounced.

'I thought I was a soldier,' I overheard him say once, 'but I wasn't, I was a complete balloon.'

These days, Liam's politics were of a more constitutional bent. A cousin of Rita's was married on to an in-law of Eddie McAteer, leader of the Nationalist Party. A decent spud, in Liam's opinion, but no pushover: *Eddie can fight his corner with the best of them.*

The man himself had been speaking down in Limerick on Friday night, there was a report on the meeting in the *Irish News* which Liam had folded open on the bar and which he fell to reading as he sipped his beer.

'He has a great way with the words, all the same, our Eddie,' he said after a time, smacking the page with the back of his hand.

I had glanced at the report myself. Eddie McAteer assuring the people of Limerick that things were looking up in the North.

'"A faint feeling of lightness in the air",' Liam read. 'I like that.'

The door opened. Bob Wallace, 'the Buddha' (we were fond of our nicknames in the International), a bookie's runner from Sandy Row, came in brushing ash from his shoulders and his great bald head. I made a move, but Jamesie had him covered.

'Bush, Bob?'

Bob nodded serenely, placed his hands flat on the counter and half closed his eyes in anticipation.

'Talking of air,' said Hugh to Liam with the barman's instinct for steering conversation away from politics. 'How's the young fella getting on?'

Liam's son had started work the month before with British Oxygen over in Castlereagh.

'Well,' said Liam. 'Very well, I'm glad to say.' And he blessed the company again for saving his son's working life.

At the far end of the bar the Buddha stared, rapt, at the whiskey Jamesie set before him.

'I never thought I'd see the day when you were thankful for British anything,' Hugh muttered, forgetting himself, and Liam winked – *Ah, now* – and I wondered what memories were locked away by that brief shutter.

I left them to their talk and joined Jamesie at the till.

'What happened to you last night?' he asked me.

'Didn't fancy it,' I said. 'I was feeling a bit wrecked.'

'Didn't fancy it? *Nurses?* Fuck sake, wee lad.'

The nurses had started coming to the hotel restaurant on Sunday nights some time in the autumn, after five o'clock Mass round the corner in St Malachy's. There were six of them lived together in a house off the Lisburn Road. They had been timid and ill-at-ease to start with, barely looking up from their plates while they ate, cutting dead their conversation the moment a man came within half a mile of their table. Little by little, though, they loosened up. They began to call in, in twos and threes, the odd week night when they weren't working and even to venture down to the Blue Bar beforehand for a drink. Jamesie had been making up to them for weeks and had finally wangled an invite to a twenty-first birthday party the previous night. The old suave routine, he told me. Never fails.

'Know that Karen one,' Jamesie said now, 'know with the black hair? Fuck me, you want to see her dance – the diddies on her? I'm not kidding, she'd have your eye out.'

Bob the Buddha, having contemplated his glass for an exact two minutes (I never was able to determine which came first, the baldness or this habit of meditation), breathed a heavy sigh, downed the whiskey and went out.

Odd? As two left feet anywhere but a bar.

A moment later, a pair of men in business suits entered the room from the inside stairs, talking as though they were accustomed to having to compete with several dozen voices and accustomed nonetheless to being heard. The slightly louder of the two (though I wouldn't have staked money on that) was a guest from Dublin who had checked in an hour after the Vances on Sunday night. Fitzgerald, or Fitzpatrick, I wasn't sure which, for he had insisted from the outset that everyone call him plain Fitz. And everyone did, in the International and across the road in the City Hall where he spent that small portion of each day when he actually ventured out of the hotel. Which isn't to say he was idle. Since his arrival, I had seldom known him to be alone. He had lunch with one councillor in the dining room, afternoon tea in the lounge with another, met a third and a fourth for dinner and rounded off his day in the Cocktail Bar over brandy with a fifth. No, Fitz was far from idle. I had pieced together enough of his conversation in the past days (OK, so with a voice like his it didn't take a detective) to know what this was all about: jobs. British Oxygen notwithstanding, Belfast as ever was light a few thousand. Fitz in his modest, if voluble, way was offering to make up a little of the shortfall. 'Super-garages' was the term being bandied about. Now I wouldn't have known a super-garage if I'd found one in my soup, but I was certain of one thing, Fitz was the first person I had ever met, outside of the City Hall of course, who believed in the coming of the Belfast Urban Motorway.

That's right, Belfast – Urban – Motorway: B.U.M.

I suppose I had been dimly aware of the B.U.M. for almost as long as I had been aware of Belfast itself. At odd intervals throughout my childhood the initials would make an appearance in the headlines of the local papers, complete with artists' impressions of roads raised on stilts, curving through the unrecognisable city, and futuristic cars disappearing into tree-topped tunnels. *M-plan to speed Ulster into 21st century claim.* My parents taught me to be sceptical, they had been reading such stories since the end of the war, at least, and sure enough the next day the headlines would be taken up again with the more mundane stuff of factory closures and constitution-in-crisis claims.

Everything in our newspapers was a *claim*, apart from the factory closures.

And yet somewhere those artists' impressions were taken seriously enough for their shadow to have fallen over large tracts of the inner city. Planning blight, we were learning to call it. Just when the motorway had begun to slip your mind, a councillor, or a minister up at Stormont, under questioning, would say that housing repairs *were* going to be carried out in such and such a place, just as soon as a final decision was taken on the B.U.M. Why waste money repairing what you were only going to bull-doze anyway?

They really did call it the B.U.M. in City Hall, by the way. They can't all have been stupid, so perhaps the abbreviation was meant to make the idea less intimidating, in a Frankie Howerd, *Up Pompeii* sort of way, though even then someone might have stopped to wonder what message it sent to the people whose houses were currently mouldering along the road's intended route. If they had any doubts before, there was no escaping now the fact that they were stranded up the arse-end of nowhere.

Fitz and his friend had stopped just inside the door to light cigars, it being a rule of Fitz's never to smoke until he had stepped over the threshold into a barroom. Old-fashioned chivalry, Len Gray said, adding that he had even seen Fitz crush a newly lit cigar one evening when a woman came into the Cocktail Bar. They weren't cheap either, the brand Fitz smoked: Armanda, we called them; as in leg. We had to order in more on Thursday morning. Fitz had got through in three days what we usually sold in a fortnight.

Guests with that kind of money more often than not booked into the Grand Central, on Royal Avenue, but Fitz had senti-mental as well as practical reasons for choosing the International and its close-up view of the City Hall. Sixty years back, his grandfather, just then starting to make his way in the world, had travelled to Belfast to witness the hall's grand opening. He wasn't alone; there hadn't been a building to match it anywhere in Ireland for half a century.

While standing at the balustrade of the great horseshoe stairwell, craning his neck to marvel at the mosaics lining the enormous dome a hundred feet above, he became aware of a hand resting against his. Glancing down, he found that the hand was attached to the slender wrist of the most beautiful girl he had ever set eyes on. When she realised what she had done, the girl blushed to melt his heart. Her name was Edith Banks and she had come up to Belfast that morning from Saintfield, County Down. Fitz's grandfather determined then and there to marry her. Though he was expected to pass the night with relatives in Drogheda, he left the City Hall in search of a place to stay in Belfast. And the first place he saw was the International, or as it was then called (and if ever there was an omen it was this) the Union. When he tried to book a room, however, he was told that not only was the Union full, but there wasn't a bed to be had in all of the city. In his sudden dejection he was on the point of walking away, leaving Belfast altogether (for at that moment the thought that you could marry a girl you had talked to for no more than fifteen minutes seemed preposterous), when the hotel proprietor herself appeared.

As chance would have it, the proprietor was a Kilkenny woman, like his own mother, and the long and the short of it was that she offered to make him up a cot in her office. There he slept and the following morning took himself off to Saintfield and found Edith Banks and secured her hand in marriage.

'So now,' Fitz said when he told this story, 'if ever I hear hotheads below in Dublin cursing the union I have a quiet smile to myself, for without *the Union* I wouldn't be standing here.'

And if I tell you that I had seen Nationalist as well as Unionist councillors, sometimes both together, join in his enjoyment of the punchline, you will maybe understand something of the

International in those days; or at least of the rarity of someone coming into town talking about jobs and the B.U.M.

Fitz's big laugh – bigger, if anything, than usual this morning – exploded from him again now, as he finally satisfied himself his cigar was lit and approached the bar. I counted down the seconds to the slap on his companion's back and placed myself at their service.

'Gentlemen.'

Fitz reached for his wallet. The other man stopped him.

'Ah, ah.' The man wore a Rotary Club tie, the narrow end hanging half an inch lower than the broad. He made a move for his own wallet; Fitz took hold of his wrist.

'Put that away, Trevor.'

Trevor refused, Fitz persisted. There followed more lunges for pockets, more laying on of hands, till at last Trevor brought the tussle to a halt.

'You wouldn't want to offend me now?'

Fitz signalled reluctant surrender.

'Paddy,' the victor said and held up two fingers.

'Paddy it is,' I said.

Fitz wandered off to choose a seat. Trevor (I recognised him vaguely) peered at the tariff card (was it Noades you called him?) and counted out money on the bar. I set down the glasses of whiskey (yes, *Councillor* Noades) and was just filling the water jug when Stanley came bustling in. He pulled up short, as though remembering he didn't want to be seen to be hurrying, scanned the room and, not finding who he was looking for, slumped at a table against the wall and faced the door.

'Do you want to check that?'

The man in the Rotary Club tie, whose name in that instant I had quite forgotten, moved coins across the counter to me.

'Yes,' I said, scooping them up. 'No.'

In the mirror I watched Stanley remove and carefully fold his overcoat, then tap an untipped cigarette on the table top and light it with a Swift. He pinched a crumb of tobacco from his bottom lip and rubbed his fingers over the ashtray. An unfeasibly long time seemed to elapse before he released the smoke from his lungs. I watched him inhale again to see would he repeat the feat and, when he did, carried on watching to see could he do it a third time. I might have watched him smoke the entire cigarette had Jamesie not suddenly been at my side.

'Look at your man.'

'Hm?'

'No Drink over there.'

'He's only in the door,' I said.

'Bollocks,' said Jamesie. 'He's no intention of buying anything, I know him. That's three times this week.'

Actually it was four times, though on two occasions he had bought a drink eventually, or should I say had a drink bought for him, both by the same goateed Englishman with the piercing voice (an actor, had to be), which is how I caught Stanley's name.

'Maybe he's waiting for someone.'

Jamesie rested a hand on the counter and turned his head exaggeratedly, taking in the whole bar.

'I'm sorry, was I away when they put up the waiting room sign?'

'Jamesie,' I said, 'you're a real laugh a month, do you know that?'

Jamesie smiled without mirth. I went out from behind the bar before he would. Stanley was looking at his watch as I approached.

'You all right there?'

He started and pulled his sleeve over his wrist.

'I'm just …'

'No,' I said, backing off. 'Of course.'

Jamesie was standing, arms folded, watching me. I shrugged, he shook his head, I walked down the room to cast an eye over the toilets. Like the toilets needed it. The floor was still slick from the morning's mopping and the urinal gleamed like something grand and civic. I did a quick spot check in the mirror: four, but none of them bad and nothing on my nose or chin. I grinned to see my teeth. So-so. I thought maybe I was all right looking. (It wasn't that I hadn't had my moments, in the last six months I had had plenty, but I would be fooling myself if I said looks had much to do with most of them.) I hoped that all right would be good enough.

When I left the toilets a minute later, Stanley had a brown lemonade in front of him and Jamesie's face was set in a self-satisfied smirk. Hugh and Liam Strong were still deep in conversation. I went back behind the bar and picked up Liam's *Irish News*, trying not to look at Jamesie or Stanley. Avoiding the first was easy, avoiding the second was much, much harder.

There were moments, even on a Saturday morning, when a bar seemed far too public a place to have to work in.

4

I never had any intention of becoming a barman, it was something into which, you might say, I had inadvertently *fallen*. That at least was the way my parents saw it. They had hopes for me, my parents, or they had once they had got used to the idea of me being around at all. I was a late child, not so much an afterthought, I always suspected, as a complete oversight. By the time I was born both my elder brothers had already left school and my mother and father had begun to contemplate an un-encumbered middle age; who knows, maybe even a little fun. My earliest memory is of sitting in an armchair by the gas fire looking across the room to where my parents sat, side by side on the settee, looking back at me. I'm ashamed to confess that even now I am vague about their lives before I arrived, there had just been so much of them and we never did get into the habit of talking a lot. Their own parents were all four dead and their brothers and sisters, of whom, I was reminded each Christmas when the cards massed on the mantelpiece, there were many, were so far flung as to be practically invisible to me during the years of my growing. I knew that Things Had Been Hard when my parents were first married, though this complaint seemed so general to people of their age that it added little to my understanding: in the thirties they had gone without to feed their children, in the Blitz they had sheltered under the kitchen table while landmines exploded at the top of the street … You know how it goes. They lived in the usual run of rented rooms and kitchen houses, collecting friends and porcelain cats in more or less equal measure, and finally moved, as many people of their generation were then moving in those post-war years, to a brand-new Corporation estate on the outskirts of the city, where in the front bedroom of their two-bedroom maisonette I was born, too suddenly for medical assistance, nine months to the day after they received their keys.

Andy and Edna, my father and mother (even their names when I at last learned them seemed to me inseparable), outstanding in only one respect: in this most God-obsessed of cities they had lost their religion. It was not that they were atheist, or even agnostic, at least not actively; one had been born Catholic, the other Protestant – in the absence of grandparents I was never quite sure which was which – but it was as though when they met their native faiths had somehow cancelled each other out.

No church marked my arrival into the world and I have left instructions that none is to mark my leaving.

My schooling was, it's true, Protestant, in so far as it had any religion at all, but even that struck me afterwards as simple expediency, the local State primary being a mere two-minute walk from our flats. Only once in my childhood do I remember either of my parents discussing the religious divide that so vexed the rest of the population. It was, Andy – or perhaps Edna – said, like choosing between turnip and swede.

I was always Daniel in those days. I hated the name and dreaded the start of each new school year when I had to stand up in class and say it out loud. For two or three days beforehand I would be covered head to toe in hives; the smell of calamine lotion would not wash away until the leaves began to turn and the nights drew in.

A day or two after my eighth birthday a family called Speed

moved to our street from somewhere over by the shipyard; two girls and a boy, Dave. There was a mother but no father, we said *he* was in prison, it was easier to understand than divorce. The girls were maybe only twelve and thirteen, but they seemed to me entirely grown up. Dave was ten and obsessed with his willy. He dropped his shorts when old grannies were walking past, trailing their shopping. He pissed in puddles in the rain. It gave you a brill tickle in your tool, he said; we took his word for it. He brought his sisters' bras out for the rest of us boys to inspect. Somebody got the hold of one of them and threw it at me. The strap went over my head. For the rest of the afternoon, none of the other boys would go near me.

'Stop it,' I told them. 'Yous aren't funny.'

Dave pointed out the girls' bedroom window and said if we waited across the street on a particular night we could see the two of them undressing. He said they had asked him to tell us. I could hardly sleep for thinking about it. I came out in hives again. But the strip show never happened, someone more nervous than even I was must have blabbed. I was told I wasn't to play with Dave any more. His mother broke down crying one afternoon in the VG and, like that, the family were gone again.

For a long time afterwards, if I met boys from another part of the estate and they asked my name I'd say, without hesitation, it's Dave, Dave Speed.

You don't see hives anymore. Maybe they found a cure.

My brothers were away from home before I was old enough to remember them ever having been there. One was in the merchant navy and brought me curious tin toys on his infrequent leaves in Belfast, until one year he didn't show up at all, after which he became just another Christmas card on the mantelpiece. Colin, he was called, the same name as a tin duck I still have in my bedroom, sitting astride a tricycle wearing a red jacket and a helicopter cap. Mick, the younger of the two, was a short, balding man with glasses. He chain-smoked Gallaher's – he worked in the factory – and sat blinking at me through his little private cloud whenever he called, as much at a loss as my parents for anything to say.

'*Go Modern – Go Gallaher's*,' I would chirrup, and sometimes to shut me up he would give me sixpence.

'Go get yourself some sweets.'

I got to know Mick a bit better later, in the International. I had to ask Hugh to show him the door one night when he insisted I put everything on the slate. He seemed much shorter to me by then, certainly a lot balder. Five years after that he was dead, like a lot of other people in this story.

I don't mean to suggest that my brothers were considered failures. They never wanted for work, never to my knowledge gave our parents any bother. By the standards of the time in fact they were relative successes, it was just that over the years the standards changed.

The name thing aside, primary school was a breeze. I was made library monitor and put in for my eleven-plus a year early. My mother decided when I passed that I should go to university. I was a child, you must remember, of the Butler Age: free education for all. My father, more cautious, spoke of GCEs and The Bank, but both seemed agreed I would go far and in fairness to them I did at first give every indication that I intended to. I was bright, if not quite, in the slightly more luminous company of grammar school, dazzling; homework, such was the atmosphere in a late-fifties maisonette with parents the wrong side of their own half-centuries, was practically an entertainment to me. When I was thirteen I won second prize in a County Antrim essay competition and got my name in the paper. Neighbours stopped my parents in the street to congratulate them. My parents were beyond proud. It was all I could do after that to keep them from nailing my report cards to the telegraph poles.

O Levels came and went and were passed and to my parents' eyes at any rate I was still on the right track. But something had happened to me. I grew moody – moodier than was strictly necessary for a healthy adolescence – and unhappy. Andy and

Edna, if they noticed, didn't comment. My mother returned from the city one autumn day with a Queen's scarf she had bought off a stall in Smithfield market. I became unhappier still. It was some months before I was able to identify the cause of all this misery. His name was Gregory, we sat together in a couple of classes, but we could hardly be said to be close. My first reaction on discovering that I fancied him was disappointment. There was so little about him that was attractive; his face was pinched, his nose, which was all cartilage, was red the year round, with cold in winter and sunburn in summer. He played the *tuba*. I found a girl in the year below and made myself fall in love with her. We went to the pictures together and exchanged long letters between classes. I took her back to the maisonette one afternoon when I knew my parents were out and we had a sort of sex. It felt fairly wonderful. But then I began to think about Gregory again, his pinched cheeks, his red nose ... the way he played the tuba.

I knew as soon as the A Levels were over that I wasn't going to university. I fretted for days over how to break it to my parents – I would denounce the exam system as a conformist tyranny, I would go to England and leave a note, I wouldn't tell them at all but pretend I had got the grades and spend the next three years wandering the Ulster Museum – and in the end I crossed my fingers and hoped that *something* would happen before the middle of August.

I hadn't long to wait. The leavers' dance was arranged, that year as every year, for the evening before the last day of term; a chance for pupils and teachers to step out of their seven-year roles and meet as adult human beings. (There were always rumours in advance of old scores being settled – hatchets were routinely mentioned – but somehow the threatened showdowns never materialised.) It was one of our better Junes, my classmates and I got pissed in a park before making our unsteady way to the school dining hall. The teachers assembled there appeared to be every bit as drunk as we were, the younger men frankly eyeing up the girls. Boys formed huddles to the side of a table where minerals were being sold, spirit bottles could be glimpsed being slipped back, none too surreptitiously, into sports jacket pockets; known smokers were directed to an area around the fire escape doors by a woman teacher who had enjoyed – boy, did she enjoy it – the reputation of being the strictest in the school. Later she was spotted having a sly fag herself: St Moritz.

There was beat music and twisting, pelvises ground together during the slow dances. It was, to use the phrase that was just then beginning to filter through to us from across the water, all very permissive. And it was as the party was reaching its height that the Unpleasantness – as my mother referred to it ever after – occurred.

I kissed a boy. OK, so it was a long, long kiss, but that was all I did, I kissed him. Not Gregory. Gregory hadn't even turned up for the party: summer cold, his nose must have been a sight. No, this was someone, something, wholly unexpected. He would probably still say, as he said at the time, that he was unused to alcohol, that he had been given a tin of beer and he was confused, that it was in any case an emotional time and that I had come on to him. And perhaps I did, though that's not the way I remember it. (I am five-foot six, he had been a useful prop forward.) My memory is of wandering the empty quadrangle together and finding a place to sit away from the lights and the music and the smell of Bacardi and Miranda Orange. I remember us side by side, our backs against a low wall, our shoulders touching, and thinking that words seemed suddenly weighted. I remember taking my shirt off.

Did I forget to say that earlier? I took my shirt off. It *was* a very good June.

Maybe it was that caused the problem as much as the kiss, me all topless and pressed against him when we were discovered by Mr Reynolds and Mrs Gibson as they scrambled up the grassy slope from the playing fields. At any rate, when Mr Reynolds pulled us apart I was the one Mrs Gibson slapped. My companion began to cry. (He's a barrister now, and a very good one I hear he is too.) After that things became a bit muddled. I don't recall what all I said, though I do recall I felt heroic, then Mr Reynolds slapped me too, and then there were other teachers running across the quadrangle and I was taken to the headmaster's office to where in due course the police were summoned. By midnight when I was deposited on my parents' doorstep I was cautioned, expelled and headachingly sober.

We sat through the night in the front room of the maisonette, Andy, Edna and I; we sat through most of the following morning, discussing in our stop-start way My (now reduced) Future. Around dawn it was decided that I should leave the country altogether and go to stay in one of those places where the Christmas cards came from, but then, just after the milkman had left, my parents became worried that this would only expose me to more temptation, or rather, as they were determined to think of it, corrupting influences. I kept telling myself, you're seventeen, you don't have to go along with this, but the truth was I had no better idea myself what I might do. There were few enough role models around in Belfast in those days.

The mobile shop had long since been and gone out of the street when my father rose slowly from his chair and said *Clive White.*

My mother was horrified.

'Clive White's a publican.'

'Used to be.'

My father began searching in the sideboard for the biscuit tin that served them as family archive.

'He's something in hotels now.'

'Hotels?'

My mother's hopes rose visibly. I pictured myself in a bell-hop's uniform, elevators clanking up and down. My father found the piece of paper he was looking for and strode towards the front door.

'Pyjamas,' I said.

He glared at me a moment then veered off, right, into their bedroom and reappeared a short time later dressed.

'But what will you tell him?' my mother asked.

My father looked at the back of the door as though the answer might be written there.

'A story,' he said, and turned the handle decisively.

I don't know what story my father told Clive White – Second Cousin Clive, as I was now encouraged to call him. My father was not a practised liar and Second Cousin Clive, when I finally met him, turned out to be as wide as a row of houses, someone to whom the truth was an interesting variation. Nevertheless, when Andy arrived home from phoning him he looked like a man who had clutched at a straw and was amazed to find he had the makings of a lifeline.

'Clive says he'll see what he can do.'

I decided not to hold my breath, even my mother appeared less than convinced, but there are things in this world far more unpleasant than two boys kissing and by the beginning of the following week Belfast had lurched a step nearer to its unpleasant future (or perhaps I mean past) and I was sitting in the manager's office of the International Hotel with Second Cousin Clive's testimonial in my inside pocket.

5

Stanley succeeded in eking out his lemonade for a full sixty minutes, despite Jamesie's several attempts to remove his near-empty glass. *Sorry, is that not finished? Only it looked like it was finished.* Each time the door opened he straightened up expectantly, and each time hunched forward again and looked at his watch. He put the watch to his ear a couple of times too and at one point took it off altogether and wound it. He smoked two more cigarettes out of his pack of ten, holding on to the smoke, as it seemed to me, longer with every drag. In between cigarettes he flexed his fingers repeatedly, a tic I had marked on his previous visits to the bar, though now grown so alarming that his hands at times appeared to be in heated discussion with one another, more than once, I could have sworn, to the accompaniment of stifled yelps. Even Hugh, who was not normally given to passing judgement on customers' foibles, couldn't resist commenting out the corner of his mouth:

'They're coming to take me away, ha-ha, hee-hee ...'

And then, a little after ten past twelve, a young woman dressed smartly – if unusually, for Belfast – in black slacks and polo neck came in and crossed the floor to where Stanley sat. They talked briefly, the woman handed Stanley a note. Stanley appeared from his expression to ask a question. The woman shrugged and turned on her heel. As she passed me again on her way to the door I recognised how completely bored she was by the whole business. I set up my drinks and took the money and when I lifted my eyes from the till Stanley was disappearing up the steps to the street.

If you want to know the truth, part of me was not sorry to see him go, or maybe I was just not sorry that whoever it was he was to have met, whoever sent the note with the bored postgirl, had failed to show. Aside from anything else his presence had become just too distracting, especially with Jamesie hovering (once or twice I worried that he had noticed me looking too long and not hard enough in Stanleys direction); but I was panicked as well, for there was no telling when, or even if, I would see him again.

Fitz's friend, Councillor Noades, was hailing me from the other side of the room. I was halfway to the table when he shouted his order:

'Another couple of Paddys, there's a good lad.'

Returning to the bar I picked up Stanley's glass and ashtray and I thought, people pass through your life and away and all you are left with are lip-rings and butts and a number, if you are lucky, scrawled on a beer mat. Remnants. I hardly had to strain at all for the tears I blinked back.

A soap moment, Hugh would have said.

(There was a night, during the summer, we had been run off our feet, but were too wide awake to go home; Jamesie and I stayed on talking to Hugh, and Jamesie, being Jamesie, asked him right out why he had never married.

'Oh, don't worry, I had my chances. Engaged and everything, I was.'

'So what happened?'

Hugh gestured with his impeccable hands to the darkened room.

'She said I was spending too much time in bars.'

'Bars? Bitch. I hope you decked her.'

I thought for a moment Hugh was going to deck Jamesie, but all he did was fetch the coats, 'You know what the doctor said to the man who thought he was a bar of soap? That's Lifebuoy.')

As it happened, for the next couple of hours there were too many other glasses to fill and ashtrays to empty for me to give Stanley more than a passing thought. The usual Saturday lunch-time glut. Customers coming in today with little bits of ash clinging to their clothes and hair. At least it made for conversation.

'Did you see what happened to Brand's?'

'What?'

'A fire.'

'A *fire*?'

'Huge one.'

'At *Brand's*?'

'Yes.'

'No?'

Bangor Ron had come down to help with the lunches. He was still Bangor, even though the other Ron – 'Bessbrook' – had been gone from the hotel years before half the people working there now had even started.

The soup of the day was chicken; I hated the fatty smell of it, the separated beige-gold look of it. Needless to say we sold gallons of the stuff.

'Cheer up,' a woman told me as I dunked the ladle into the urn for the umpteenth time. 'It might never happen.'

'It just did,' I said, handing her the bowl.

Len Gray, the bar manager, stuck his head round the door once or twice to see how we were getting on.

'Yous are busting today, fellas.'

Busting wasn't the word for it. The punters just kept on coming. Jamesie, Hugh and I worked around one another, ducking, sidestepping, keeping an eye out for each other's pints of stout. We made a good team when we didn't think too hard, and bar tending at such times had about it a sort of art and grace.

A pint of Export.

A bottle of Toby.

A soup and a salad sandwich.

Two Guinness, a Vat 69, a vodka and white, a glass of lager and lime, a fizzy orange and a Castella.

Same again.

Put another wee one in there.

Jamesie – Hugh – Danny Boy – when you're free …

Just as *Grandstand* was about to start, some wag hopped up on a chair and switched over to UTV. A guy on the screen held up a teacup and said something I couldn't hear; subtitles appeared in what I thought might be Irish. A chorus of voices howled for the return of BBC. The wag stepped back on to the chair, his hand hovering over the tuner.

'Are you sure, now?'

The chorus was sure: 'Turn the fucking thing over!'

'Have it your own way,' he said. 'But we'll all have to learn to speak it one of these days.'

As Belfast bar banter went, this struck me as being a bit close to the bone, though nobody else seemed in the least put out. Only much later, chancing to read down the weekend listings, did I realise that the language I had seen on the television was Russian.

Like I said, sometimes I was a total wanker.

Slowly at first, and then with a sudden rush for the doors, the bar three-quarters emptied. Again, this was normal Saturday practice. I glanced at the clock already knowing where the hands were pointed: two-fifteen. All around Belfast at that time on a Saturday, football worked its purgative magic on the city's clubs and bars. Every Saturday the Reds, the Whites, the Blues, the Crues and the Glens, the big five Belfast teams, drew men in bafflingly large numbers to freeze their balls off on open terraces, swearing never after this week to return, forgetting they had sworn the same thing last week, while countless hundreds others turned out themselves, their only warm-up a couple of pre-match hot whiskies, to huff and puff around the parks and sloping playing fields of the city. Football. You could nearly admire it if it wasn't all so perfectly pointless.

Still, I suppose it gave the bar staff some respite.

Hugh was stuffing banknotes into grey cloth bags when I came back from the storeroom with my coat.

'Half-three OK?'

It was longer than a normal lunch break, but then this was far from a normal day. I had come in expecting to work till six and would be lucky now to get away before midnight.

'Half-three's fine,' Hugh said.

Jamesie was erecting a tower of dirty tumblers on the draining board.

'Nurses,' he said, as though that explained something.

I left the basement by the stairs next to the boiler room, emerging into an uncovered passageway behind the ground-floor cloaks and toilets. At the bottom of the passageway a gate opened on to Donegall Square Mews and just short of this was a door, currently ajar, into the bar of the Damask Room. I ducked inside. The tables were laid in readiness for the four o'clock reception – a big one by the looks of it, a hundred and twenty or thirty: three long rows running up the room, interrupted briefly by pillars, then carrying on to the far wall where they joined the top table, at which Michael and Janet were currently conferring while smoothing whipped egg-white over chips in the icing of an enormous wedding cake.

Michael said he didn't know sometimes where people got the money. Michael, Janet said, had taken the words out of her mouth, a thing which Michael was forever doing to Janet, though she didn't seem to mind in the slightest. Michael and Janet had been with the hotel since the Union days when receptions on this scale were unheard of. Both were married, happily so, as far as anyone could tell, but at work they were inseparable. They were each as shortsighted as the other and it was a toss-up which was the more forgetful, so that between the two of them they seemed only ever to have one pair of glasses, which they were always swapping back and forth. They inclined their heads now, talking low, enveloped in the wintry light from the back windows.

'Ah, love's young dream,' I piped up, the sort of meaningless thing you do say when you work in a place with sixty other people. I don't know what I expected – an exasperated smile, perhaps, certainly not the start that Michael and Janet gave. Their heads cracked, the glasses (I think Michael had been wearing them last) came off, I dived behind the bar.

'Danny Boy?' Janet said. 'Is that you?'

'Who do you think it is?' said Michael, from a position close to the ground, and then I heard the Master's voice.

'Is there a problem?'

'No, no problem,' Michael said, and though I couldn't see Janet I knew she would be nodding the head off her shoulders.

'Good.'

The Master could stretch the word out so long there was scarcely a bit of good left in it by the time he was finished.

'Yes,' he said and I could picture him walking down the room checking on the place-settings. 'Goo –'

I hugged my knees squeezing my eyes tight shut. His tread came nearer.

'– oo –'

The anticipation was more than I could bear. I leaped to my feet.

'Michael, that's you OK for mixers ... Mr Rogan.'

The Master had stopped with one foot still shy of the ground. I focused on a point a little to the left of his ear. Michael was handing the glasses to Janet.

'Mixers,' I repeated. 'I was just counting: big wedding.'

The Master swayed slightly, taking in my duffel coat. I cast about for an explanation, found none; I felt a burning urge to pee.

'Oh please, God,' I prayed, in defiance of my parents, 'make him look away.'

God, or whoever it was controlled the wind, obliged by causing the door behind me to slam shut. The Master glanced aside, I saw my chance and scooted across the room to the main door. 'Got to run.'

His voice reached me as I gained the corridor beyond – 'Danny, I wanted a word!' – but I decided I was far enough away to pretend not to have heard.

The kitchens were doing their usual Saturday afternoon field-hospital impersonation, all boiling water and blood and blades on bone. Lunch was barely over in the dining room, the remains binned and carted off, and upwards of four hundred wedding guests would be landing in looking fed between now and the commencement of dinner at half past four. How the chefs coped, let alone *catered*, was beyond me. There were feats performed in hotel kitchens day and daily that would have had John Wayne pushing back his hat and whistling in awe.

Barney was sitting on a stool by the cold store in his woolly hat and scarf, nursing his foot with gloved hands.

'Marian?' I asked him. Barney nodded.

'Came up behind me in the still room. Didn't spot her till it was too late.'

He stamped the air with his uninjured foot.

'Nasty.'

'I'm sure it's broke.'

'I'm sure it's not.'

He attempted to stand and sat straight back down again.

'No?' he said. 'Well, it's dislocated or something.'

'You shouldn't provoke her.'

'I know, but I can't help myself.'

At last he felt able to venture a few steps.

'Were you cold,' I said, 'or were you heading out?'

'Both,' said Barney.

We walked back through the kitchens. 'Master's on the prowl,' I said.

Barney peeked out from the service door to check that the Damask Room was clear, then we crossed the dance floor in front of the touched-up wedding cake and finding the gate on to the mews unlocked left by way of it.

'How much time do you have?' I asked Barney.

'About half a fag's worth.'

We were only occasional smokers, Barney and I. Well, it got us out and about.

A nylon curtain was flapping from the open window of one of the rooms on the second floor. A hand reached out and pulled the curtain back inside. The window shut. Behind the condensation a man appeared indistinctly, naked to the waist. Barney had started into some story about a Difficult Customer and a Steak Sent Back.

'God,' I said. I was still thinking about the man at the window. 'You're kidding me.'

Out on Linen Hall Street the commercial day was already on the wane. The solicitors and insurers who occupied the old linen warehouses had shut up shop for the weekend and traffic here was sparse and bound for out of town. A couple of streetlights burned with a pinkish glow, though whether they had recently come on or had not switched off from the night before I couldn't tell. We stood on the pavement, passing a cigarette between us. Barney's story ground on.

'"Not well done?" Chef said. "Tell him you don't get any more well done without a congratulations card."'

'Amazing,' I said. 'Unbelievable.'

Three boys, the youngest no more than five or six, hurtled up James Street South from Bedford Street, panting, glancing over their shoulders as they cut across the road between cars and carried on, guttied-feet pounding, up the mews. I looked down the way they had come. Half a minute passed, nobody appeared. Still the damp slap of their feet echoed. Still Barney talked. On the other side of the street a woman dressed all in pink took a photograph of the back of the City Hall, the gates of which stood closed to traffic. She looked about her, winding the film on, and at the same moment that I recognised her as the photographer from Brand's Arcade, she latched on to Barney and me, raised the camera, snapped, then calmly turned the corner and was gone. Even Barney paused at this.

'What was that about?'

'Search me.'

We walked to the end of the street. Through the curved colonnade of the cenotaph next to the City Hall, I thought I glimpsed a pink hat on the west of Donegall Square, but the traffic here was heavier, the pedestrians more numerous, I might have been mistaken.

'Maybe she fancied us,' Barney said, though the notion clearly baffled him.

'Maybe she'd nothing better to photograph.'

'More likely,' Barney said.

We had stopped beside the Windsor Café. A warm buttery smell rose from the basement windows with the sound of women's voices. *And I says ...* – You didn't – *I did* – Good for you – *Here's me to him, do you think I was born yesterday?*

Across the city, church bells rang their first warning to hotel workers. Not long now. Not long now. A dog trotted by, looking purposeful.

Barney returned to work by the front door, which was asking for it I told him, though he wouldn't listen, and I decided to take a turn around the town. I suppose I was searching for Stanley and, while I didn't admit as much to myself at the time, every street I walked down without finding him at the end of it was a disappointment.

(And what would I have done if I had met him? Mumbled and blushed and hurried on, of course.)

Fire engines were still in attendance at Brand's, though fewer than earlier, their hoses dead skins cast on the footpath. The morning's crowd too had diminished to a few onlookers held by the arcade's aspect of smouldering inside-outness. The excitement over, it was just another January Saturday afternoon. Sale signs in store windows further along the street urged shoppers to hurry, hurry, hurry: last few days ... *Must end soon* ... but nobody I saw was in any great rush.

I wish I could describe for you Belfast as it was then, before it was brought shaking, quaking and laying about it with batons and stones on to the world's small screens, but I'm afraid I was not in the habit of noticing it much myself. What reason was there to, after all? It was simply The Town. I could give you the statistics you might find in any book – population, industry, numbers of churches and bars – or I could tell you that a week before the events I am describing I had woken in a room not a quarter of a mile from the City Hall to the sound of chickens fussing in the yard below. Only in recent years had the journey on foot from southern tip to northern fringe – from extreme east to far west – ceased to be a comfortable stroll; even now few people I knew missing their last bus home would have dreamed of taking a taxi. The B.U.M. was to change all that, of course. The B.U.M. was to give us four-lane, *six*-lane carriageways in the sky, primary distributor routes, ring roads – inner, outer and intermediate – with flats where there used to be ratty houses, growth centres where now there were small outlying towns. We were going to be modern tomorrow, but for today the city was little different from the city I had been born into. Ask me then did I like it and I don't know that I would have understood the question; you might as well have asked me did I like breathing. If I had seen other cities I would have understood that Belfast was in its way beautiful, as it was I reckoned there were probably better places to live and probably places a whole lot worse.

I spent forty-five minutes on its streets, too broke, two days after pay day, to spend much of anything else. Once in a while I said hello to someone I knew from the estate or the hotel, I made eye contact with a man looking in the window of Mullan's bookshop, but his wife joined him before I could tell whether there was anything to it. I bought a fruit scone in Inglis's and because the girl at the till was attractive in a kind of boyish way, I went back and bought another one. I did what I often did in the break between shifts, I killed time. The afternoon wasn't getting any warmer; a quarter of an hour early, I went back to the International.

The Blue Bar was quiet, less than a dozen customers. Horses paraded through fog on the TV screen. Nobody paid them much attention. Jamesie was on his own behind the bar, standing, when I came in, with his arms hanging loose by his side. He didn't move a muscle as I lifted the hatch and took up position beside him.

'Cold enough out there,' I said.

'Uh.'

'Been like this since I left?'

'Uh.'

'When's Hugh back?'

'Uh-uh.'

I looked at his face. The light didn't appear to be on.

'Jamesie, are you all right?'

He smiled, at no one in particular, then grabbed my upper arm and pulled me to the corner of the counter nearest the door.

'Sted.'

'What?'

He grimaced at me to keep my voice down.

'The first table,' he said. 'It's Ted Connolly. *Bap.*'

'The Roker Wank –'

Jamesie showed me his fist, then, smiling, turned and walked back along the bar. I followed him, hands clasped behind me. At

44

a table four feet from the counter two men were talking about butter; at least, one of them, a gaunt fifty-year-old in a neat but unmistakable chestnut wig, was moving half a pound of the stuff backwards and forwards on the tabletop while the other tossed a pound block from hand to hand. The wrappers were cream with green lettering. Dairy Pride. Sitting across and a little aloof from these two was, I now recognised, the mystery *Racing Post* reader I had seen this morning in the lobby. I jerked my head and Jamesie returned with me to the other end of the bar.

'Tall fella?' I asked.

'Blond one.'

'He's not blond.'

'Not blond? Course he's blond.'

I stole a glance. The butter juggler (who to my mind was more fair than blond) set down the Dairy Pride and raised his glass to show us it was empty.

'Order,' I said. Jamesie's arms went limp again.

'Jamesie,' I hissed, then took over myself.

'A pint of Bass,' Ted Connolly said. 'And ... ?'

His companions looked at their glasses without enthusiasm. The great man arched his eyebrows. They were sandy and, when he raised them like that, seemed almost to disappear into his freckled forehead. He waved a hand.

'Just the Bass.'

Jamesie, passing behind me, said with some admiration, 'Four in an hour.'

I drew the pint and carried it to the table on a tray. Ted Connolly made no attempt to pay. The aloof man showed me his room key at the same moment as he leaned into the conversation.

'Look at George Best.'

'Charlie has a point,' said the third man. 'Look at George.'

(I can tell you, from where I was standing, peering down on him, that when he nodded his wig remained perfectly still.)

Whatever it was Ted did look at, wrinkling his eyes, it produced a smirk. Besides the butter, there were a few bedraggled sheets of paper on the table and a twenty-deck of Cadets, wet at one corner. I picked the cigarettes up to wipe underneath. Ted took the box from me and popped it in his jacket pocket. The ashtray was full. I set it on the tray and left an empty one in its place.

'Did he smoke all them himself?' I whispered. Jamesie nodded and I began to understand his change of heart had nothing to do with football.

I washed glasses. Jamesie sliced lemons. On the TV the horses ran from thick fog into thicker fog. I watched for a moment to see would they come out, but they never did. A result flashed up. For all I knew the jockeys had dismounted and drawn straws. A Tele Boy came in from the street, tugging a newspaper from the pile under his arm and folding it in a single movement. They were all Tele Boys, no matter what their age. This one was pushing forty. He clocked Ted Connolly straight off. *No*, he seemed to say beneath his breath and then glanced about as if for confirmation that this was some sort of joke, but he went on standing anyway, a yard in from the door, furled newspaper poised between forefinger and thumb like a knife about to be thrown.

'*Tele*,' he said, going through the motions. 'Sixth. Late. *Tele*.'

Ted was juggling butter again. The Wig set his elbows square on the table and with his hands traced a shape in the air that might have been a football or might have been the whole world.

'It's the way of the future.'

'Doran's right,' Charlie said. 'At least give it some more thought.'

Ted contemplated his glass, swallowed a third of his pint. The Tele Boy pointed the paper as if to ask, *Is it you?* Ted Connolly shook his head. The Tele Boy smiled. *I didn't think so.* He had started for the door when Ted snatched up a pound of Dairy Pride, raising it above his head like a trophy.

'*Moo* taste Dairy Pride. Try it, you'll never put another butter ...' Charlie and Doran had begun a kind of rhythmic nodding which they broke off suddenly as Ted jabbed his own head forward. '… *on your bap.*'

The two men exchanged glances and smiled. The Roker Wonder looked from one to the other, then threw his head back laughing.

'It's rubbish,' he said.

'Of course,' the Tele Boy said from the door. 'It all is.'

Charlie and Doran shifted in their chairs. Ted drank down the rest of his pint and, still laughing, exited the bar towards the inside staircase. No sooner was he gone than a clatter of footsteps descended the street stairs. The door thumped back against the wall and half a dozen men sporting red carnations in their lapels laid claim to one end of the bar. A few moments later half a dozen more, distinguishable only by the colour of their flower, arrived and crowded at the other end. Each influx was followed by an equal number of women who distributed themselves in smaller groups around the tables. The McAdam/O'Brien wedding party had arrived. Someone slapped a fiver on the bar.

'Six Guinness, four Bacardi, two cokes, a gin, a vodka and a split tonic.'

'Here we go,' Jamesie said, and I approached the group at the other end.

'Gentlemen. What can I get you?'

6

'Gentlemen. What can I get you?'

'Drunk, fast.'

My first day, my first customers. Two London journalists with an hour to put in before the taxi took them to the airport. They had been in Belfast three days and had seen, they said, all they could bear to see sober. Eager to please, I served them doubles, neat, refilling their glasses the instant they were empty. If I say so myself, I got them drunk very fast indeed. I got them close to paralytic. As I was helping one of them to the door, he turned his lolling head towards my face.

'Where the fuck are we?'

'The International.'

'What the fuck is that?'

'It's a hotel. In Belfast.'

The journalist missed his footing; his eyes struggled to focus. 'How the fucking hell did we end up here?'

Would you like the short answer, I wanted to say, or the long answer? All the same, I could see his point.

* * *

I search my memory, but I have no firm recollection of ever having set eyes on the International Hotel before the June day I first resisted the temptation to click my heels at the top of the front steps and asked the small woman with the red-rimmed eyes behind reception to direct me to the manager's office.

'Marian,' she said and blew her nose. 'Don't mind me. I'm not always like this.'

The interview was nothing like as terrifying as I had expected; it was scarcely an interview in the proper sense of the word at all. Mr Rogan, the Master, as I would soon learn to call him, was sombre and distracted. Several times while I was in the room the phone rang. The Master listened in silence.

'Thank you,' he said. 'I appreciate your phoning.'

And after each call he sat for a moment staring at his desk, before rousing himself and shifting papers.

'Where had we got to?'

Nowhere in particular, and we might have remained there the rest of the day had not Len Gray arrived, late and apologetic, and asked to see my reference. He ran his eyes down the page, gnawing on a rag nail.

'I'd like him to start tomorrow,' he said.

The Master nodded. The phone rang. Len and I slipped away.

'You know we're desperate,' Len said when we were outside the door. 'Clive or no Clive, that's the only reason I'm taking you on.'

I say I had never seen the hotel before (come to think of it, I had never till then seen the back of the City Hall), but I had heard of it. In the previous few days, in fact, the whole country had heard of the International so often that my parents had serious doubts when Clive White got in touch through a neighbour telling them what he had found for me. Tragedy has a way of tainting a place.

And necessity has a way of overcoming most reservations in the end.

'What *else* am I going to do?' I asked my parents.

Andy and Edna, I think, were shocked, not by my insistence so much as by the simple unaccustomed fact of my voice. *I* was shocked. I said more to them that evening after the interview than I did in the course of an average year. Well, I didn't say much beyond that one sentence, but I said it over and over.

'OK, OK,' my father said finally.

He switched on the television as if to signal that from now on we would leave talking to people who were paid to do it, thank you.

'We *are* happy,' my mother whispered to me. 'As long as it's what you really want.'

Oh, it was what I wanted all right. My initial impressions of the International may have been brief – the atmosphere more than a little subdued – but they were enough to seduce me entirely. The rich pile of the carpets, the drapes dripping reds and golds, the vast ceilings, the chandeliers, the sheer *unnecessariness* of it all … how could a young man fail to be impressed?

Exactly.

I am told that the Savoy Hotel in London takes its name from the count who built his palace on that very site in the Middle Ages, and that in Paris and Rome many old palaces themselves were converted to hotels when their owners hit hard times. It was this lingering opulent quality I had fallen in love with. Forget the cinema – or picture palace, as my parents still sometimes referred to it – in a hotel you could act out the fantasy yourself.

The Union Hotel was the first hotel in Ireland to offer hot and cold running water in every room.

So Nancy O'Connor said. Nancy O'Connor worked in the Union as a chambermaid in the years before the Great War, though long before that she remembered Annie Owens, the hotel's proprietor, coming with Mary, her cook, into St George's Market, where Nancy's mother had a stall, and personally overseeing the buying of vegetables.

'I saw her many's the time give back a solitary potato out of a couple of stone because she didn't like the look of it.'

This would have been 1903 or 1904, for Nancy was not yet ten. The Union then was a small affair, little more than a private house with extra beds for guests. Priests, a lot of them, and the odd commercial traveller from across the water. When Nancy went to work there six years later there were eight rooms and four staff living in the hotel along with Annie and her two younger brothers, who had come north with her from the family home in County Kilkenny. The ground-floor lounge was already there, much as it was when I knew it, and there was a small bar on the first landing in which Annie would sit for a strict hour every evening and talk to her gentlemen guests about affairs of Church, State or marketplace as required.

'An hour was all she dared allow herself,' Nancy said. 'Annie Owens could have run rings round the lot of them if she'd been bothered.'

In time, Nancy married the night boots, a Scot named Ross, and took a house in Little May Street, a minute's walk from the hotel. Within weeks she was pregnant. She left Annie Owens's employ and, though it was not her intention, never went out to work again. The war was on. Ross joined up and was killed in the Crimea with peace already declared (Nancy never did understand exactly where the Crimea was, still less what her husband had been doing there), leaving Nancy with two small boys to bring up on her own. The first died in infancy, the second survived only as long as the start of the next war, lost when the liner on which he was a waiter was sunk in the north Atlantic. In between times Nancy had a third child, a girl, Violet, whose father's name she never divulged. The girl was born blind and palsied, a punishment, some said, behind Nancy's back. Nancy got to hear what they were saying anyway. *TCs*, she would whisper in Violet's ear when they passed such people on the street: Twisted Christians; and mother and daughter would laugh like sisters.

Others, more open, advised her to give the child over to an institution, but Nancy would not be parted from her. For nearly thirty years she devoted her waking hours to Violet's care. They kept little other company, but one afternoon a week walked together the short distance to the Union Hotel where they took tea in the private rooms of Nancy's former employer.

Throughout this time, the Union had continued to grow in size and reputation. Another floor was added, an adjacent property annexed: every couple of years, Nancy said – more renovations. Annie Owens's brothers were long gone from the hotel, successful businessmen now in their own right; a nephew was climbing the ladder in Washington DC on his way to becoming an aide to President Eisenhower. Annie Owens herself had become a woman of wealth and standing and counted among her friends several bishops and a cardinal who presented her with his own ring in recognition of her steadfast loyalty to the Church. Yet in spite of her devoutness she never once passed judgement on Nancy. Judgement was for God alone and Annie Owens's God, Nancy liked to think, had more serious matters to concern himself with than a young mother, deprived of a husband, looking for solace.

Violet and Annie Owens died within a week of each other in the summer of 1950. The Union Hotel passed to Annie's eldest brother. Nancy was fifty-six years old, but felt as though she had lived three lives. For want of anything better to do, she took to drink. She said she thought it would either fill her days or end them. Hugh, who was working then in the Kitchen Bar on Victoria Square, remembered her at that time as a very loud drunk with a fondness for young men to whom she would attach herself, often physically, and offer her services in return for a large gin. Services which, Hugh was happy to report, in defence of mankind, or that portion of it which frequented the

Kitchen Bar, were never availed of, though endless drinks were stood her.

If you threw her out one door, she would come straight back in the other. This could go on for hours. The Kitchen Bar regulars dubbed her Yo-YO'Connor. The staff, eventually, left her alone.

In time, Hugh went as senior barman to a house on the Stewartstown Road, several miles distant from Nancy's haunts, and gradually ceased to hear reports of her. He had long since written her off as dead when he walked in for his first shift in the International to find her dozing over a bottle of stout in the corner of the Blue Bar. She had come back, she told him, to where she had been happiest. In fact, she was sitting in what, in her day, had been a neighbouring warehouse.

The intervening years had calmed her somewhat, though she was still an old soak. She was three years older again and virtually pickled when I started work there and she adopted me.

'You don't have to pretend with me,' were the first words she addressed to me: 'Nancy knows.'

I pretended, anyway, that I didn't know what she could possibly know. Late at night, however, leaving the Blue Bar, she would pause, unsteadily, at the door and sing to me. Always the same song, always 'Danny Boy'. It had been sung to me before, of course, but never with such subversive delight. Coming from Nancy's mouth, the calling of the pipes was unambiguous, at least to my reddening ears. To everyone else her cracked performance was just another big bar-laugh, my discomfort no more nor less than anyone else's being serenaded by a seventy-two-year-old lush. Which was why, though Nancy died, inevitably, if mercifully suddenly, something under two months after I met her, the Danny Boy tag stuck fast.

Nancy, I think, sometimes mixed things up; *made* them up, even. Certainly she never told me the same story, the same way, twice.

But she told me this story and swore to me it was true. During the war, the English traitor Lord Haw Haw named the Union in one of his broadcasts from Germany. British morale was crumbling, he claimed, disaffection was rife, and, as if to prove it, in Belfast the IRA were meeting in the Union Hotel to plot against the detested Churchill government. Actually, the only people Nancy could remember meeting in the hotel in those days were a group of writers, *reds* a lot of them, she didn't doubt, but it was the Nazis themselves, not the British, they wanted brought down.

One night the writers had as a guest speaker a minister of the Czech government in exile, and at the end of his talk Annie Owens presented him with a Czechoslovakian flag – in Belfast, in the middle of a world war – so that Nancy wondered if there wasn't a cupboard somewhere in Annie's rooms stocked with the flags of every country on God's earth against just such an eventuality. Tears welled in the man's eyes as he took his seat. Tears welled in Nancy's as she told me.

When the war ended and the communists came to power in his country, the minister killed himself by jumping from a balcony of the government palace. Annie Owens lit candles in St Malachy's church. The Soviets spread stories about the dead man of course, called him a bourgeois reactionary, an enemy of the people; all the usual names. A week before she died, Annie Owens told Nancy she had never ceased imagining the poor man leaping to his death, clutching the flag she had given him, like a useless parachute.

Nancy couldn't be sure that this episode had anything to do with it, but, if you asked her, Annie Owens was never quite the same woman after the war. The Union itself seemed altered, certainly its reputation plummeted. Perhaps it was just age, perhaps for all the renovations it had simply not been able to keep up with changing times.

Long afterwards, though, Nancy couldn't help wondering whether Lord Haw Haw wasn't in some way connected with the funny name the hotel had begun to acquire in certain parts of the city.

The danger with propaganda after all is that some people will hear in it what they believe in any case to be true.

*

If only I'd known some of this on my first day, I might have earned myself a half-decent tip from those drunken London journalists before they fell into their taxi and out of my life for ever.

Next!

7

'Four pints of Double.'

'Three pints of Tennents.'

The McAdam/O'Brien party drank. In the half hour before they ascended to the Damask Room, the till never stopped. Jamesie and I flung ourselves about like tennis players, every serve met by an instant return.

'Two rums, two vodkas, two cokes.'

'A Bass and a Bass shandy.'

More drink!

In the way of all wedding guests they were free with their tips. Odd pennies, thruppenny bits (Irish and British: small and silver or angled and old gold), tanners, here and there a shilling, once a florin from which the dead king's head had been all but erased, were left in the shallows on the bar and were scraped, resisting, into a pint glass whose contents gave off an ever more potent smell of alloy and alcohol. A good Saturday could keep me in pocket money for the whole of the next week. Even a bad one would get me a couple of packets of fags, or a drink or three when work had ended and we were loosed on the City That Can't Stay Awake. Too late for most of the nightclubs and ballrooms, we would hunt down private parties or bars with elastic hours. We were well known of course, the International was a big fish in our provincial pond. And we were kindly treated, even seven months on from the events of the previous summer. The International barmen. It was a sort of fame, I suppose.

I found myself watching a pint pot fill. Three men of more or less identical age and appearance looked at me expectantly across the counter. I had not the first idea which of them the pint belonged to. For a moment, in the Blue Bar's perpetual electric night-light, I could not even be sure whether it was afternoon or evening. The three men continued to look at me.

'Guinness?' I asked, holding up the glass. The men shook their heads as one.

'Anybody order a Guinness?' I shouted past them. Not a body answered. It happened, I told myself; not often, but it happened. 'Pint of Guinness?'

'Ah, go on then.' The middle member of the trio before me tendered the necessary. 'Since you've poured it.'

The men's faces split in triplet grins. I smiled back, eventually, and resolved that the next drink any of them ordered would come out of the slops tray.

Hugh returned from his break and stood on a chair to turn the telly over to the wrestling. Mick McManus with some guy's head gripped between his thighs, the referee kneeling on the canvas: *Do you yet? Do you yet?* Going for a submission, they called it. Personally I preferred tag, the Royle brothers in the light trunks, which didn't budge an inch, no matter how many times the brothers were dumped on the canvas or flung headlong across the ring. What material could cling so closely and yet never, in all the bouts I had witnessed from behind the bar, give the slightest hint of what was inside?

McManus tightened his grip, his opponent's body bucked and writhed, the referee spoke into his contorted face: *Do you yet? Do you yet?* The spectators ringside were on their feet howling for a result. (I felt a cry rise in my own throat, but choked it back in time. One of these days I was going to forget myself entirely.)

The Roman games, I fancied, must have looked and sounded something like this, at least the Roman games as I understood them from Tony Curtis films, though it was the thought that this contest was going on in some northern English town, not a million miles from the town where I stood watching, that gave it its special attraction for me. Men laying hands on one another's skin, bodies pressed tight together, sweating and grunting. *Do you yet? Do you yet?*

'Submit,' Jamesie shouted at the television. 'Submit before McManus farts and kills you.'

'You're feeling better,' Hugh said.

'It's work,' Jamesie told him. 'It agrees with me.'

'Aye, well you'll be feeling tip-top by the end of the night, then. I've just had a word with Len, a couple more's rung in sick. We're on our own here.'

'In that case,' Jamesie said, throwing down the cloth with which he had been wiping the counter, 'I'm taking my break now.'

A wee man with a big nose and a long list scribbled on a beer mat pushed through to the bar.

'All yours, Danny Boy,' said Jamesie, but he had only been gone a matter of moments when he came charging back into the room.

'Have you seen?' he said. 'There's a flipping horse and carriage out the front.'

The McAdams and O'Briens and their friends jostled for the doors. I looked to Hugh who scanned the emptying bar and nodded and I followed those guests who had taken the shorter, outside route up to the street. At the top of the stairs I stopped and gripped the handrail.

'Fuck me.'

'Wild, isn't it?' said Jamesie.

Wild was mild. I don't know where you would have hired a carriage like that in Belfast, unless the Brothers Grimm had opened a place. The bodywork appeared to have been iced rather than painted, so that I wouldn't have been surprised if the coachman had broken a door knob off and fed that to his horse, instead of the apple he was holding in the flat of his hand. The horse's plume was pure pink candyfloss.

The bride and groom had remained in the carriage for the benefit of the cameras; she pushed back her veil and pressed her cheek against his at the open window.

Jamesie and I both let out low whistles.

They could have arrived in a motorcycle and sidecar and still have been beautiful.

'Anne, Joe, this way …' The carriage rocked like a row boat as they changed position. 'That's lovely.'

The Master waited, hands clasped behind his back, at the end of the red carpet, rolled down the front steps for all newlyweds. The bride's father meantime paced about looking at his watch every few seconds, in the manner of a man who was not used to control being taken from his hands. The coachman, chatting to Jamesie once all the fuss had died down, said he thought at one point on the slow journey from the church that the father was going to get out of the car ahead and pull the carriage himself. I had seen him about the hotel several times in the previous week, and heard he had been in several times more, wanting to know where every penny of the money he was spending was going, though by all appearances he wasn't short of a few bob. The joke doing the rounds was that he had even asked one of the chambermaids to help him try out the nuptial bed.

At last the bride and groom were able to step down from the carriage. The Master now came forward and shook them both by the hand.

'Mr and Mrs O'Brien,' he said, and the assembled wedding guests whistled and applauded. Cars driving by tooted their horns. A shiver ran from the horse's right ear to the end of its plaited tail which flicked against the stays.

'Whoa, boy,' the coachman said, as though it was part of his script.

The bride's father lit a cigarette and blew a grateful stream of smoke into the January air.

Mr McAdam needn't have worried. We were big on weddings in the International. Weddings in fact had been the saving of us in the past and the management were not likely to forget it. Francis, the assistant manager – Mr Simmons as he asked us, apologetically, to call him when he was on duty – had described for me once the sad wreck the hotel had become by the end of its days as the Union: rooms lying unlet from one month to the next, even at the height of the tourist season. Businessmen nowadays were as likely to hop on a plane back to England at the end of the day as stay over, and the priests who had once provided such reliable business no longer came in the same numbers now that Annie Owens and her cardinal's ring were gone.

'It would've given you the creeps some nights. And the smell...? There was air in those corridors I'm sure hadn't circulated since before the war.'

If the hotel had closed ten years ago, Francis was convinced, few people would have noticed, let alone cared.

'You'd never have thought then that all this would have been possible.'

Possible was a word Francis used a lot. Possible was the word that had helped elevate him to assistant manager. Where others saw impenetrable difficulty, he could always find a chink of light; the turnaround in the hotel's fortunes had made an unwavering optimist of him.

The second best thing the new owners had done, he said, was change the name. ('I mean, 1960, it was a whole new world.') The *very* best thing they had done was bring in the weddings, and not just for the well-to-do; parties started coming from all over the city and from all walks of life to the International. The money these receptions generated did no harm, of course, but for Francis it was more than that. There was nothing in the world so hopeful as the sight of two people starting out together and that transmitted to the hotel itself: staff, customers, passers-by must have picked up on the …

'Vibe?' I said.

Francis nodded uncertainly. 'Mm.'

More car horns sounded. A big, cream-coloured Hillman, got up in satin ribbon, turned into the street. As the last of the McAdams and O'Briens tailed the bride and groom up the red carpet and through the front doors another wedding was already arriving.

Downstairs again, the wee man with the big nose now had a long line of drinks in front of him and was asking Hugh for a hand to carry them up to the Damask Room. I leaned over the bar for a tray and told Hugh I would take care of it. The man went on ahead of me, but so slowly that I caught him on the third or fourth stair, leaning on the banister.

'The old lungs,' he explained and hauled up something grey into his hanky. The tray of drinks weighed on my wrists as I tried to fall in with his slow ascent. 'Nice wedding?' I asked.

'Oh, the best, the best.' He coughed again, then carried on behind his hand. 'They're big people, you know, her people – McAdam the bookies.'

I hadn't heard of them, though I said *right* as if I had.

'Whereas nobody in our family ever had that,' he clicked his fingers and I noticed now, from its fraying cuff, that his suit had seen many years' service. 'But they couldn't have made us more welcome, they could not now.'

The rate he was going I was worried the reception would be

half over before we arrived, but I was forgetting the bride and groom would have gone to their room to freshen up (amazingly some people seemed to believe that was all they did do) and wait till everyone was seated before making their grand entrance. I spotted Tim Cassidy, another of the barmen, in among the stragglers outside the function room.

'You on here this evening, Tim?'

'If I don't collapse first,' he said, and right enough he wasn't exactly the picture of health.

'Have you the strength to take these in for this gentleman?' Tim smiled weakly as I handed him the tray. The little guy touched my sleeve.

'Put that in your pocket.'

I looked down at his closed fist.

'It's only coppers, I'm afraid.'

'You don't have to,' I said. I was thinking about what he had said to me on the stairs. I was thinking about his suit.

'Sure,' he said, and pressed the coins into my hand, 'if you only did what you had to you'd never do anything you wanted at all.'

Well, when you put it like that … I accepted the money and started back down the Long Corridor. Paula, the new waitress, was on the payphone at the far end by the basement stairs. She fumbled to replace the receiver as I drew near.

'I thought you'd have been away on by now,' I said. It was the first I'd really spoken to her. Her reply was directed towards the telephone.

'They want me to work late.'

'It's the flu,' I said and she nodded at the wall. I should have left it at that. 'You know you can use the phone in the office if you're ringing home.'

Not even a nod this time. The colour rose in her cheeks and my own came out in sympathy and in shame. Listen to yourself, I thought. Ringing home. What age are you?

'It's OK,' unfortunately, was what I said.

She turned a look on me, quick and defiant.

'I'm glad you approve.'

'I didn't mean it like that.'

'Yeah, right,' she said, and then with a rustle of her uniform and a flash of her plastered heels she was gone.

Oh, bollocks. Bollocks arse and tits.

The wrestling had been switched over in my absence in readiness for the football results. Soon all attention would be on the box and the irritating chitter of the teleprinter. (Irritating to me: I had no doubt Jamesie was sat in a neighbouring bar, pools coupons in hand, hanging on its every inky pulse.) I slid the evening paper out from beside the till and laid it on the bar. *Woman Dies in One of 4 Ulster Fires.* There was a picture of the dead woman's house off the Ormeau Road and a larger, indistinct one of a fireman in the wreckage of Brand's Arcade. Sarah Chesney, wife of William Chesney, Brand's caretaker, told how she climbed on to the roof of her fourth floor flat and was rescued by 'a handsome fireman'. Obviously not the fireman in the photograph, even allowing for the poor picture quality. In Larne, ten people had been rescued from a blaze in a house on a council estate. What was it with all these fires? A column on the far left-hand side reported the deaths the night before of three American astronauts in a fire on board Apollo 1 at Cape Kennedy. That at least wasn't altogether a shock; as Hugh said, rockets were things they used for killing people in the war. Halfway through I skipped down to the final front-page headline: *Orange 'Concern' at Bishop's Visit.*

Now here was something I recognised. The story had been smouldering away on the inside pages for most of the last week. The Bishop of Ripon, wherever that was (Ripon to me was a racecourse), had made noises about reuniting the Anglican and Catholic churches. He had been invited to speak in Belfast and apparently some people weren't too happy at the idea. The Evangelical Protestant Society were demanding a meeting, to put the Bishop straight I suppose. To be honest, I hadn't taken much notice at first. I had other, less theological matters on my mind, and besides the Evangelical Protestant Society and their ilk were against a lot of things, from Sunday football to the B.U.M. You think I'm kidding? The Evangelicals *really* had it in for the B.U.M. The B.U.M. was going to require central planning, which meant less power for local Unionist councils, which meant, to the Evangelical Protestants, *juggernauts* of iniquity trundling in. They had it all worked out. I only wish I was kidding.

Everyone knew the Evangelical Protestant Society were fruit-cakes, but as fruitcakes went they were harmless enough; soon, though, other Protestant societies, not wanting to be outdone, began voicing their opposition to the Bishop of Ripon and it was only a matter of time before the loudest voice of all joined in. On Thursday the Reverend Ian Paisley threatened street demon-strations if the Bishop's visit went ahead.

Ian Paisley was basically a joke that became less funny each time you heard it. In fact he was so unfunny now it was starting to hurt, very badly. Whether he was dropped on his head when he was a baby or what, his eyes saw catastrophe at every turn; catastrophe for Ulster that is, or more particularly, catastrophe for the Protestant people of Ulster. The Papist hordes were closing in. Our Prime Minister, Terence O'Neill, who had once visited a Catholic school and spoke meekly of reform, was the arch-traitor. Paisley marched around the country trying to convince the Protestant people of Ulster that they were in need of his salvation (a statue of Nelson was blown up in Dublin on the fiftieth anniversary of the Easter Rising, which helped him no end) and, while most ignored him, not a few of them came along every Sunday to the church he had built for himself, to be scared more. Others joined his Ulster Constitution Defence Committee and the Ulster Protestant Volunteers and marched around the country behind him. A handful formed a volunteer force of their own. The previous May a letter was sent to the papers declaring war on the IRA and its splinter groups. It was news to most people that there was enough of an IRA to splinter. The letter was signed Captain William Johnston, Adjutant, First Battalion, Belfast UVF. Late one night in June, this handful, sorry, *battalion* had ambushed four Catholic men coming out of a bar on Malvern Street off the Shankill Road, shooting one dead and badly wounding another two.

Among those arrested for the murder was a Hugh Arnold McClean who, according to the police, said in answer to the charge: 'I am sorry I ever heard tell of that man Paisley.'

Ian Paisley insisted he had never heard tell of Hugh Arnold McClean or his organisation, even after O'Neill quoted speeches in which Paisley had thanked the Ulster Volunteer Force for their support. Paisley's a minister, so I suppose he wouldn't have lied. Even so, like some quack doctor whose cure is worse than the illness he is treating, he had succeeded in raising the temperature of those months.

And here he was stoking the fires again; and now the Orange Order was getting involved. I didn't hold out much hope for the Bishop of Ripon.

A customer tapped the bar with a two-bob bit. I served him and went back to leafing through the paper.

Bun boycott has no effect on sales: bakers. Bread prices were up and the Portadown branch of the Housewives' League had called on women not to buy cakes and buns in protest. A spokeswoman contradicted the local bakers and pronounced the boycott a great success. She was asking now for housewives in other towns to follow the Portadown lead. You only had to walk down any high street in Northern Ireland and see the mountains of iced diamonds and coconut fingers and cream slices and jammy doughnuts in the bakery windows to understand there were fortunes at stake here. We Northern Irish were fond of our sticky buns, all right. As the man said, every tooth in our dentists' rubbish bins was sweet.

The trickle back had now begun of those lunchtime drinkers who had taken themselves off to play football. Some, I could only assume, had been dropped off by ambulance and helped down the steps by their team-mates. One fella, his face the colour of an overripe tomato, made it no further than the stool nearest the door before collapsing.

'How did you get on, Neville?' a friend called out to him.

'12–1,' Neville managed to croak and it would have been an unnecessary cruelty to ask him which team had notched up the dozen. The friend contented himself with a gentler jibe.

'*12*? Are you sure it was football yous were playing?'

The trickle grew, became a torrent. There was a run on hot toddies and pints of lager. Twice in ten minutes Hugh had to go and change a barrel, leaving me to work the bar on my own. Across the counter was a solid wall of faces vying for my attention. The first time it had happened to me I nearly lost my nerve altogether. By this stage, however, I had established a few simple rules for myself, and anyone who called me 'son' was served last.

'OK, OK, yous'll all get a drink, wait your turn,' I shouted. I could be quite butch when I wanted to be.

After the second barrel change, Hugh had to call for glasses to be returned to the bar.

'I never thought I'd say this,' he told me, 'but I wish Jamesie was here.'

Only the classified results saved us from being overrun completely.

Doran and Charlie, the Dairy Pride duo, were sitting exactly where Ted Connolly had abandoned them, the wrappers on their blocks of butter now greasy and grubby. I guessed it had not been their idea to transact business in this way. I guessed they were neither of them too familiar with the insides of a bar on a Saturday afternoon. They gazed about them wistfully at the crowd gathered in the Blue Bar greeting each new football result with whoops and groans. The sons and husbands of the women they wanted to buy their brand. A small cheer went up for the

Sunderland score. They had stuffed Brentford 5–2 in the fourth round of the FA Cup.

'Bap's going to Wembley!' someone shouted.

Doran's neck twitched; his wig didn't move; his neck twitched again and the spasm ran all the way to his fingers, sending a sheet of paper fluttering from the table to the floor. A customer standing at the bar bent to retrieve it and I glimpsed what appeared to be a cow, or a bull, on its hind legs, wearing a red and white striped football jersey. There was writing underneath. I saw the customer's lips move as he handed the paper back.

'*Moo* taste Dairy Pride,' I imagined he was saying. 'Try it, you'll never put another butter ... *on your bap.*'

Actually, I thought, it was quite catchy.

*

Those men gunned down on Malvern Street, by the way. They were all barmen. They worked in the International. Peter Ward was eighteen when he died. I turned eighteen a fortnight after he was buried, a fortnight after I started work in the hotel.

8

As soon as Jamesie returned, not a penny better off than when he left, I phoned Mrs Sullivan in the flat below my parents' and asked her to tell them I wouldn't be home for dinner. My mother hated using Mrs Sullivan's phone – there were only two people had phones then in the whole block – but sometimes it was just unavoidable. I made a point of ringing whenever I was working late. Mrs Sullivan didn't mind and though my mother would declare herself mortified that I had disturbed the poor woman yet again I knew that she was thankful for the call. And of course by showing that I tried when possible to keep her informed, I earned myself a little leeway at other times.

'I didn't want to be waking Mrs Sullivan,' I'd say. 'It was near one before I was finished, there was nobody there could give me a lift.'

In fact, the duty manager waited every night till the last member of staff was ready and dropped us all home. I had not bothered to mention this. My parents in any case would not have expected a manager to act as taxi driver for employees. An actual taxi, of course, was a reckless extravagance and out of the question. On such nights they believed I stayed in the staff house in Atholl Street. And occasionally I did.

Our lives together had quickly settled back into their normal tight-lipped routine after the Unpleasantness of the previous summer. Nothing more was said on the subject once my parents' initial shock had passed. Perhaps they thought my own shock had cured me of my unwholesome desire. Perhaps they thought, like most people in most places with most things they don't like or understand, that if they didn't talk about it it would simply go away.

Their worries for my safety in the International lasted no longer than it took the police to track down the men responsible for the Malvern Street shooting. Two other murder charges were brought against them: an elderly woman killed in a petrol bombing, a man shot off the Springfield Road. All the city's recent loose ends tied up in a matter of days. Such was their relief that Andy and Edna were able to joke with me about the bottle thrown at the Queen and Prince Philip's car as it was driven past the International on their visit to Belfast early in July. I had not been on the staff long enough to know anything worth knowing about the woman who threw it – a chambermaid called Iris, from Salford – though the feeling seemed to be that she was not in full possession of her senses.

'She's no sense of direction, that's for sure,' my mother quipped. The bottle had missed its target by a mile.

Iris's offence in any case paled next to that of the labourer who minutes later hurled a breeze block from the top of a building on Great Victoria Street, damaging the radiator of the Royal car, and even that, when the fuss had died down, was hard to take too seriously. I was told years after, though I never saw it myself, that one journalist covering the visit had filed an eye-witness's account insisting that the breeze block had in fact come from the direction of the *Grâce à Noël* delicatessen, which establishment did not then, or ever, exist in Belfast.

In the absence of a family Bible my parents had always turned for comfort and reassurance in troubled times to the *Reader's Digest*.

It was in that good book, a week after Iris had shied her bottle, that one or other of them came across a potted life of Cesar Ritz, who, the story revealed, had started his working life as a waiter in a Swiss hotel. In no time at all, some of Andy and Edna's old ambition for me revived. I might only be pulling pints now, but at least I was pulling them in one of the best hotels in Belfast. Neighbours who had once shared in my essay-writing glory were given to understand that I had made an astute career move, learning a lucrative trade from the bottom up.

It was not my parents' fault that they had never spent much time in hotels. Hotels to their minds meant money – didn't the *Reader's Digest* say so? – and money, being beyond scrutiny, conferred a sort of respectability on all their goings-on. I had not been working in the International long before I began to arrive at a somewhat different conclusion.

Hotels are places where people go hoping for sex. Newlyweds, of course, and second-honeymooners and dirty-weekenders; but they were far from alone. Businessmen, in my short experience, considered infidelity as something of an unavoidable occurrence at some point in their career and rather than wait for temptation to wear them down gradually, the majority seemed inclined to seek sex out and have done with it. Time and again. Any hotel worker will tell you of guests making discreet enquiries about finding 'company' for the evening and there isn't a chambermaid in the country hasn't had to back out of a door double-quick after catching sight of couples going at it in the bedroom mirror.

Sunday morning was the worst. Staff in the International referred to it as the earthquake shift.

I got to know several of the prostitutes who dropped in to the bars of the International now and then looking for trade. Journalists, they reckoned, were the most fun to be with, in part no doubt because out-of-town journalists in Belfast in those days were as rare as hens' teeth. Farmers were the worst tippers. Farmers, in fact, were more or less always best steered clear of.

Maybe it was the anonymity a hotel offered, maybe it was the luxury, the feeling of indulgence, maybe it was that people away from home drank more than they were used to, or maybe it was a carry over from coaching days when sharing rooms and even beds had been common practice: a sort of fuck-memory but whatever it was you couldn't escape the fact, hotels *aroused*.

On the Thursday of my second week I found myself in conversation with a rather jaded-looking Liverpudlian guest called Frank. He had stopped into the Blue Bar after dinner for a quick drink before hitting the town, but he was back again by half-nine declaring the evening a washout.

'It's the holidays,' I said. They're all away to their caravans.'

He told me he normally enjoyed coming to Belfast, he always met (he held my eye a second then focused on the tip of his cigarette) interesting people.

'In Belfast?'

I laughed. I don't know why.

'Don't act surprised.'

My stomach, when he said this, seemed to contract, with alarm I think. I busied myself about the till, turning his words over in my head. They could mean anything, they probably meant nothing at all. It was a slack night; when I ran out of things to occupy me I returned to Frank at the bar.

'Have you friends here, then?' I asked.

'A few,' he said. He appeared to have recovered a little from his dejection. 'Very good friends.'

I don't remember what I did in the moments before he spoke again.

'Actually, one lad I know puts me in mind of you a lot.'

My stomach contracted still more, but it wasn't fear I was feeling now.

'Really?'

'Really.'

I stayed where I was, hand resting on the counter, though the way I was leaning I was getting a cramp in my forearm. I wanted him to understand that I was in no hurry to cut this conversation short.

'Mark,' he said, flicking ash.

I pretended to think.

'Can't say I know him.'

'Oh, you'd like Mark,' Frank said.

'I'll look out for him.'

'Do.'

He was completely at his ease now, his hands, between drags on his cigarette, clasped around his right knee. I collected glasses from the counter and made sure we weren't attracting attention. Walter was engrossed in the television, lip-synching the actors' lines; Alec was stealing sly looks in the mirror at his hairline. When I turned back Frank asked me did I ever go to Liverpool. I told him I didn't. That was a shame, he said, we could have a right laugh, the two of us.

'Next time you're here,' I said, but Frank pulled a face.

'That could be months.'

We looked at each other.

'What about tonight, when you're finished?'

I shrugged.

'I have a bottle in my room,' he said, then noticing the panic in my eyes perhaps, added, 'Or in the morning – I don't go till lunchtime – we could get a cup of tea somewhere, have a chat.'

I met him in the café in Great Victoria Street station. I had managed only two or three hours' sleep and for a long time as he tried to engage me I could do no more than stare out the café window at the ragamuffin sparrows pinching crumbs from under the beaks of slow-headed pigeons. There was a strained note in Frank's voice, and not a little impatience. Eventually I returned his gaze.

'I don't know what I'm supposed to do,' I said.

His hand moved across the table stopping just out of reach of my own.

'Don't think about it,' he said. 'Just talk to me.'

So I talked, babbled probably, and Frank listened. Half of what I said was a surprise even to me. I seemed to make out that my entire life had been guiding me towards our meeting here this morning in the station, and who knows, maybe it had. All the while Frank kept one eye on the concourse clock. When he suddenly stood up, I went to get out of my seat, too.

'Not yet,' he said. 'In a minute.'

I watched him walk to the men's toilets. I watched the people passing, buying newspapers and flowers, hurrying to make trains. I waited maybe two minutes before leaving the café and going after Frank.

A few months later I was in the garage of a house in Dunmurry where a party was going on, with a rosy-cheeked guy who had been giving me the come on. We did it standing up against a workbench, wasted on vodka and cider, climaxing without thrill. I asked him his name as we straightened ourselves for going back indoors.

'Mark,' he said.

I asked him did he know a Frank, from Liverpool, and he told me yes, he did. And I laughed then.

'He's such a liar,' I said. We didn't look a bit alike.

Frank had been telling the truth about one thing though. Walking back towards the International that day in July he had said that the most important lesson I could learn was to be alert at all times. Men like us, he said, were scared, a lot of them, and with good cause. You might get no more than a glance, a gesture, a half-sentence, before they shied away. You never knew what you might miss if you weren't quick to pick up the signs.

'Use those eyes and ears of yours, believe me, it will happen.'

And it had happened, not as often as I might have wished, but often enough: a glance, a gesture, a half-sentence, just like Frank said.

The job helped. I was careful, of course, but I was curious too. Some part of me even enjoyed the subterfuge. That what I was doing was illegal did cross my mind, but it was the Sack, not the

Law I most feared. Anyway I had grown up in a place where all sex was considered dirty; furtiveness seemed a necessary part of it.

I was careful, but I was prepared to take a risk. I visited rooms. A phone call was all it took, prearranged: a pint of this or a bottle of that to room number whatever. I would knock on the door and sometimes to add to the excitement I would say the magic hotel words, 'Room service!'

I was careful … And now and then I was reckless, not even bothering with the drinks charade, just getting into the lobby lift in my break and walking straight down the corridor to the room in question as though it was the most natural thing in the world.

There had been women as well, the odd time. Why not? I was just eighteen, I was having fun, and once you switch on there is no telling what signals you will pick up. I didn't ask any of the other staff, male or female, if they were doing similar things, and none of them, if they were, offered to confide in me, which is perhaps no surprise. Whether I was alone or not, though, you have to understand there was nothing especially attractive about me, save this one thing: I worked in a hotel and I looked as if, were you to ask me, I wouldn't say no.

And was I proud of myself? Truthfully? Yes (hey, I was the International champion of the one-night handstand), I was proud. Until the Vances came along.

At six o'clock there is a brief lull. The various weddings are in their various function rooms and the late afternoon drinkers have gone home for a nap or a wash or a fry or a fuck or whatever it is that revives them enough to be back down town by eight.

Jamesie reads from the paper, ' "The Grove, Shore Road, from Monday, first showing outside London: *Night Games*." Big X.' When it comes to Xs, size matters to Jamesie. ' "This Swedish shocker …" ' He looks up, awed at the coincidence of two of his favourite words … '"is the most controversial film to hit local screens for some time. The story of a depraved mother (Ingrid Thulin) whose house parties result in her son having an aversion to sex, which he decides to exorcise during one final party. Definitely not for the squeamish."'

Jamesie's smile is that of a man who has never known a squeam in his life.

'What do you think, boys?'

'I think you should see a doctor,' Hugh says.

'What about half a dozen nurses?'

Hugh comes over to help me lift a bottle of Smirnoff on to the optics.

'Wee lad wouldn't know what to do with them,' he mutters.

'What's he saying? What's he saying?' Jamesie asks, then decides on the one response that will answer all eventualities. 'Ask your ma, Hugh.'

He's out on the floor wiping tables before Hugh can turn and get his hands on him.

'God forgive me,' Hugh says, 'but I hate that bastard.'

A kid who looked about fourteen and small for his age stuck his head round the corner and said Len wanted a word with me next door. I glanced at Hugh for permission even though he was in no position to refuse it.

'Go on ahead,' he said. 'I'll not kill this moron till you get back.'

There were maybe nine or ten customers in the Cocktail Bar, most of them residents, all of them over sixty. Len was stood by one of the copper-topped tables when I went in, laughing at something which a man puffing on an ornate blond pipe had just said. (I guessed it was him said it from the way over the next minute or so he kept removing the pipe stem from his mouth, repeating a phrase to each member of the company in turn and wheezing anew.) I waited just inside the door. The kid waited beside me, a tray rucked under his right arm. His hair had been combed into a side parting and plastered down.

'You new?' I asked, not looking at him.

His only reply was a sarcastic snort.

'It's just I've never seen you.'

'So? I've never seen you either.'

We were both staring fixedly at the table of the unending joke. Len's ears were red with the effort of maintaining his grin.

'How old are you, anyway?' I asked.

'Old enough,' he said.

'Oh, yeah?' I said. 'Old enough for what?'

'Old enough to know people who'll slap your chops if you don't shut up and leave me alone.'

Len was at last trying to disengage himself.

'You cheeky wee bastard.'

'You spotty big cunt.'

The kid moved off to take an order as Len approached me, still unable to shake the smile entirely.

'You met the boy, then?' he asked me.

The boy? I looked at the kid again, and then out the corner of my eye at Len. I could see no resemblance.

'The wife's sister's son,' Len said. 'This flu gets any worse I'll have his younger brother in as well.'

'Right wee fella,' I said.

Len nodded.

'Isn't he?'

He was manoeuvring me towards the door as he spoke till eventually we were out in the hallway. Len's left hand hovered about the side pocket of his bar manager's white coat.

'Is everything OK, Danny?'

'In the Blue Bar?'

'In general.'

I thought for a moment.

'Fine,' I said, and only then decided everything was. 'Absolutely fine.'

The hand went into the pocket and withdrew a pale blue envelope with my name written on the front in purple ink.

'That American couple left this in at the office. The Master asked me to pass it on to you.'

I stared at the envelope, unable to bring myself to touch it.

'You sure there's nothing I should know about?'

I shook my head and persuaded my hand to take the envelope. Len, though, jerked it back out of my reach.

'Only, the Master thought it looked a bit, you know, *odd*.' The phone was ringing in the Cocktail Bar. 'And I have to say ...'

The kid appeared in the doorway.

'Uncle Len, some fella called Fitz for you.'

Len narrowed one eye at me, then thrust the envelope into my hand.

'Here. Get back to work.'

'I'm going,' I said and went, like a shot.

The Blue Bar was still half empty. Hugh and Jamesie were side by side behind the counter as though they had never exchanged an angry word in their lives.

'Hugh,' I said. 'Have I time for a quick smoke?'

He glanced up and around the tables.

'Well, as long as it is quick.'

'You'll hardly even notice I'm gone.'

I leaned one shoulder against the wall to the right of the front door and lit a Number 6. There had been a shower earlier, but now the evening was clear and chill. A taxi halted on the street above me and a man and a woman skipped up the steps to the hotel entrance. I turned the Vances's letter over in my hands a couple of times before slipping my finger under the flap and ripping it open. The Duke of Wellington peeped out over the ragged edge. I peeled the fiver back and saw another one behind it. Behind that was a folded sheet of paper the same colour as the envelope. I flipped the cigarette into a puddle at the foot of the stairs, too heartsick to smoke any more. The cigarette landed on its end against the bottom step and extinguished the slow way, from the filter up.

9

Bob and Natalie Vance had booked in for the last full week of January, Sunday to Saturday. They were from Albuquerque, New Mexico: *You know*, they told us, *the place where Bugs Bunny is always taking a wrong turn*. ('I thought that was Des Moines,' Walter said, in the voice of Bugs's distant cousin. 'There too,' said Bob Vance.) I would have put them both at about forty, but they were the kind of tanned-skinned, sun-blond Americans with whom it was hard to tell. Their daughter back home was a college sophomore, whatever that meant.

Americans as a rule didn't come to Ireland for the weather, certainly not in January, and sure enough Natalie soon let it be known she was trying to trace her great-grandmother's people, Murphys from Bally-something, which didn't exactly narrow it down. They had spent two weeks trawling around the South before someone, maybe to see if they were really as clueless as they appeared, informed them there were a few Bally-somethings up north they might investigate too. They left the International on the Monday morning full of optimism, despite Marian's best efforts to prepare them for possible disappointment, and returned that afternoon claiming success. They had got lost in their hire car looking for the main road out over the mountains and had wound up in the very place they were trying to find, not three miles from the city centre.

'Ballymurphy,' Natalie told Marian, and Bob repeated it like a TV gumshoe explaining the solution to the mystery.

'Bally? *Murphy.*'

I asked Marian what on earth she had said to them.

'What do you think I said? "Gee, that must be the place right enough." '

All these years later if I think of Bob and Natalie Vance with any pleasure whatever I think of them sitting in their Albuquerque ranch-home surrounded by their only daughter – thirty years on from her sophomore year – and her suntanned children and, who knows, maybe their suntanned children too, looking at photographs of a Belfast housing estate under lowering January skies and saying, 'Never forget, kids, where you came from.'

Mostly, though, I think the Vances were playing Marian, me and the rest of the International staff for fools all along.

The Vances were surprised by Belfast. I would go so far as to say they were tickled to find a city of any size here at all. Dublin they knew plenty about – James Joyce and Molly Malone – but Belfast ...? Folks back home didn't sing songs about it and the Vances couldn't remember ever having seen the city in the movies. Natalie in particular kept on about how *cute* everything was, as though Belfast was a doll-sized version of the real thing. From what I saw those first couple of days – the little winks and smiles that passed between them, the under-the-table nudges – she and Bob regarded the inhabitants with the same mixture of affection and amusement. Nothing is too serious in a toy town. And of course they were in a hotel. A hotel is already a holiday from the everyday world.

Wednesday it rained, all morning and into the afternoon. Bob and Natalie abandoned their plan to drive back out to Ballymurphy and came down to the Blue Bar right after lunch, choosing a table smack in the middle of the floor. Up till then I had not considered either of them to be big drinkers. They showed up in the bar at the same time each evening and tackled their single pints of Guinness like they would ice-cream floats (I'll swear they were expecting to be given spoons), sipping, savouring, where all around them people opened their throats and swallowed. That afternoon, however, they were on the shorts, whiskey for him, vodka for her, and they weren't hanging about: every twenty minutes or so, *Same again, Danny Boy.* These were more or less the only words I heard them speak and as time went on I began to wonder whether they had had a falling-out, for they were edgy as well as silent, preferring to look anywhere but into one another's eyes.

It was half-day closing in town. A group of guys had come in, shop assistants, who got together every Wednesday afternoon for a few pints; not much older than me, I suppose, nor much better paid probably, but all fancying themselves a bit with their John Temple pound-a-week suits and Herman's Hermits fringes. And not without reason, one or two of them. They made a lot of noise, as they usually did the longer the afternoon went on, slagging one another off, cracking light-blue jokes. I noticed Natalie smiling to herself at some of the things they came off with. A couple of the guys noticed too. Their voices got that bit louder, their cracks that bit cruder. Bob sat with his back to them, his hands clasped behind his neck, frowning with the effort of not hearing. Natalie sucked in her cheeks and played with her glass. After a few minutes of this Bob pushed back his chair and walked to the bar.

'Same again, Danny Boy.'

One of the shop assistants took the opportunity of her husband's absence to shout across to Natalie asking where she was from.

'Albuquerque.'

'Alba whatee?'

'*Quer*que.'

'Albeseein'ye,' another of the guys shouted, pointlessly, over the top of her, and his friends laughed. Natalie shook her head, still half-smiling, and pushed a matchbox a couple of inches across the table with the side of her index finger. Bob was following the exchange in the mirror, mouth shut tight, chewing on the inside of his lip. As he arrived back at his wife's side with the drinks, stooping to set them on the table, someone called out, *Howdy.* Natalie's fingertips brushed the back of her husband's knee. He looked at her briefly before turning.

'Howdy,' he said, and the next thing I knew he and Natalie were pulling up chairs to the other table and Bob was offering to buy everyone a drink. Everyone accepted, that round and the next. Each time Bob returned from the bar he had been squeezed out further on to the periphery of the group and Natalie drawn further into its centre. The way it looked to me, the Belfast guys were taking it in turns to keep Bob occupied while the rest attempted to flirt with his wife. Bob appeared not to notice, Natalie not to mind, but just once or twice, I was nearly certain, I saw something too swift almost to be called a glance pass between them. It was still only three o'clock. The drinks were piling up on the table, the guys beside Natalie were moving in closer, one had slung an arm across the back of her seat; their friends out on the edge either forgot or just stopped bothering to distract Bob.

Despite the rain and early closing, or because of them, we had by this time a pretty good crowd in for a weekday afternoon. I was aware all at once of how boisterous the whole room had become, and how muggy. I was not overexerted, though I was on my own, and yet my shirt felt damply uncomfortable where it was stuffed into the waistband of my trousers. Natalie Vance had a beer mat in her hand and was fanning under her chin. The noise from that part of the room seemed suddenly to drop away as the young men packed around her raised their glasses and tried to find their mouths. Natalie stretched her neck, rolling her head back against her shoulders. The young men drank deeply.

'All right!'

Bob Vance's voice was so loud, so unexpected, the guy to Natalie's immediate left almost bit a chunk out of his pint glass. Bob was on his feet, one hand outstretched, the fingers too agitated to perform the snap he appeared to be trying to make. Natalie, though, was already on her way out from behind the table to join him, struggling to get her heel into a shoe that had somehow worked itself off her foot. The shop assistants looked after them blankly a few moments and then spluttered into the pints Bob had bought them. They could not see, what I could see, that Bob and Natalie were laughing too as he gripped her elbow guiding her out of the bar.

I could have kicked myself for being so stupid. What I had mistaken earlier for ill-humour had been simple boredom. From the moment they arrived in the bar, the Vances were *itching* for diversion of a particular kind: an adventure to get themselves worked up for going back to their room. The blood was thumping in my ears (because, what can I say, it had got to me watching them) and I could almost hear in it the headboard banging against their wall. *Fuck me, fuck me, fuck me.* So I was surprised, to say the least, when barely an hour later they landed back into the Blue Bar and sat up at the counter, like two people with urgent business still unfinished.

I know your game, I wanted to tell them.

'What'll it be?' I asked, archly, I thought. 'Same again, or something different?'

Bob checked with Nancy, who shrugged.

'Same, I guess.'

So much for arch, I guessed.

I got them their whiskey and their vodka and left them to it. Most of the shop assistants had had their fill and gone home in the hour the Vances had been away. Those that remained shouted slurry greetings, which Bob dismissed with a wag of his head and Nancy ignored completely. She had her eye on a couple, solicitors from an office in Chichester Street, standing a little way off, closer together than was necessary and apart from their colleagues. I had seen them both in the bar at various times with other partners. The woman, at least, I was fairly sure, was married. I don't know whether this conveyed itself to Natalie Vance, or whether in her current mood everything had taken on an illicit character. She crossed and uncrossed her legs, dispatched her drink and was swinging round in her seat to order another as Stanley entered the bar, sloughing off his sodden overcoat and shaking it out the door behind him. Rain had run down the back of his neck; he opened his shirt collar rubbing at his nape with a handkerchief. The handkerchief was yellow with a dark green check, his neck, when he had finished rubbing, red and tender-looking. He sat down, facing the door as ever, and lit a fag. Inhale ... exhale. My chest rose and fell in time. I suppose, if you were on the lookout for that sort of thing, it might have been taken for a sigh. I can think of no other explanation for the expression on Natalie's face when, only a fraction belatedly, I gave her my full attention. Her mouth was a twisted pucker. Well, Danny Boy, it seemed to say, who'd've thought it?

I gave her a look of my own: *like you're one to talk.*

It is not vanity that makes me say that for a time then Natalie followed my every move as I worked the bar. I knew I was being re-evaluated and I was not embarrassed by the scrutiny. Between the two of us we managed to wrestle into submission some fairly major moral, ethical and – let's not kid ourselves – aesthetic objections, and all without another word being spoken. Stanley's English friend had arrived by now and the two were deep in conversation, which didn't exactly disincline me.

Bob, who was conducting his own reconnaissance of the bar, had noticed none of this and Natalie for once was giving him no hints, though from what I'd already seen of the two of them in action there is no saying that this inattention too wasn't contrived. Whatever, when next his glass was empty I was right in front of him, waiting.

'Same again, Danny Boy.'

I pointed to the clock.

'This will be the last you get from me,' I said. 'I'm knocking off in half an hour.'

Natalie couldn't stop herself, she laughed short and sharp. Bob looked from her face to mine as the penny finally dropped.

'Half an hour?' he said, and I nodded. Natalie was already gathering her things.

Room 304.

Natalie let me in. She had undressed to an ivory-coloured slip and for a moment I had to fight against the faint revulsion I had always felt when confronted by women's underwear. She closed the door behind me.

'Bob, honey, he's here.'

The way she said it, I might have been a neighbour come to see the new patio they'd had laid. Bob came out of the bathroom wearing only his trunks. He looked heavy inside there, like he'd been waiting for this a long time. He picked up a bottle from the bedside table. Johnny Walker.

'Drink, Danny Boy?'

'No thanks,' I said. The first of the flu victims had called in sick that morning. I had put myself down for an extra hour in the evening to help out. 'I have to keep a clear head.'

Hugh would have been proud of me. My hands were spotless too.

Natalie walked round the bed and took the bottle from Bob.

'No more drink.'

Without another word, she lay out on the bed pulling the slip up over her head and I thought, there is no way I am ready for this and I tried looking everywhere but at Bob as his trunks came down over his hips and his fingers slapped the underside of his downward-pointing erection by way of encouragement. Natalie looked back at me over her forehead.

'You ever done it with two people before?'

'Not at the same time,' I said, though I could more truthfully have said not even in the same week and oh, God, I was starting to feel very, very uncertain, but Bob and his Albuquerque cock were poised above Natalie and I wanted so badly to watch them, even for just a minute – she had placed her feet on the bed now and her legs were two sides of a V with Bob in between lowering himself and I swear I thought he was never going to get there and I didn't know suddenly whether I wanted to push him aside or her aside or push them both together but I was over by the bed myself and Natalie's hands were tugging my belt and Bob said shit and fuck and baby and Natalie said shush, over and over again.

I didn't see the Vances at all on Thursday, though then again I didn't go out of my way to find them. I understood they would need a little time to readjust. I know I did. We had done something intimate and outrageous together; it wasn't easy to balance the one against the other, still less to revert overnight to being hotel guests and hotel barman again. All the same, a day and a half seemed to me to be about long enough. The resilience of youth. So when I arrived back from my lunch break on Friday afternoon and bumped into Bob coming out of the dining room I suppose I expected some small recognition of our complicity, a slight awkwardness perhaps, but no more and definitely not the look of near terror which spread across Bob's face, draining it of colour. Natalie followed him out of the dining room, closing her handbag. Seeing me, she laid a hand on her husband's sleeve and her eyes made a dumb appeal I was unwilling to try to understand.

I had always thought shaking with rage was just a figure of

speech, but I shook then; it took me most of the rest of the day to stop.

Standing by the door of the Blue Bar under the empty mile-high January Saturday-night sky, I had begun to tremble again as I bent a match out from its book, struck it, cupping my hands to protect the flame, then, when I was sure it was strong enough, touched it to the corner of the Vances's envelope. The paper browned and curled. I held it pinched between forefinger and thumb until the heat seared the rims of my nails and I had to shake it free to burn itself out on the ground. When the last wisps of smoke had cleared I dragged a foot over the ashes and then all that was left was a grey smudge.

Through the door of the bar I saw Jamesie scratch the front of his trousers as he laughed to himself at something in the paper. Hugh leaned back, like an artist, initialling with a capital H the pint of Guinness he was drawing. These draught dispensers were only a matter of months old and already Hugh was an expert. Another little twitch of the tap – not too much – stop; watch; twitch.

I had to tilt my head to keep my eyes from brimming over. And it was through this inverted haze that I saw the woman with the pink suit and hat for the third time that day. How long she had been watching me over the street-level railing, I didn't know, nor could I tell whether she recognised me and to be honest I wasn't about to ask; this time I was the one who scurried away.

*

I owe it to Barney, who got it from Marian, who was just then coming off duty, the story of what happened next. The woman in the pink suit and hat, handbag on one wrist, camera on the other, appeared in the lobby as though picked up by the wind and dropped there. The veil had begun to detach itself from one side of her hat. A curious polka dot on the shoulders of her jacket turned out to be soot, for when she absentmindedly dusted herself she left a dark line across her right collarbone. Marian at first was not unduly concerned; if there was one thing sitting at the reception desk of a hotel taught you it was not to judge a book by its cover, however eccentric that cover might be. (Marian had been on duty the night Dave Dee checked in – sunglasses at nine o'clock! – and a nicer fella you couldn't meet.) Besides there were, as ever, a hundred and one other things going on: people passing to and from the cloakroom, parties making their way from the lounge to the dining room, residents wanting directions or asking were there any calls, and still Marian was trying to get away, because if you weren't careful you could be trapped there all evening, especially on Saturday, especially four weeks after Christmas when it seemed everyone in Belfast would rather be anywhere except at home for another night. It was Nicola, her relief, who in a quiet moment drew her attention to the woman again.

'Is she all right, do you think?'

The woman had moved now across to the sheet of foolscap tacked to the lobby wall listing the evening's functions. Marian leaned over the counter and spoke to her. 'Can I help you?'

The woman took no notice but continued with her scrutiny of the functions list. Marian, her coat already on her for going home, came out from behind the desk.

'Were you for one of the weddings? The last of them started over an hour ago.'

This time the woman responded.

'I just wanted a photo.'

Marian glanced at her watch.

'Well, now, it could be … which wedding was it? It could be half-eight – nine – maybe later.'

Something in the woman's manner now alarmed Marian. She was smiling, not listening. Marian had the unsettling feeling she had seen her before, earlier in the week, hanging around outside the hotel. 'It's a long wait.'

'No,' the woman said and pointed at the list. 'I want a photo of this.'

'And then,' Marian told Barney, who told me, 'she only goes and hands me the camera and says, "Would you mind?" *Mind?* The hair was standing on the back of my neck. "No," I said, "of course I wouldn't," but the next thing she says, "Hold on, we should have flowers, do you not think?" And she goes over and yanks a couple of carnations from the vase at reception. If you'd seen Nicola's face. "Hey," she says. "You can't touch those." Your woman waves at her as if to say there's no need to get excited. "I'll give you them back in a minute," she says. She's laughing, like, not crazy laughing or anything, just like she's having fun. Even so there's people stopping on their way into the dining room and staring – some guy keeping the lift doors open to give the people in there a look – and I'm standing there like a prune holding her camera, wondering which of the two of us isn't wise and thinking it'd be just my luck if the Master was to come waltzing round the corner, which of course was the worst thing I could have done, for you know what he's like, you no sooner think about him than there he is and there he was and oh, brilliant, I'm saying to myself, why didn't I just walk out the door the second the hands hit six and leave Nicola to deal with this.'

The Master held back a moment trying to take everything in (after all he had been working in hotels a lot longer than Marian) and only when he was certain that something wasn't right did he venture a pace forward and say in that too quiet voice of his, 'Perhaps I can help,' looking from the woman with the flowers to Marian with the camera, and his smile that said, Well, I'm waiting.

'And God alone knows what would have happened next,' said Barney to me, 'if yon fella Bap Connolly hadn't stepped out from somewhere and took the hold of your woman's arm and said, "I wondered what was keeping you," and led her off downstairs to the bars. Marian and the Master both stood looking after them and were still standing there when your woman comes running back up the stairs. "Sorry," she says and takes the camera from Marian and hands the Master the flowers (now, *there* was a photograph, Nicola says) and then off she goes again after Bap.'

10

It was from Barney that I also learned that Fitz and Councillor Noades were having dinner that evening with Clive White.

'I didn't know Fitz and your Clive were such big buddies,' Barney said.

Neither did I, though, if I'd thought about it, I suppose it could only ever have been a matter of time.

Clive White's parents, my own parents told me, had nothing, and their parents before them had even less than that. This was not intended as a put-down, but as a testimony to my second cousin's pedigree. They were good people, Clive's people, was what I was asked to understand. In working-class Belfast, poverty and purity went hand in hand and the highest tribute you could pay a family was that they were poor, but they were honest. Clive early on arrived at the conclusion that being the second was scant compensation for being the first. Honesty, he thought, ought to earn its crust like everything else. He ran errands for elderly neighbours, helped out in corner shops; he played the comb and paper for cinema queues on the Oldpark and Crumlin Roads. The earnings he sank into clothes pegs, bought off a tinker for a penny-ha'penny a dozen and sold door to door for a modest tuppence. Before he was quite twelve years old he was already lending money to school friends, charging interest at a strictly biblical five per cent, but he realised he would be a long time becoming rich by being scrupulous. He started to explore honesty's outer limits, a territory where the pure light that had guided his forebears turned distinctly shady. On leaving school, at the earliest opportunity, he toured the country with a man called Titch, selling crockery from the tailboard of a lorry. Titch supplied the lorry and the crockery, Clive the innocent salesman's face. Titch's own face carried a scar running from the corner of his mouth to his left earlobe, an early lesson in the necessity of shutting up shop and driving the minute your wares were shifted.

Clive learned fast; fast enough to figure out he could do better on his own, though he stayed with Titch almost four years, by which time he knew Northern Ireland inside out. He developed a special fondness for border towns and border people. He admired the pragmatism that could wish the boundary away at the same time as profiting from its existence; he loved the way a cow, say, became less and more than itself when translated across the invisible line and concluded that the only worth a thing had was the amount you could persuade a body to part with for it. Still only twenty, he took the lease on a second-hand shop in Belfast's Gresham Street – a sign above the door said 'Since 1850', which was possibly true for the building itself – and quickly gained the reputation of not caring too much how long the goods he bought had been in their current owner's possession, nor how they came to be there to begin with. Early enquiries from the police revealed a willingness to cut profit margins to the bone when dealing with members of the Royal Ulster Constabulary. Naturally he prospered. At twenty-five he became licensee of his first bar, a dingy but popular affair in the heart of Belfast's docks. The clientele was rarely the same two nights running. Ships and crews came and went, opening Clive's eyes and ears to as yet undreamed of ways of making money. He provided a little side room, at a price of course, to people passing through with business to conduct. Boxes and crates came in by the back door full, and empty were broken up for the barroom fire. He was flexible about closing time, never more so than when the docks' police, finishing a late shift, were in need of a place to have a drink and unwind. Other, bigger premises followed – there was a short-lived interest in a nightclub – but Second Cousin Clive was still of the opinion that he was seeing too little return for his hard work. He decided that the real money lay not in selling the drink over the counter but in selling it into the bars. Using some of the contacts he had picked up during his time in the docks – and renewing old acquaintances along the border – he now established himself as an importer of wines, beers and spirits. His own drinking was increasingly confined to hotel lounge bars, many of which he was, before long, supplying. Barely out of his twenties, he mixed with the better class of businessmen, comfortable in the knowledge that their arrival at respectability, like his own, had not been achieved without cutting a corner or two along the way. Even then, he knew, they were not above doing a deal if one was going. He let it be known that he was broad-minded about the use of his firm's lorries and cultivated certain city councillors whose brief included road construction and slum clearance. (He had made a nice few bob out of the M1 extensions around Portadown and his appetite was whetted.) So, when Fitz landed into town with his talk of investment and the Belfast Urban Motorway, it was not long before Clive White got to hear of it and not long after that before he made an appearance at the International. I think the expression is *like a fly to shite*.

I later found out that he had been hovering around as early as Tuesday morning, though it was Friday afternoon before I saw him myself. Business had just been wound up for the week across the road in City Hall and notice posted for the monthly council meeting the following Wednesday. Both the hotel's bars were loud with the indiscreet conversations of local politicians, all block loans and valuation lists ... and Malvern Street. A motion had been proposed to start clearing houses there. Road-widening for the B.U.M., was what I gathered. I didn't enquire too much. Malvern Street was not a subject anyone in the International wanted to dwell on, though we didn't always have a say in the matter. Only the day before, Rocky Burns, a crony of Peter Ward's killers, had been back in court appealing a firearms conviction.

Fitz was in the thick of the councillors, being tugged this way and that, from Blue Bar to Cocktail Bar and back, looking, I thought, for once a little bewildered. I seemed to hear with his ears all those harsh importuning Belfast voices, *C'm'ere ... Fitz! C'm'ere I want you ... C'm'ere now.* Clive White could not have timed his entrance any better. Materialising just inside the door, drink already in hand, with many smiles and nods to the left of him and the right, he steered his unhurried, unwavering course to Fitz's side. Within minutes neither man was anywhere to be seen.

It turns out, though I did not discover this until some days after, that the two spent most of the rest of Friday evening in the lounge bar of the Royal Avenue Hotel. Padraig Nolan, a barman there, told me they were joined late on by a couple of young women.

'And I mean young. If they hadn't been sitting with Clive, I'd have asked to see their birth certificates.'

A taxi arrived around midnight and the four left together, Fitz linking arms with both girls: party, Padraig got the impression, which perhaps accounted for Fitz's great good humour that Saturday morning when I saw him again in the Blue Bar. Clive White, by all accounts, was in even better humour. He had strolled into the lobby a little before lunch and flirted with Marian. He asked her was I behaving myself and told her she wanted to keep her eye on me. Marian, who had apologised to me once, unnecessarily, that my second cousin gave her the creeps, told him she was well able to look out for herself and Clive White said he didn't doubt it, didn't doubt it for a minute. Nicola got the same charm treatment when Clive returned for dinner. She was still a little agitated by the commotion with the woman in pink and was not displeased by the attention. She looked at Clive in his handsome grey suit, a precise triangle of white hanky peeping from the breast pocket, the camel-hair overcoat that hadn't cost him fourpence over his arm, and she thought how nice it was to see someone who had made the effort. He put her in mind of that English actor who was forever in the papers these days – Oliver Reed; not her type exactly, but impressive nonetheless. It would have been an insult to ask a man like that if he was dressed up for a special occasion; even so something in his manner suggested that tonight was a bit out of the ordinary.

'Shall I get someone to take your coat down to the cloakroom?' she asked.

Clive White squeezed the camel hair a little closer to his side.

'No, don't bother yourself,' he said. 'I'll just keep it with me.'

It was shortly after this that Barney, his shift finished, stopped in at the Blue Bar to fill me in on all that I had been missing upstairs.

'I wouldn't like to be picking up that one,' he said. He meant the bill for the dinner Fitz and Noades and Clive White were just tucking into. 'They've two bottles of champagne ordered up.'

'Ah,' said Hugh, nudging past me to the till, 'the world is ill-divid.'

'Isn't it just,' Barney said, and tugging his scarf up round his ears walked to the door, looking poor but honest and pleased enough with everything except the weather.

*

The bar had begun to fill again. The air was rich with the Saturday night smell of soaps and unguents and slim panatellas. Hugh's mate Liam Strong was back in with his wife, Rita. Rita's hair, set that morning, had an armour-plated look about it. I tried to imagine Liam running his hand through it and then looked at

Liam and tried to imagine Rita wanting him to. There had been talk when they first came in this evening of them going to see *Dr Zhivago*.

'Again,' said Liam.

'What do you mean, again. We missed the first half-hour the last time because I couldn't get you out of here.'

'So,' said Liam, lifting their drinks and winking at Hugh, 'we'll go and see the first half-hour.'

Already though they were installed in their corner like people who had no intention of moving for the rest of the night. Another couple, Acheson I think their name was, had taken the table next to them, the husband shoulder to shoulder with Liam. The two men dropped the odd comment to each other out the sides of their mouths, the women leaning in every so often to talk across them. And there were other familiar faces; at certain moments in the Blue Bar it was easy to forget that there were four storeys of hotel above your head, and residents wandering in looked now and then like people who had turned up at the wrong party. I was beginning to let myself relax into the flow of the evening when Stanley was there again before me, glancing all around the room, not so much for a free seat I guessed as for one that was occupied by a person he recognised. Recognising no one, he perched on the end of a banquette next to two old boys from the Markets who came in every weekend to argue with each other.

'I don't like to tell you,' Hugh said, 'but you just topped that pint of stout up with ale.'

'Frig.'

I poured the head of the pint into the slops tray and then the whole lot down the sink. I put another tumbler under the tap and by the time I was able to leave it settle Jamesie already had Stanley in his sights and was striding down the bar towards him.

'Have you change for the cigarette machine?' the woman I was serving asked.

'*What?*'

'Change for the cigarette machine.'

I took the money from her open palm.

'You might have said.'

'I did, just there now.'

Jamesie was leaning across the counter, chin resting casually on his hand.

'And a box of matches,' the woman said.

I nodded, said nothing. It was too late now. I put as much distance between myself and Jamesie as I could possibly manage.

'Who's next?' I called, louder than was necessary. When I dared look again Jamesie was dribbling lager into a half pint glass which he gripped in his right hand so tight I thought he might break it. Catching my eye he softened his hold and extended his little finger effeminately.

'Next!' I shouted.

When we met at the till a minute or two later, Jamesie told me the whole story.

'Recognise that fella?'

It was useless to pretend.

'Yes,' I said.

'Remember this morning?' Jamesie was going for the full build-up. 'Remember I said he never bought a drink? So I seen him sitting down there now ...'

We moved apart briefly, went to our customers, returned.

'... sitting there like a drink was the last thing on his mind, and I thought, no you don't, it's Saturday fucking night. So I leans across and I says, Can I help you?'

Hugh walked by with four pints in his hands.

'Are you two on go-slow?' he asked.

'Do you see anybody waiting?' Jamesie said, then in the next breath, 'And do you know what he said?'

'A glass of lager,' I said, not wanting to give him the satisfaction of a punch line.

'Did he fuck!' Jamesie was delighted. 'Do you *know* what he said? A glass of water. A glass of fucking water!'

Oh, Stanley, I thought, you absolute prick. Jamesie carried on talking and serving.

'Here's me to him … Four shillings, thanks … Here's me, a glass of water? Certainly. Would you like that in Irish whiskey or in Scotch?' Jamesie broke off a moment to savour his riposte. 'Irish or Scotch. Pick the bones out of that!

'Anyway, he thinks a minute, his hands jigging about the way they do, and then he says, Actually, I think I'll have a half of lager. Actually, I think you're right, I said. Well I could've but I didn't, I was letting him off.'

And for the next few minutes each time I passed him, Jamesie was muttering to himself: 'A glass of water. A glass of fucking water.'

Stanley sat by the old boys from the Markets, fidgeting with his drink, an expression on his face of the purest misery. If I could have gone out there I would have given him a shake and told him to stop making it so hard for me to fall in love with him.

Len's nephew, the tiddler, slipped in behind the bar for a word with Hugh.

'Somebody should put a bell on that wee fella,' Jamesie said. 'I was nearly picking Brylcreem out of the sole of my shoe there.'

Tim Cassidy was taken bad with the flu and was asking to be sent home. Len wanted somebody from the Blue Bar to go up and lend a hand in the Damask Room. Hugh had to bend down to reply.

'Tell Len … Tell your uncle I can't spare anyone. It's going to be mustard in here, you can see yourself.'

('Maybe if you lift him,' Jamesie whispered.)

The kid shrugged and left. Hugh slapped the tap down over a pint pot.

'Tiptoes,' I said to Jamesie and we both crept around him,

shushing the till, the optics and our squeaking shoes for making too much noise.

'Yous're very funny,' Hugh said. 'I'm not having some squirt giving me orders in my bar.'

A minute later the squirt was back. Hugh leaned over again, listened grimly, then straightened.

'OK,' he said. 'But as long as it's only an hour.'

He turned to the sink, flipped on the cold water and let it run over his wrists and along his manicured fingers.

'Jamesie, Danny, toss a coin,' he said, and we knew better this time than to make fun.

Jamesie called heads, the penny came down tails.

'Jammy bastard.'

'You can go if you want.'

'Wise up,' Jamesie said. 'You won, didn't you?'

There was no point arguing with him. They mightn't have been obvious to everyone, but Jamesie had rules and you had to abide by the decision of the coin. Besides, the tips were now up in the function rooms and I could talk my way out of all the nurses' parties in the world, but Jamesie would never have forgiven me for not accepting my luck in getting a cut of a second pool. I left Stanley with his quarter-pint of lager, still waiting for whoever it was he had been waiting for since half-eleven this morning (I let myself believe his face fell further as I rounded the corner out of the bar), and hopped up the stairs to the Long Corridor.

Cecil the night porter was standing by the cloakroom hatch fumbling at the knobs of a large tape recorder, watched by old Hamish the cloakroom attendant. As I approached, Cecil, his ear resting almost on top of the machine, jabbed the play button. There was a loud hiss. Cecil jerked back. A woman said, *Cecil, you've that too far away from the TV.*

'Norma,' Cecil explained. 'And I had not it too far away.'

He turned the volume to a whisper, jabbed another button and the tape ran forward from one rickety spool to the other. The next time he pressed play he took care to listen in first before turning the volume back up.

'... engines from as far away as Lisburn ...'

'That's Ivor Mills,' I said. Cecil grimaced at me and I fell quiet looking with him and Hamish at the flittering brown tape.

'Cecil Parker,' (Hamish glanced up at him, Cecil nodded) 'you arrived on the scene shortly after the fire broke out?'

A boy's voice shouted *Linfield*, there was a scuffle, Cecil said, 'I did, yes'. There was a moment's silence.

'And the fire had already taken quite a hold?'

'It had, yes.'

'So ...' Ivor Mills searched for a question. 'Would you say the people inside had a lucky escape?'

'I would, yes.'

Cecil stopped the tape. Hamish gave an appreciative whistle.

'Is that it?' I asked.

'What do you mean, is that it?' Cecil placed a protective hand on the tape recorder. 'That was on the *news*.'

'They'll have heard that all the way over in Omagh,' Hamish said. If it had been anyone else I would have suspected a joke, but jokes were not in Hamish's nature.

'Strabane,' he added helpfully, though it was clear from Cecil's expression that this was no help at all.

(He was in a world of his own in that cloakroom, Marian said. Jamesie, more direct, would shout sometimes from the bottom of the stairs, 'Hamish, you can come out, the war's over!')

The door of the Damask Room opened. A plump man with a napkin still tucked into his belt made haste for the adjacent toilets. His lead was followed a second or two later by four more men in a tight pack. The formalities were over. By the time I entered, the lower tables were already being cleared away and the guests were dragging their chairs towards the sides of the room.

Those guests, that is, who weren't already at the bar. I ducked under that counter like Audie Murphy.

'Sorry, I'm late,' I told Lar the lone barman. 'Heard you were having a spot of bother.'

Flashes came from the far end of the room where the photographer was still busy with the top table. I could make out neither bride nor groom, but saw Michael and Janet standing on the sidelines, watching over proceedings like a third set of parents.

The band began tuning up to the left of the bar, a drummer, a seated guitarist, a double bass player and a singer I thought I recognised from the entertainments pages, who sat for the moment beside the guitarist, the bulbous end of a microphone resting on her knees. A saxophone lay across a third chair and a man, dressed like the other musicians in a pale-blue shirt and knitted tie, hunkered in a corner of the low stage adjusting the tripod of a music stand.

'Who's the group?' I asked Lar.

'Thelma Beckett. Apparently the groom wanted Deirdre and the Defenders, but the bride's father wouldn't hear of it.'

'You wouldn't get music stands with Deirdre and the Defenders,' I said.

'Some would say you wouldn't even get music,' said Lar.

The main lights went down on the room and there was a second rush for the bar as guests tried to get a drink in before the dancing started. Thelma Beckett rose to her feet. They were small feet and made to seem even smaller by the back-lift of her stiletto heels on which she stood a touch over five-feet tall. Two bluish spotlights fell together on her microphone, catching the sequins stitched into her dress, another came to rest just short of the room's central pillars and waited there until the bride and groom walked into it at the same moment as Thelma began to sing 'Moon River'. The couple waltzed, happier than any couple might think they have a right to expect, the spotlight followed them down the maple floor towards Lar and me, then drifted with them across the face of the stage where the band played and Thelma sang, dream-makingly, heart-achingly, and the rainbow's end was her dress as she moved her weight from one minute foot to the other and back, and the rainbow's end was the slow-turning mirror-ball suspended above the heads of the four parents as they swapped partners and joined their children on the dance floor.

It was a relief when the saxophone at last let go of the melody and the drums and double bass upped the tempo. The floor filled with shuffling couples, leaving me to get on with the business of selling drink to men who would not or could not dance.

The groom had been separated from his new wife and after being passed from one mother to the next and dallying briefly to twist with a dubious but finally delighted aunt, he arrived in the middle of a ruck of his mates at the bar.

'Congratulations,' I said.

He grinned in a way I could imagine would inspire devotion.

'Give this man a pint before he dies of thirst,' one of his mates said, and half a dozen hands vied to pay for it.

'The first one's on the house,' I said.

'You'll not be getting out for too many more of those!'

'Not at all! He'll put his foot down from the start, won't you, Joe?'

Joe only grinned again. He brought the glass to his lips and kissed the rim like he might the back of his bride's neck, the insteps of her stockinged feet. The friends cheered and he drank.

The bride arrived a minute later hitching her crystal nylon shoulder straps as Joe's friends made way.

'See your Uncle Fred,' she said.

Lar poured her a Babycham and she said, 'I shouldn't,' and lifted it anyway. Little clots of make-up had formed in the damp creases at the sides of her nose. I imagined the slope of her bottom under her dress where the groom's hand rested, the cool clamminess of exertion, and I envied them each the other when they kissed.

After an hour, the bar traffic became more sedate and one of the waiters came in behind the counter with Lar to let me away. Half-talking, half-singing, Thelma Beckett told how the candy-coloured clown they call the sandman tiptoed into her room every night. I never heard her dreams begin.

11

Gallant Ted Connolly, having rescued on a whim the young woman he now knew to be called Ingrid Titterington ('Plarmed and cheased,' he said), ordered his fourth pint of the still-young night, his eighth since lunchtime – not to mention the several large tumblers of whiskey he had drunk in his room for dinner – and fell head-forward-on-his-chest asleep after one wondrous gulp. Ingrid waited to see would he wake, then glanced about to see had anyone noticed him drop off. A bored boy who looked like he might be awaiting the arrival of his first pubic hair rubbed the back of his head against the flock paper by the Cocktail Bar door. Behind the counter, a man in a white coat inserted the blunt end of a pencil into one veiny ear. Among the customers conversation was as low as the light from the half-moon fittings on the barroom walls. Whether it was politeness or what, no one so much as glanced at the footballer snoring gently at Ingrid's elbow.

Immediately prior to his passing out, Ted Connolly had been explaining to her the potentially hazardous complications of a septic toe, an explanation that she was mostly sure had nothing to do with dressing up as a cow, though it had followed on quite seamlessly from that topic. In the previous ninety minutes Ingrid had had replayed for her the highlights and lowlights of the current Sunderland league campaign and been given – strictly off the record, now – a gloomy forecast for the remainder of the season. She felt as though, were Ted's injury to be longer than predicted healing, she could slot in quite comfortably to the Sunderland forward line in his place and anticipate every pass and feint of her team-mates. She herself had contributed little to the conversation. Ted Connolly (he told her early on he didn't care for the nickname Bap) had quickly forgotten to be intrigued by what she had been doing in the lobby of the International that attracted such attention, or why she had being doing it. Which suited Ingrid just fine. She was glad of the opportunity not to think for a while, but now Ted was asleep and showing no immediate signs of waking and Ingrid's mind was let loose to wander again. She waited a few moments more and then, taking her camera and her bag, followed the direction of her thoughts upstairs towards the Damask Room, which was how I came at last to meet her face-to-face as I pushed open the function room door.

I had a pretty good idea then what was going on and Ingrid, I think, knew it. She took a pace back, performed a half-turn and then came back to face me; it was all she could do to keep from smiling.

'It's the letter burner,' she said.

Her ears stuck out a little, but maybe that was the hat. I don't know where her veil had gone.

'I thought I'd enter into the spirit of the day,' I said.

She looked at me, puzzled.

'Brand's.' I pointed to the camera. 'I saw you there this morning.'

I was conscious that I was keeping myself between her and the Damask Room's smoked-glass doors.

'Yes,' she said, 'I've been …'

'And at the back of the City Hall. You took a picture of me and my friend.'

She peered at me more closely.

'I was wearing a duffel coat, you probably wouldn't have made the connection ... the bow tie and everything.'

'No, I remember now.' She seemed quite pleased by this. 'Isn't that funny, you're in my collection.'

'You'll have to send me a copy.'

I thought she looked doubtful, then realised from the sudden burst of music that the door had opened behind me. Mr McAdam, the bride's father, sidled past us into the toilets. I decided it might be a good idea if we didn't hang about there too much longer. I took a gamble.

'This wouldn't be about Joe, would it?'

She pressed her lips tight together and I worried that she might be about to cry, but I couldn't have been more wrong. She held my gaze as she shook her head and her eyes remained quite clear.

'He should be so lucky.'

The toilet door was yanked back. The bride's father nodded to us out of his bride's father's reverie.

'Evening.'

I replied for both of us and thrust my hand out to my new acquaintance before she could add anything of her own.

'I'm Danny,' I said.

She frowned, thrown for the moment.

'*Danny*,' I repeated, waggling my fingers.

'Ingrid,' Ingrid said, and placed her hand in mine. I was already walking.

'I've got to get back to work,' I said. 'In the Blue Bar, have you been there? You'd like it. Everybody likes the Blue Bar. You should come in for a drink.'

We were halfway down the stairs before I let go of her hand.

'I suppose you think that's clever,' she said.

I thought about lying, decided against it.

'A bit,' I said.

A guest pushed by, heading up. Ingrid carried on down a step. I tucked in behind her.

'You can't stop me going back up there,' she said over her shoulder.

'No,' I said, 'but I don't think you should.'

She turned abruptly on the bottom stair.

'Why?'

'Just because.'

'Great argument, Danny.'

She threw up her hands in an ironic gesture of surrender, her thumb caught the brim of her hat and sent it skidding across the floor. Her hair was a dirty fair and flat. She glowered at the hat as though it were a living thing. I think she would have been happy to leave it where it lay.

'Bloody hat, I should never have bought it. Even the woman in the shop said so.'

She pushed her fingers through her hair. It fell back limp against her cheek.

'The suit's lovely,' I said.

'Thank you. Swiss Arcade. It's hard to know what to wear.'

I picked up the hat and she took it from me, cuffing the crown with the back of her hand.

'Stupid thing.'

She paused at the door of the Cocktail Bar. I remembered what Barney had told me about her and Ted Connolly.

'Are you with someone?'

She shook her head and followed me into the Blue Bar. I pointed her to a free seat, but before I could ask her what she was drinking Hugh called to me:

'Danny Boy. Two pints of Double. Fella in the corduroy jacket.'

As soon as I was able I took Jamesie aside. 'Listen, the woman just came in, in the pink outfit … Don't let her see you looking … Sitting under the telly.'

Jamesie scanned the mirror until he found her.

'Would you keep a wee eye out for her?'

'You sniffing?'

Old suave Jamesie.

'You are, aren't you?' And this time, instead of saying the word he performed the action, hoovering the air with his nose. There was no way I was going to convince him otherwise.

'OK, I am, I'm sniffing.'

Jamesie smacked his lips. He put an arm round my shoulder. I was reminded that he hadn't been home to wash or change since yesterday lunchtime.

'Don't you worry, Danny Boy, anybody tries to make a move on her ...'

'Jamesie, just let me know if she looks like she's going to leave.'

It was standing room only now. I couldn't see Stanley anywhere. I hadn't really expected to, which isn't to say I hadn't been hoping. I sought out Ingrid through the crowd. Above her head Gary Cooper or Randolph Scott, I could never tell them apart, worked a guy over with his bare knuckles. Ingrid saw me look her way and smiled. I don't know if I smiled back; I was half wondering whether I might be able to make her fall for me. I was surprised at myself. Ingrid crossed her eyes and leaned back against the wall. Randolph, or Gary, whichever was in *High Noon*, wound up for the killer blow. *Biff.*

12

Ingrid Titterington, she confided in me a few weeks later, before she disappeared off the face of the earth, or went to Enniskillen, as Hugh maintained, made it her business the summer of her sixteenth birthday to sleep with as many boys of her acquaintance as she was able to. Her ex-best friend, Judith Waters, had pronounced her frigid one afternoon on the bus home from school, since when Ingrid had endured endless taunts and slaggings from Judith's new friends who seemed to Ingrid to number by now almost the entire fourth form girls.

She started the Monday of the first week of the holidays with Norman Pavis, Judith's boyfriend (Judith, she decided, was welcome to him: smelly dick), and carried on, the following Thursday, with Ian Sinclair round the back of the changing rooms at the King George V playing fields, Sydenham. Barry Lemon did it with her more or less non-stop two Saturday nights later on the carpet of the McAteers's front room where Ingrid was babysitting the McAteers's dead-to-the-world toddler, Sue, and did it with her again, frantically, the next morning in the long grass just out of sight of his own back garden while his parents called up and down the street telling him to come on and get into the car or they were going on holiday without him.

Walking home alone later that morning Ingrid congratulated herself on her flying start, calculating that at the current rate she should reach double figures by the middle of August. She even thought she was beginning to enjoy it. And then, just when she least wanted to, she found herself falling in love.

Albert Kennedy had taken over the Co-op milk float from his Uncle George, who had woken up the neighbourhood every morning for a decade with his smoker's cough and had finally died a fortnight before of lung cancer. Albert was lean, long-legged and eighteen and from the day and hour Ingrid saw him, standing at her front door in his brown overall with the leather satchel slung across the chest, she could think of no one else.

'No cream last Sunday?' he asked her. 'That's five-and-four, then.'

Barry Lemon came back from the Isle of Man with his dick practically poking out of his trousers, but he was ten days too late. Though he pleaded with her and cajoled, though he took to standing at dead of night under the lamppost outside her bedroom window and even threatened to tell her parents (till Ingrid pointed out that whatever her father did to her, he would definitely beat seven kinds of shite out of Barry), Ingrid was unbending. She didn't care any more what Judith Waters called her, she didn't care if her tally of lovers never got above four – and in truth she was sorry now about the first three – she wanted Albert and Albert alone. The only problem was that Albert did not want her, though as he was at pains to explain the night she followed him around the neighbourhood on his collecting round, he had nothing against Ingrid personally, it was just that his heart was already pledged elsewhere. Albert Kennedy, it turned out, was the best-looking Seventh Day Adventist in Belfast; girl-friends, in the church or out of it, did not at present figure in his plans. If there was one thing the experiences of that summer had taught Ingrid, however, it was that all teenage boys could be won round sooner or later. (NB Judith Waters, twenty-five seconds in the case of Norman Pavis.) So, like a penitent going to prayer, she dragged herself out of bed every morning before it was quite light and waited at the open blinds for the battery-powered whine of Albert's float. For two weeks he delivered the family's daily pinta right into her hands, torn between answering her daily more complex theological questions and carrying on with his rounds, before finally he caved in and asked her would she like to sit up with him in his cab so that they could talk more. As she walked out to the milk float Ingrid saw two dogs sniffing and baying over a knot of Kleenex at the base of the nearest lamppost. Barry Lemon had not yet given up.

Albert Kennedy ceased to be a Seventh Day Adventist early one August morning in a secluded corner of Ormeau Park. He had dropped Ingrid off at the park gates before swinging round into Ravenhill Avenue and the Co-op depot, and then returned on foot with the intention of explaining to her the precise date of the Second Coming. The next morning, while everyone else was at work, they slipped back to Ingrid's own house – Ingrid's parents own double bed – and the next morning and the next and by the time Sunday came around Albert had barely enough energy to stagger to the nearest Episcopalian church, where his conscience slumbered untroubled through the booming empty sermon.

Ingrid was the first girl of her year to get engaged. Her parents were pleased. Even Judith Waters deemed her worthy of a new respect.

'Haven't you done well for yourself, snaring him?' she said.

Already, though, Ingrid had ceased to regard snaring Albert Kennedy as much of an achievement. *All I did was open my legs.*

After the bliss of those summer mornings bumping through the east Belfast streets in the milk float, the thrill of falling, being in love was curiously void of excitement. She looked at the joyless faces of the women on the streets where she lived. Married one and all. It wasn't Albert she had trapped but herself. And Albert too had changed. He watched her jealously, wanting to know where she had been, who she had been talking to, what

111

she was thinking. Ingrid swore that as soon as she got out of love with him she would never let herself fall in love again. It took her two years to engineer the fight that led to Albert asking for his ring back. Afterwards she couldn't understand why it hadn't occurred to her earlier. One day when Albert, finding her daydreaming by a window, asked her what she was thinking – 'Truthfully?' she asked him. 'Truthfully …' – she told him she was remembering the boys there had been before she met him.

Things, not surprisingly, were pretty gruesome for a while, still she comforted herself that she was a wiser person for the whole sorry business.

Ingrid had found work in a draughtsman's office and went to the tech on day release to study mechanical drawing. She was paid a pittance to begin with, but it was her money to do with what she would. She signed up for evening classes in art history and photography, she subscribed to magazines and periodicals, poetry and politics, and saw every film, good and bad, in Belfast. Her friends now were other tech students; she went with them to the Maritime round the corner from the college, to the Orpheus and the Boom Boom Room. R'n'B was their thing and Ingrid would dance until her hair collapsed in damp bangs and the teeth ached in her head. There were boyfriends, of course, but strictly on her own terms. She liked the touch of a man's hands on her waist as they stood kissing outside a ballroom, once in a while she liked letting herself be undressed, the cold slap of her nakedness before she was entangled in arms and blankets, but after a few weeks she would bring the affair to a polite end. Pangs – and she did sometimes have them – were preferable to the slow souring of romance. Besides, times were changing, or such at least was the conclusion she had drawn from her magazines and periodicals. In one of these she read the oath of allegiance sworn by the free citizens of Aragon in the Middle Ages to their king:

> We who are as good as you, swear to you who are not better than we, to accept you as our king and sovereign lord, provided that you observe all our liberties and laws; but if not, then not.

If not, then not. It seemed to Ingrid as good a principle as any to live by. She cut the article out and pinned it to her bedroom wall.

She met Joe two days after her nineteenth birthday at a party in a firetrap of a flat off University Street. Joe had just graduated from the art college and was going to be a major painter, i.e. he had fuck all money, less even than the fuck all most of Ingrid's friends had: fuck all at all. He lived on crisps and apples and was famous for having made a single black coffee last two days in a city centre café. Apparently he'd left the half-full mug behind a radiator overnight. He smoked most of the packet of cigarettes that Ingrid had bought for the party. She bought another box when she met him for a drink the next day and he smoked most of those as well. Ingrid didn't mind, she had just been awarded a pay rise with the promise of a bigger one when she finished her course the following June. Anyway, she enjoyed talking to Joe. He argued with her that Ellsworth Kelly was a more important painter than Jackson Pollock – everything you needed to know about him, it seemed, was summed up in the precise sliver of white border down the left edge of Broadway – and said that Andy Warhol would be remembered more for his haircut than his canvases. A lot of what he said was bravado – he'd rather eat his own leg than compromise his art to make a fast buck (Joe liked to talk as though he was in Greenwich Village) – but she accepted that this was a necessary part of the process for him, before he could convince anyone else he had to convince himself. Ingrid was convinced from the day, a week after they first met, that he showed her his paintings. They were in a damp shed at the bottom of somebody's garden on the Cliftonville Road. Joe was paying thirty shillings a week for the use of this 'studio'. The windows were hung with greying net curtains tied in a knot to admit a weedy light. For warmth he had a paraffin heater, which gave the place the air of a thwarted picnic. The sheets of hardboard he painted on were solid blocks of colour with titles like *The gods dispute their divinity*. Ingrid didn't pretend the

113

paintings meant anything to her, but there was a rigour in their execution that she could only admire.

Interests weren't all they shared. They were both, they discovered early on, the oldest child in a family of four; both had two sisters and one brother. Both, though this came out much later, lost their virginity at the same age. Spooky. The dissimilarities, however, were what really made Ingrid's hair stand on end.

Joe's family hailed from a market town in county Tyrone. He and his two sisters and one brother had grown up in a three-bedroom house his parents shared with his mother's own father and mother and their son, Joe's uncle, also called Joe. His parents had had their name on a council waiting list since they were married and each time a child was born they called at the council offices to see were they any closer to the top of the list, but always it seemed there were people whose need was more urgent. It wasn't that there were no council houses to be had, there were, just not in Joe's parents' part of town. And it wasn't that Joe's parents cared particularly which part of town they lived in, they didn't care about anything beyond getting a house of their own; but the council cared, the council cared very much. The council had ward boundaries to think of, majorities to return where no majority existed. It was a hard old job, people didn't know the half of it.

Ingrid was not stupid, though you didn't need to be especially clever to see that more than one local government in Northern Ireland could not have stood without the aid of substantial rigging, even so she was staggered by the cold calculation that crammed two families – three generations: four children and five adults – into the one house.

'It could have been worse,' Joe said. 'The toilet could have been inside taking up room.'

They were spending more and more of their free time together. They told one another about the people they fancied and if either had a date they would meet the following day to go over the evening in detail: what way did he kiss? What did her hair smell like? How far did you go? Joe called Ingrid his buddy and she liked that. They were buddies for some months before they found themselves in his room, a forty-minute walk from his studio shed, removing each other's clothes, all their buddy fingers thumbs, and lying in bed locked in a shocked embrace, hardly daring to breathe for fear of touching more. The second time they slept together they had no such inhibitions, but tore into making love with a ferocity that would have embarrassed them both had they been with anyone else. He screamed, she screamed, the people in the rooms either side hammered on the walls. They were a little surprised, disappointed even, when they were finished, to find the ceiling still intact.

Of course they weren't seeing each other, not *seeing* seeing. It was a kind of friendship-with-sex thing. All the same they soon stopped talking about fancying other people.

That Christmas Ingrid bought Joe a present. The previous few wintry weeks he had been trekking across town to the Cliftonville Road each day in the same windcheater he had been wearing when she got to know him in the summer. He would arrive in the city to meet her in the evenings, shivering and blowing on his hands, scarlet with cold. There was a tweed overcoat Ingrid had been looking at in the window of Anderson McAuley's, not cheap, but she was due a Christmas bonus; she let herself be persuaded that Joe would accept the gift as a share in her windfall. The parcel sat on the seat between them their last night out before he went back to Tyrone. She had wanted him to open it, but now, seeing his stricken expression, hoped desperately that he wouldn't. Joe obliged her by not so much as glancing at it once. Ingrid was not entirely sure how he managed to smuggle it out of the bar without her seeing.

She didn't hear from him again for a fortnight. Then, coming out of Mooney's one January evening with a girlfriend, she bumped into him as he hurried through the rain towards Arthur Street. He still had on the windcheater. Ingrid's friend took herself off to look in a shop window.

'When did you get back?' Ingrid asked.

'Sunday. I was going to call you at work.'

Ingrid shrugged.

'You're soaked,' she said.

'I missed you,' he said and then he kissed her.

He wore the overcoat eventually. Thanked her for it too, but told her she shouldn't have. She said she knew, he said but *really* she shouldn't have.

'I *know*,' she said. 'But it does look gorgeous on you.'

It was around then that Ingrid realised she was in love and though on some level she understood it was a necessary condition of love that each time felt like the first time, she began to think she could never have truly loved Albert Kennedy. She was nervous, naturally, this was not what she had planned for herself, but she watched as Joe arrived at the same conclusion, as surprised, she believed, as she was, and she thought if ever love had a chance it was this love, so softly entered into.

Through spring and into summer she sat at her desk in the draughtsman's office, a model of conscientiousness, rewarding herself with certain minutes in the day when she would lay down her pencil and think of Joe. Nights they stayed together she held on to him and when he recounted to her his disappointments, the paintings that had not come off, the galleries unwilling to take a risk, she told him that she was certain his time would come and told herself that even if it never did she would be there to make sure he was always able to carry on. He had at last allowed her to buy canvases for him and sometimes when money was impossibly tight he accepted without complaint her gifts of brushes and paints: an investment, she assured him, against the day when he was rich and famous.

Towards the end of September a thunderstorm took the roof off the Cliftonville Road shed. The owner said there was nothing for it but to knock it down and build a sturdier one. He let it be known he would be looking double the money if Joe wanted to return there to work. Joe, needless to say, didn't have double the money or anything like it and when Ingrid offered to pay a percentage he lost the rag shouting at her that he wasn't a charity case yet. He moped around for a week or so, too forlorn to search out another studio.

'What's the point? They're all too dear.'

And then Ingrid really was in no doubt that she loved him, because even as she wanted to slap him, her heart ached to see him so despondent.

The evening of the day she decided to move out of home and rent a flat – two bedrooms, 'You're going to have to pay your way,' she would say, 'but you'll have your own place to paint' – he met her after work, hopping from foot to foot, from the kerb to the road to the kerb again. He had run into a friend from art college whose parents had a cottage in Donegal which he could have for nothing till Christmas or even Easter. Ingrid tried hard to be pleased. She thought about mentioning the flat idea, but he was so full of Donegal and the solitude and the light that she let it go. When he gets back, she told herself.

'Can I come and visit you?' she asked.

'Every weekend.'

'How about every other weekend?'

'It's a deal.'

Only when he had gone did she notice how much of her old life she had let slip in the last few months. She was too late to sign up for her night classes, so she joined a camera club which met every Tuesday behind a barber's shop in Lower Garfield Street. Ingrid was the only woman and the only member under thirty. Her presence seemed to unsettle one half of the men and titillate the other half. After three weeks the discussion turned to hiring a life model – the same life model, possibly, as last year? – and Ingrid decided to forget to go back.

She wrote to Joe two or three times a week, not love letters exactly, though there were nights when she allowed her longing for him to saturate the page, but letters nevertheless intimate with the minute details of her days. And to begin with Joe wrote back.

He even returned to Belfast at the end of the first month, saving her the trouble of taking a Friday off work to travel to Donegal. Ingrid couldn't remember a better weekend; for days after his departure she felt the ghostly shape of him reaching right up into her stomach. In her euphoria she took the plunge and rented a flat. One bedroom, but the sitting room was enormous, with a south-facing window where you would have no trouble imagining an easel. Soon afterwards Joe's letters stopped. She waited a week before calling at her parents' house, but there was nothing there for her either. She wrote every day asking Joe was he all right; she hunted down his Belfast mates to see had they had any word.

'You know Joe,' his mates said, and even as she said yes Ingrid wondered if she really did.

In the end she contacted his mother and father: *Excuse me for writing like this, but I'm a friend of Joe's and I was just wondering* … It was obvious from the first line of his mother's polite reply that his parents had never heard of her. The second line was even worse. They had seen Joe the previous week, with Anne. He was looking very well, if a bit thin. Anne was a lovely girl.

Still trembling, Ingrid walked straight out to the post office, the letter mangled in her hand, and telegrammed the cottage in Donegal, demanding to know what was going on. She went two nights without sleep, and got into trouble for dozing off at her desk. When she arrived home from work on the third night an envelope lay waiting for her in the hallway. Ingrid took the envelope into the flat and set it on the mantelpiece opposite the south-facing window. She made herself beans on toast, a pot of tea, and ate her meal sitting on the sofa looking anywhere but at the fireplace. Then she washed the dishes. She picked up the letter at length as though its contents were a matter of no importance. She was eating a dry cream cracker, one unbroken edge of which jutted from her mouth, forcing the corners into a tight grin. The letter was one long apology. Ingrid read to the point where he told her that he and Anne were to be married ('I don't know how to say this, I need her'), then folded the letter and the cracker crumbs into the envelope and placed it back on the mantelpiece. She was halfway to the bathroom when she threw up.

'I never want to go through another couple of months like it,' Ingrid said to me. This was late March; she had heard on the grapevine that Joe had gone to work for Anne's father. 'I'm only lucky I didn't lose my job, though God knows it was a close-run thing.'

She got a doctor's line for the first week, but she was twice as bad by the end of it as she had been at the start. The boss turned a blind eye for a day or two more, then called her into his office.

'This isn't good enough, is it?' he said.

He was thumbing through a pile of line drawings. Ingrid tilted her head trying to see what it was he wasn't happy with. He slapped his hand down, making her jump.

'You're on another planet, wee girl.'

He wasn't a bad sort, Ingrid's boss, but she hated it when he lost his temper; even more, she hated it when he called her wee girl.

'You're a good worker, I don't want to have to let you go.'

He was leaning forward across the desk looking up into her lowered eyes. Ingrid drained them of everything that might betray her.

'If I find out all this is over some boy ...'

Ingrid remained silent. The boss straightened up, shook his head.

'Have it your way, just don't say I didn't warn you.'

He had returned to the drawings on his desk. His hair was combed back, the strands straight as telephone wires over his freckled scalp. Ingrid imagined him at his bathroom mirror and wondered how he convinced himself he was other than he was, an unimpressive man. He would be here until he retired, but she only had to keep her head and sooner or later she would move on to better things. He was right, she was a good worker.

The boss glanced up again as if to ask why she was still there.

'Nothing like this will happen again,' Ingrid said. 'I promise.'

In retrospect, she said, she had probably begun planning the wedding day that afternoon as she left his office. There were times indeed in the weeks that followed when the plans were all that held her together. *Now don't get maudlin*, she'd scold herself. *You've got to make sure and do this right.* She would have to dress for the occasion, of course, something bright; it was a celebration after all. And she would have to take photographs: preserve the memories. Yes, there would have to be photographs, from the beginning of the day to the end. She wanted to have a complete record of how her world looked the day she gave up on love for ever.

13

Half past eight on a Saturday evening in a busy bar. A blessed
time, I used to think – before McGurk's, before McLaughlin's,
before the Four Step Inn, the Mountainview Tavern, the
Crescent Bar, before Loughinisland – the time when you were
most likely to feel yourself in communion with other bars in
other cities and towns and villages too small to merit a mention
on the map. In grander hotels than ours, in gin palaces and
lounges and saloons and corner bars and houses where it was still
possible to comprehend how fine the line had once been between
private and public, people were gathered at half past eight on a
Saturday night, money in their pocket and a drink in their hand.
Good people, bad people and people no better than they ought
to be. The week's end. I could never find it in me to dislike this
hour, no matter how swamped we were, no matter how raggedly
the night might conclude. There was an ease that settled on a bar
then, a smoothness like a machine oiled, not too well, but just so.
Everything at half past eight on a Saturday night felt earned. It
would break your heart if you let it.

At eight thirty-one in the Blue Bar a glass smashed; a hush
descended like a fire blanket; Tommy Cooper said *What? What?*
and the studio audience laughed; a hand went up in the far left

corner of the barroom, a shout accompanying it – 'Accident!';
Tommy Cooper's shoulders shook, the tassel on his fez shook;
the conversations in the Blue Bar reignited.

'Spillage!' Hugh called.

I was closest to the hatch. I dropped to my hunkers and
stepped out Cossack-style on to the other side. 'Gangway,' I said.
'Gangway.'

I had said at least another twenty by the time I returned from
the store behind the Cocktail Bar with the mop. The man who
had dropped the glass was laying towelling mats on the blue vinyl
seats, where drink had splashed. A woman standing by the table
held the hem of her lavender dress; a stain spread darkly between
her wide apart knees. Her laugh was loud and hoarse.

'Oh, heavens, Myrtle,' she said. 'Look at the state of me.'

Myrtle I took to be the woman in the cultured-pearl necklace
who was hoisting her bottom out of the way of the towelling
mats and working a knuckle into the corner of each eye. Every
time she thought it safe to prise her lids apart she would take one
look at her friend and splutter with laughter again.

'Fi,' was all she could say, unable to muster the strength to
voice a V. 'Fi.'

Vi performed a little dance for my benefit.

'Sir, sir, I *did* put my hand up but it came through my fingers.'

A tear appeared on Myrtle's cheek. The man with the mats
was red in the face, whether from embarrassment at spilling the
drink or at Vi's antics I couldn't say. I decided he and Vi were
husband and wife.

'It just slipped out of my mitt,' he said.

'You're not the first person ever broke a glass in this bar,' I
told him. I picked the larger shards of the pint pot off the floor
and set them in the ashtray.

'Watch you your fingers on that glass,' he said, to me I
thought, until I heard Vi's voice mocking:

'God, and there was me just about to grab the hold of it.'

Bending over I spied the glass's thick base against the wall, upright amongst the butts and betting slips and bits fallen out of sandwiches. I fished under the seat with the mop. The glass came out reluctantly. When I was finally able to reach it with my hand I found there was still drink in the bottom.

'There you go, Chester,' Vi said. 'He saved you some.'

Most names I find, no matter how unlikely, cease to be a surprise the second after they are spoken. Chester's came to rest on him like a borrowed bowler hat, ill-fitting, faintly ridiculous. He sighed as though disheartened by the reminder of it. I tried to transfer the glass, liquid and all to the ashtray. Two inches short, the beer spilled over my fingers. Chester offered me his handkerchief.

'Thanks, I'm fine,' I said, and swirled the mop around the beer-darkened carpet. The strands grew grey and twisted. I spun the handle until the mop head formed a tighter ball and then forced it against the sieve in the stern of the bucket. The liquid that dribbled on to the galvanised base seemed incommensurate with the amount that had been spilled. I tested the carpet with the toe of my shoe. Beer bubbled up dirtily. I swabbed some more. Again the yield, when I squeezed the mop into the bucket, was meagre. Too bad, that would have to do.

'You all right?' I asked.

Vi made a drinking motion with her arm and nodded towards Chester.

'He wasn't all right to begin with,' she said. Chester smiled, resigned, and not for the last time I suspected, to being the butt of their humour.

'I can't think how I did it.'

'It's a bar, things break,' I said again. 'Don't worry yourself.'

As I was taking the mop and bucket back out to the storeroom I saw Ingrid come away from the counter carrying a drink.

'First of many?' she asked.

'I hope not.' I nodded at the glass in her hand. 'You?'

She wrinkled her nose.

'Nah. This is me and then I'm off.'

'Home?' I asked, and then took a dunt between the shoulders that nearly sent me, the mop and bucket flying.

'Sorry, fella.' A big hand on my upper arm righted me. 'Some ignorant gaunch knocked me into you.'

I had stumbled several feet from Ingrid, who even as I located her again was being forced back further by the jockeying that followed the bumps and shoves.

'Let me know when you're going,' I called to her, telling myself that I only wanted to make sure she did in fact leave the hotel.

Ingrid cupped a hand behind her ear.

'When ... you're ... going,' I repeated and this time she nodded like she'd heard me, like she meant it. I faced into the throng shouting, 'Gangway. Mop coming through.'

A path was cleared before me.

Out in the back hall Ted Connolly was standing uncertainly, writing on a napkin. Before him, blocking my way, a silver-haired woman, dressed as though for a particularly low church service, jigged like a schoolgirl, her eyes level with the footballer's slow-moving hand. At the top of the stairs a man waited, inspecting his shoes. Ted ground the biro to a full stop. The woman snatched the napkin back and read the inscription aloud.

'To Dermot and Dorothy with ... fondest regards, Ted Connolly.'

She practically skipped up the stairs.

'Look what he wrote, Dermot.'

Dermot looked everywhere but at the napkin which he shoved into his pocket unexamined. Ted Connolly went on standing, swaying a little, holding the pen out, and for a moment I didn't know whether to carry on forward or go back the way I had come. The mop shaft clanged against the side of the bucket. The famed fair-haired bap swivelled on its thick neck. Ted eyed me narrowly as though wondering was I the reason he had come out here in the first place. He wagged the pen a couple of times, struggling to remember. I struggled to say something, anything.

'Good result yous had the day.'

The wagging pen fell to the floor and I thought maybe I'd said the wrong thing. (It was Sunderland he played for? They *had* won?) Ted's stare drifted from me to the pen lying crosswise on the beige and blue tiles. I set the bucket down, scooped the pen up and reached out my hand to return it. His face suddenly cleared. He took hold of my wrist and signed my cuff, then handing me the pen turned and walked back towards the Cocktail Bar.

'Moo,' he said. Or maybe it was 'more'.

Jamesie offered to buy the shirt off me, or at least the cuff. He tried pressing his own cuff against mine to see would the signature transfer.

'You can make out the b,' he said, scrutinising the blue smudge, then frowning: '*b?*'

'Why don't you just ask him yourself?'

'I wouldn't give the man the satisfaction,' Jamesie said, but when I offered him the pen Ted Connolly had used he accepted it readily enough. For weeks afterwards he carried the biro clipped into his shirt pocket and, when he had occasion to, he didn't so much take it out as flourish it:

I bet you a million pounds you'll never guess whose pen this is?

Hugh had nipped out to the toilet. Oscar moved into position on the other side of the bar from me. Oscar was a deaf mute, from over Annadale direction. He sometimes had a couple of mates with him, but not tonight.

'Oscar,' I said. 'What'll it be? The usual?'

I wasn't sure if he did lip-read, as Hugh insisted, or whether he had just figured out we couldn't be asking him anything else.

Oscar gave me a wink. Oscar had a beautiful wink that tugged one corner of his mouth into a shy smile. I flipped on his pint and took the coins he slid across the counter.

125

'To the penny,' I said.

Oscar always had the right money. I suppose it cut down on the need for conversation. I gave him his drink, he gave me his wink. Hugh came back from the toilet.

'That's evil,' he said. 'That isn't natural.'

'What?' I asked.

'In there.' He pinched his nostrils. 'It would kill you stone dead.'

It was the one thing about working in bars that Hugh found hard to stomach. Some people he swore saved the shit up until they got into our toilets. Some of them, he once went so far as to say, came in here for no other reason.

'They'd think it was worth the few bob for a pint not to have to do that at home.'

'I suppose he shits roses,' Jamesie said to me under his breath.

'And the noises ...' Hugh went on as the Gents door opened and we all looked up to see Stanley step through it. He must have been in there a quarter of an hour or more.

'I might have known,' Jamesie muttered, suddenly on Hugh's side. 'Dirty bastard.'

I was at the tap next to Jamesie, our pints neck and neck.

'Jamesie,' I said, 'would you give over and leave the fella alone.'

I set my pint down and scraped the head with a knife. Jamesie took the knife from me and levelled off his own pint.

'What's it to you?' he said.

'He's harmless,' I said.

'As long as you don't strike a match around him.'

A thruppenny tip lay on the bar. I pressed it into Jamesie's hand.

'Here, get yourself some better crackers next Christmas.'

'You being funny again?' Hugh asked, passing behind us and nudging Jamesie.

'Amn't I always?'

Hugh returned and laid his hand on Jamesie's shoulder.

'Do you want the truth, son?'

Liam Strong was back up at the bar. His eyes were glassy and his ears seemed redder, thicker.

'The truth never did anyone a bit of harm, now,' he said.

'No?' said Jamesie. I could see him weighing up the opportunity, but in the end he let it pass. 'Whatever you say, Liam.'

Through a gap between the people waiting on drinks I spotted the two old boys from the Markets, half turned away from one another, huffing. Beside them a fella and girl had somehow managed to squeeze into the space previously occupied by Stanley. The tight fit didn't seem to bother them. The girl wore white nylons and had crossed her left leg over her boyfriend's hand. I thought of her alternately tensing and relaxing her thighs. I tensed my own. My mind must have wandered, the next thing I knew someone had come to stand in the gap and was trying to attract my attention.

'Sorry,' I said, and only then focused on the person. Stanley.

'No hurry,' he said, which was as well, for I needed a moment to recover from the shock.

(I forced myself to think about the smell in the toilets, if you must know. At least it damped down the heat I had felt rising to my cheeks.)

'Half is it?'

I was already taking the glass from the rack. Stanley pursed his lips and frowned as though faced with a momentous decision.

'Oh, go on,' he said, keeping up the act. 'A pint.'

Jamesie and Hugh were both busy. I thought I might as well go along this road a bit, see where it led. I paused with the half-pint glass midway between the drainer and the tap.

'I wouldn't want you doing anything you were going to regret now.' I raised an eyebrow; I had been told that the effect was quite fetching.

'I try never to regret anything,' Stanley said, still in jest, I was fairly certain, though I chose to believe the remark contained a grain of truth.

'A pint it is, then.'

I watched the lager pour. Stanley folded his arms on the counter and watched along with me. He had a double crown, I noticed, hell for cutting, I'm sure, but the kind of thing nonetheless I could happily have fooled with for hours. A single black hair grew where his nose joined his brow. My bottom lip tingled and I caught it between my front teeth. I knocked the tap off. If I say so myself, it was a very good-looking pint, no drips.

'How's that?'

I held my hand out for the money and was disappointed when Stanley offered me one end of a ten-bob note. I would count the change into his palm if need be just to get a touch of his skin. When I turned back from the till, though, Stanley had a cigarette in his mouth and was frisking himself for a light. I held on to the coins for as long as seemed defensible then set them on the bar. I was aware of Jamesie close behind me. Stanley was still slapping his coat pockets.

'Here,' Jamesie said, throwing a book of matches on to the counter.

'Thanks,' said Stanley, as surprised as I was.

He struck a match and Jamesie ducked.

*

If this were a film, if I were the director, I would cut from Jamesie's duck to a cork popping in the dining room upstairs and not care that the two were not strictly speaking simultaneous. Of the goings-on up there, Clive White's dinner with Fitz and Councillor Noades, I can speak with confidence only about those things my workmates witnessed – actions without accurate times, words without context – and what I have been able to reconstruct from the evidence of later events. But I will take my own liberties in the telling; I think I know my second cousin well enough.

So, some time between a quarter to and nine, Fitz, Clive

White and Councillor Noades were resting between courses, drinking Asti spumante (Barney had not looked closely at the bottles' foil wraps), while Priscilla Coote cleared their table. Clive White was no stranger to Priscilla either. Her husband had worked for him for a time in the docks bar. A very short time. The way I heard it, it was Priscilla who made her husband pack the job in. Priscilla would only say that she wasn't prepared to stand for any more of Clive's 'nonsense'. Priscilla wouldn't stand for *anyone's* nonsense. It was an open secret that if she ever ran into that Mick Jagger one she was going to clip his ear for him. There was no nonsense from Clive or Fitz or the councillor tonight as Priscilla took their used cutlery and plates. They sat with their hands in their laps. The bubbles rising in their glasses slowed from a sprint to a crawl. When at last Priscilla had gone, Fitz leaned his elbows on the tablecloth and whispered that it was a pity they couldn't have had the new girl who had brought them their soup. The councillor, who alone of the three men was currently married, allowed himself an impure smile. Clive White smiled too, though his smile had more in it of satisfaction than of lechery. The evening was shaping up very nicely. The councillor had been a little reticent when he first arrived, as though suddenly nervous at what he was getting himself into and hoping that the less he said the easier he would be able to find a way back out. After all, no matter how well he got on with Fitz, there was still the awkward fact that the man was a Southerner and though at government level there had been a noticeable thawing in relations of late between Northern Ireland and what was still generally referred to here as the Free State, such contacts did not yet enjoy much support at local Unionist party level. At local party level, in fact, such contacts were close to anathema. Of course (Clive could almost read Noades's inner wranglings in the agitation of his lips and eyebrows) business was business, but there was the added problem that the business in question – the city's first super-garage – concerned part of the Shankill Road, the Orange heartland, *the Empire's fucking belly-button*, where the redevelopment motion to go before council next Wednesday night stipulated that only houses were to be built.

That, though, was earlier. Now, his glass refilled, the councillor ventured a comment of his own about the waitresses of the International. Fitz laughed. Clive White's smile broadened.

Clive's presence here, if he said so himself, was something of a master stroke. The night before in the Royal Avenue he had rehearsed to Fitz the very objections he had watched Trevor Noades wrestling with at the start of the evening. The Shankill Road, Malvern Street in particular, was sensitive. Fitz might not know there had been bother in the area last summer. Indeed Fitz did know, shocking business altogether; and wasn't he right in thinking one of the boyos (Burns, Clive said, Burns, said Fitz) was appealing his conviction? Clive's point entirely. It was all over the papers again ... No, Malvern Street was very sensitive. There would be people – anti-O'Neill people – who would interpret *any* redevelopment as a collective punishment: breaking up the community. And for Fitz, a Dubliner, to be involved ... Clive reminded him of the recent sale of Ulster Transport Authority Hotels, and of how, after a storm of protest had been whipped up, the CIE, the UTA's southern counterpart, had been blocked by Stormont from bidding. Fitz said he remembered it well enough but didn't see what any of this had to do with him. He was a Protestant himself, after all. Admittedly, said Clive, but a southern one. What about Sir Edward Carson, Fitz asked: founding father of Northern Ireland and Dublin born and bred? Clive regretted that that would make no difference. To the voters on the Shankill Road, Fitz would be a southerner regardless. Despite what he might have heard, the Unionists didn't have it all their own way up there. There was Labour to think of and Labour weren't above a bit of populism if they thought they could scrap a council seat or two.

'So what's the solution?' Fitz asked in exasperation, and Clive White paused for a few dramatic moments before telling him.

By the time they left the Royal Avenue with the two girls Clive

White had phoned under cover of going for cigarettes, it had been agreed that Clive would make an ideal front man for Fitz's operation in Belfast. A company would be formed with an address in the city, thereby allaying the qualms of jittery Unionist councillors. Most of their qualms at any rate. Allaying the remainder – over the small matter of a super-garage in an area zoned for housing, where few of the residents owned cars – was the purpose of this evening's dinner.

'Oh, good,' said Fitz, setting down his empty glass. 'The sweet trolley.'

He raised an eyebrow at the councillor, who endeavoured not to smile for the trolley was being pushed by the young waitress they had been so taken with earlier.

Paula stopped behind Clive.

'Excuse me, sir, would you mind lifting your chair?'

A trolley wheel had become tangled in the hem of Clive's overcoat. He worked the coat free and instinctively ran his fingers down the right-hand side, to all appearances as though smoothing the nap, but in reality reassuring himself that the envelope was still in his inside pocket. The envelope contained five hundred pounds. The night before Fitz had confided in Clive that he thought he could rely on the support of half a dozen councillors and was sure they would be able to convince the necessary number of their colleagues to carry an amendment to the Malvern Street motion. In order to make his supporters' task easier, Fitz was disposed to giving them some money towards … *expenses*. Clive White thought this sounded like a very good idea, but was astonished when Fitz told him he intended to make the payment by cheque. This was not the sort of transaction that you wanted to draw attention to and cheques for five hundred pounds had a way of being noticed. (Not for the first time that night he was appalled by Fitz's naivety, though not for the first time he wondered whether this naivety might not be turned to his future advantage.) No, cash would be much better. Fitz thought this over a while. The only problem with cash, he said, was where to get hold of that much on a Saturday with the banks shut. Clive White told him he wasn't to worry, Clive would take care of it. He was reckoning it would do him no harm at all to have Fitz in his debt, even if it was only until the beginning of the week when the banks reopened. There was a great deal of money to be made here, he wanted there to be no doubt that he was in on it from the very start.

In the end, five hundred pounds was not quite as easy to come by on a Saturday as Clive had anticipated. He always made sure and kept a couple of hundred at home, the rest he raised by calling in a few old debts. It had taken him the best part of the day, wearing out his finger in the telephone dial, jumping in and out of the car, ducking in and out of bars, running up a rickety staircase here, wading through shite at the back of a scrapyard there, but he couldn't help thinking that Fitz would be impressed that he was able to manage it at such short notice.

'Oh, yes, very tasty.'

Noades was having great sport with Paula, asking her to identify every sweet on her trolley, watching as she bent over for this thing he fancied – no, he changed his mind, that one, on the bottom shelf – no, maybe the first one after all.

Clive registered the look in the girl's mauve-ringed eyes as she slid a slice of something pink and gelatinous on to the councillor's plate. Not bored, exactly, but, her timidity leeched by tiredness, light-years from impressed. He saw a chip shop, in a village in the glens, teenagers leaning against the plate-glass window who had grown up around bulls and rams and stallions. Bawdy banter, Paula laughing as knowingly as the best of them … She hadn't come floating up the Lagan in a bubble, the same wee girl.

Clive passed on dessert. He poured them all another glass of spumante, finishing the bottle.

'Your good health,' he said.

'Your health,' said Fitz and the councillor as one.

14

Jamesie let out a yelp.

'Would you quit sneaking up on people like that?'

Len's nephew (he appeared to have walked under the serving hatch without ducking) told Jamesie to catch himself on and asked to speak to Hugh.

'He's busy,' Jamesie said. 'What do you want?'

But the kid insisted his message was for Hugh and Hugh alone. Jamesie bent down level with his earhole.

'Anyone ever tell you you're an irritating little fucker?'

'And lived?' the kid asked.

Jamesie straightened up, thumbs hooked in the belt-loops of his charcoal trousers.

'What did they die of, laughter?'

Hugh had clocked the wee lad by now, but went on to the next customer regardless.

'Can I get you a comic or something while you're waiting?' Jamesie said, and the kid pulled a face like he'd heard it all a million times before.

'Cunny funt.'

'Crayons?' Jamesie persisted. 'A dodie?'

One unhurried pint later, Hugh ambled over, wiping his

hands on a linen cloth.

'Right, what is it this time?'

Oscar was signalling another drink

'Coming up,' I said, and he smiled to show he had got my meaning if not my exact words. A passable seahorse of cigarette smoke, violet in the bar-light, glided across my line of vision, little wisps of fry twisting and tumbling in its wake. I thumbed Oscar's coins uncounted into the till, watching out the corner of my eye the sketchy shoal drift in front of a Scottish geezer – something in pork butchery was all I knew – in the act of inhaling a Navy Cut; he exhaled, a single targeted jet from his pursed lips, and my fantasy was dispersed into the general murk.

'You all getting there?' I shouted.

Jamesie was tailing the kid round the corner and out of the bar.

'That was hard now, wasn't it?' I heard him say. 'Just as well you told Hugh and not me.'

'They need somebody up in the Portaferry Room,' Hugh explained to me. 'I'm sure Len thinks we're twiddling our thumbs in here.'

Stanley, his seat lost, was still standing at the bar, holding his ground despite the constant buffeting, pint glass between drinks anchored to the scuffed mahogany of the counter. He was steadying himself with his free hand for another swallow when I arrived again at that end of the bar.

'Tight fit,' I said, my subconscious seemingly hell-bent on innuendo. He mimed being crushed, goggle-eyed, tongue skewed over his bottom lip. His face, when it had recomposed itself, struck me as altogether less tense than it had been earlier. It was a look you grew to know well, working in a bar. Someone's happy, we'd say.

Mind you, you didn't often see it after barely one and a half pints. Stanley, I decided, was not much of a drinker and I wondered if he might not, after all, end up doing something tonight he wouldn't normally do.

What it was Stanley normally did do remained a mystery to me. I was fairly certain he was single and yet he did not give the impression that he was actively looking, not in the way that most single men who came into the bar were looking. Of course I was familiar enough by this stage with furtive behaviour, but Stanley's, if I was being honest, did not easily lend itself to my preferred interpretation. He grasped the base of his glass with little finger and thumb. The three remaining fingers were extended almost at right angles and moving in a way I fondly thought might be trying, independently of the rest of him, to send me a signal of some kind. I willed myself to discover the sense of it, but to no avail.

A guy squeezed through wanting change for the phone. When he had gone again he seemed, by one of those inexplicable quirks of bar congregation, to have drawn off some of the earlier pressure for space. Next time I looked, Stanley had managed to secure himself a bar stool. His cigarettes and matches were on the counter to one side of his glass and behind these he had divided his silver and coppers into two piles, though in the case of the former, maybe pile was too grand a word. I must have been staring.

'That's me,' he said, cheerfully enough: 'Cleaned out.'

I mumbled something about weekends and the next payday, but Stanley shook his head.

'No. That's me cleaned *right* out.'

He hauled on his cigarette and I thought now that what he was doing when he held on to the smoke the way he did was trying to make it last.

'That bad?' I asked and Stanley nodded.

'Worse.'

He removed three shillings from the dwarf pile.

'But, sure ...' He drained his pint and handed me the empty glass. 'Fill her up.'

I left the glass on the crowded sideboard by the sink and took the last clean one from the drainer. Some idiot was trying to tell Oscar a joke.

'Do you get it? England, Scotland, Wales and Northern Ireland are standing at the bar, looking miserable, and the guy says, "UK?"'

Oscar caught my eye and made a play of looking at the other man as though deeply perplexed.

'*You*-OK? Do you still not get it?'

Oscar frowned, left eye almost closing. The joker glanced around, saw me.

'Is this fella right in the head?' he asked.

'As right as any of the rest of us,' I said, and put Stanley's pint on.

Oscar laughed suddenly, close to the man's face. I had heard this feigned laugh of Oscar's before; even when you knew it was coming its force could take you by surprise. The joke-teller hunched his shoulders, pulling in his neck. He banged his glass down on the bar and pushed through the crowd towards the toilet, looking back and shaking his head. Oscar was laughing good and proper now, without sound. He showed me the back of one splayed hand and jerked it towards me twice. Ten minutes. Now the hand mimicked a yakking mouth. I nodded. His index finger pointed back towards his own face which performed a series of ever more exaggerated expressions of interest. I joined in the laughter. Oscar leaned his elbows peaceably on the bar, I carried the pint down to Stanley. He saluted me before taking a sip.

'Jam tomorrow,' he said.

'With the help of God and a couple of peelers.'

A saying of my mother's – the nearest she ever came to outright prayer – that my father would sometimes trump …

'With the help of God and the Great Gilhooley,' Stanley said, taking my father's words out of my mouth.

The Great Gilhooley. A music hall legend, a rabbit-from-the-hat, something-from-nothing man.

'The patron saint of tight corners,' said Stanley, toasting.

'Powerful,' I admitted. 'But not a patch on,' (conjuring another name from the collective past) 'Bamboozlum!'

136

Stanley's eyes widened, then narrowed; not for a second did they leave my face, but he was looking through me, not at me.

'Danny!' Hugh shouted.

'Got to go,' I said.

'Bam-Bam-boozlum,' said Stanley absently.

A Belfast abracadabra.

*

Bam-Bam-boozlum!

Stanley is three years old, standing on a chair in the scullery, letting on his teddy is doing the dishes.

A face ghosts across the window above the sink. Big hands under his arms hoist Stanley high into the air.

'*Bam-Bam-boozlum!*'

Stanley gives such a howl the hands set him down again.

'He doesn't know who you are,' Stanley's mother says, but Stanley knows all right, that's why he's howling.

This is his father back from the war. Now you don't see him, now you do.

Bam-Bam-boozlum!

From that night on Stanley was put to sleep in a room on his own and before too long Heather was born and then the twins, Philip and Paul, were born and by the time he was ten he could remember almost nothing of his life before his father's reappearance save for the stories his mother would tell him, stroking his hair in the blacked-out night, about the places she used to go where doves flew out of handkerchiefs, where women stepped into empty wardrobes and bearded men stepped out.

Stanley would be the first to admit he was an oddbod of a child. A hummer, a twitcher. He spent hours at a time lying on his bed with a comic up to his face, not reading so much, you would have thought if you'd seen him, as trying to disappear right into it.

His mother was always at him, *Stanley, get out into the street and play.* But the street was hopeless. Men mooched on the corner from morning to night, dressed in overalls and dungarees, looking up and down the road for work that never seemed to come. How were you supposed to play with them staring out of their long faces at you?

Stanley's father sometimes had occasion to stand out there too.

'What we need,' Stanley once heard him say, 'is another war.'

And a man from somewhere else who had stopped by to see if the view was any better from this street said, 'What we need is a proper bloody government.'

Stanley went home and read his comics and when his mother opened her purse one afternoon and closed her eyes to his outstretched hand, he started to draw his own. Four pages, thirty panels a page, each panel fully coloured. Heather and the twins helped with the colouring, reading as they shaded. Stanley couldn't draw for toffee, but his sister and brothers didn't care. They loved the fact that all his characters lived in Belfast. Tommy the Tiger Bay Tram, the Dunce of Duncairn Gardens. It wasn't a deliberate decision on Stanley's part, that was just the way it came out.

The Weeker, he called the comic, because it took him the best part of seven days to draw each one and because *wheeker* was a word they used then when they wanted to say something was really good, sticking out.

At twelve he had dreams of *The Weeker* making his fortune by the time he was twenty (*Stanley*, his mother said, *would you for God's sake GO OUT!*) and then his father got up for his fry one Sunday morning and dropped down dead on the bedroom floor. Bam-Bam-boozlum.

At fourteen Stanley left school and went out to work.

He had wanted to be apprenticed to a printer, but, for reasons which at fourteen he was powerless to resist, ended up in a shop off North Street making tea and running messages for two brothers who repaired the electrical appliances which were just then becoming more numerous in the city: kettles, vacuum cleaners, radiograms and, little by little, television sets. The televisions were for the most part big Pyes and Marconis, BBC reception only, bought from London dealers when commercial television came in across the water. You could have got yourself a nine-inch screen for ten or fifteen quid: a little pewter peephole in a wall of teak and Bakelite. Stanley's family did not yet own one so he got to know television, as it were, from the inside out. Perhaps for this reason he was never overawed by it. Time and again, unscrewing the back of a set in for repair (there was too much work coming in for him to remain a tea boy for long), he was reminded that what he was dealing with was nothing more marvellous than a complex arrangement of tubes and valves and bulbs and wires. He was not entirely immune to the attractions, but mostly he thought of television as a challenge to be mastered.

When he had been with the brothers a couple of years he moved down North Street a way to one of the new rental shops. Northern Ireland had its own commercial station by this time, Ulster Television, or Channel 9 as people called it. No home now was complete without its box. Stanley accompanied the senior engineer on his rounds. He noticed how their van was greeted at some doors like an ambulance come to the aid of a sick relative. He saw children cry when the engineer said there was nothing for it but to take the set away overnight. (*But the* Lone Ranger*'s on today!*) He saw fathers and mothers who looked like it was all they could do to stop themselves joining in. It would have made you think. It made Stanley think.

His mother worried that thinking was all Stanley ever did. *Go out*, she said. *While you still have time.*

For his eighteenth birthday he took the entire family to Blackpool. He had been saving for this holiday almost from the day and hour he started work.

Blackpool was where his mother and father were to have gone for their honeymoon, only the war got in the way.

It was the last week of August. The younger children spent most of the day at the pleasure beach. His mother seemed content to watch them enjoy themselves or to go for walks along the promenade. Stanley walked with her. He saw his first Punch and Judy show. And his second, and third, and fourth. The dog, the sausages, the baby, the rolling pin. The same every time. It irritated him vaguely in its repetitiveness, its pointlessness, but he would slow his pace anyway as he passed by, watching the arc of children sitting on the sand before the striped tent, rapt.

There was cold tongue for tea the first night in the guest house, corned beef the next. From then on Stanley and his family filled up on fish and chips at lunchtime. They went up the tower and to the pictures once. Stanley tried to persuade his mother to come with him to a show on the pier. His mother wouldn't hear of it.

'But you always used to tell me you liked shows.'

'I used to like a lot of things.' Stanley's mother had just turned forty-one. 'Anyway, you've spent enough already.'

She tried to persuade *him* to take off by himself in the evenings, go to a dance, with people his own age. On the penultimate night, more to please her than anything else, he did go out. Heavy rain had fallen earlier in the afternoon, but now the sun had come through over to the west, burnishing the rooftops and the rumpled spread of the Irish sea.

Stanley was wearing a new sports jacket and grey flannels. He had dithered before deciding to wear a tie, but once outside he took it off and slipped it, rolled, into his jacket pocket. Half a mile from the guest house he admitted to himself he had no idea what he was going to do. He went into the next café he saw and ate an ice-cream sundae. On his way out he bought a packet of cigarettes and stood for a while on the footpath smoking. Girls passed by, smelling of powder, linking arms. Boys younger than Stanley whistled at them or pushed one another into their paths to make them stop and talk.

'Watch it!' the girls shouted but stopped and talked all the same. Stanley tried hard not to feel disheartened.

A hundred yards on, he went into a lounge bar across the road from a ballroom with a board in front announcing *Dancing*

Nitely 8 'til Late. Stanley had never been in a bar or a ballroom in his life. He sipped a half-pint of mild (he hadn't expected there to be a choice), looking out through the open door of the lounge. There were fellas on the other side of the street wearing leather jackets, jeans with six-inch turn-ups. One of the fellas ran a steel comb through his hair time and again as though there was nothing to be ashamed of in the act of public grooming. Stanley hoped he and his mates weren't waiting on the ballroom opening. He hoped they weren't planning on coming into the bar. He watched for forty-five minutes before they moved en masse down the street, but by that time he had no desire to go into a dance on his own.

He ordered another half of mild. The barmaid, a tall, narrow-shouldered woman in her fifties, asked him how he was enjoying his holiday.

'Grand,' he said. He remained standing at the bar for a while after his drink was drawn, but the woman said nothing more and eventually he returned to his seat. Two young men came in, dressed alike in sleeveless pullovers and open-necked shirts. They said hello to the barmaid and passed on through a door leading to a bare staircase. A short time later three more men entered and followed them up the stairs. Stanley could hear the thump of their feet overhead, tables or chairs scraping across lino. More men came in. A few bought drinks before joining the gathering above. Stanley thought they might be playing darts up there. He had heard one new arrival ask the barmaid if this was the right place for the league.

'Go on up if you like, I'm sure you'd be very welcome,' the barmaid said.

Without realising he was doing it, Stanley had been staring at the ceiling.

'I don't really play,' he said.

The barmaid furrowed her eyebrows, but another man turning away from the bar with a glass in each hand called over to him.

'You'd best hurry, meeting'll be starting.'

Forgetting even to lift his drink, Stanley stood up and followed.

It was not a conversion, exactly. Afterwards Stanley reflected that he had been halfway down the road already.

He took a seat at the rear of the room under a heavy-draped window just as the lights were dimmed. On a table in the middle of the floor, a film projector had been set up. Its beam cut a rectangle – cream and gold Anaglypta – out of the darkness on the room's front wall. The projector clicked and stuttered, the wall-paper took on a bluish hue: a rapid countdown from five to one and then the words *Freedom! Castro's Cuba* appeared over an image of the president, his arms laden with flowers, being embraced by a pretty girl in army fatigues. Instantly the scene changed to an open-air school. Palm trees, a far-off suggestion of mountains. Another pretty girl pointed with a stick to the alphabet chalked on a blackboard. Tiny children, seated in an arc before her, bounced up and down on their backsides, mouths moving in silent unison.

A man Stanley couldn't see spoke from somewhere close to the projector.

'Eighteen months after the revolution swept them to power, Cuba's communist leaders have begun the task of eradicating the poverty and illiteracy which under the Batista dictatorship blighted their island home.'

Elderly women looked up from books spread on their laps, squinting into the camera and out from the wall of the Blackpool public house.

'Old and young alike empowered by education,' the man went on, obviously reading.

Now men shouldering vast chandeliers of bananas crossed the Anaglypta screen. They waited in line to have the fruit weighed. There were smiles and handshakes. A truck drove off filled to overflowing, odd banana fingers slipping over the tailboard. The men ran alongside waving hats frayed at the brim. The commentator said something which Stanley didn't take in. He was listening to the distant hurdy-gurdy cacophony of the pleasure beach. There was music too, closer at hand: guitars – the Shadows, Stanley thought – from the ballroom probably. Voices carried, shouts of greeting, fragments of conversation ('She said to him, you think you're too big? You're not too big yet, no, and don't you forget it'), mingling with the film's flat Lancastrian commentary, so that the revolution appeared to have been translated into a riotous end-of-pier variety, the more compelling for its familiarity.

Not a conversion, a confirmation.

'Good night?' his mother asked when he got back to the guest house.

'Brilliant,' said Stanley.

Home again in Belfast he bought himself two lengths of felt, one red, one blue. He folded the lengths in half then drew a shape on each like an oven mitt with two thumbs and cut around them with the scissors from his mother's workbox. He cut a semi-circle out of the folds, two fingers wide. Heather gave him a hand with the sewing, blue thread for the seams of the red mitt, red thread for the blue. The twins made twin papier maché balls, each with a hole let in it, and painted them as instructed, Philip's bright yellow, Paul's vivid pink. Using the finest brush he could buy, Stanley himself painted wide-eyed faces on the curved surfaces. As an afterthought he added a black moustache to the pink ball before gluing it to the blue glove and topped the yellow one with a red felt disc for a cap.

He gave his first performance kneeling behind the kitchen table.

'Hello,' he said, making his voice black-moustache gruff and

143

bending the fingers of his right hand so that the blue glove puppet bowed. 'I'm ...' He didn't know the name himself until he said it '... Rab.'

His left hand shot up. The red puppet faced Heather and the twins, arms spread wide, then moved at speed down the table towards his right hand. Stanley pitched his voice higher.

'Rab, Rab, I seen a ...'

The blue puppet pushed the red one away.

'You *seen* nothing,' (again the name just appeared) 'Jem.'

'Oh, Rab, I did,' Jem said, papier maché head twisted practically back-to-front. 'I seen a ...'

'Saw, Jem.' Rab turned to address his small audience. 'I saw, I have seen.' (Jem dropped from view, holding on to his hat.) 'Now what did you see, Jem?

'Jem?'

'Wooo,' said Stanley from under the table. 'Wooo-oooo.'

He splayed the first and third fingers of his right hand and now Rab's arms were flung apart.

'Jem, Jem,' he said, running this way and that. 'I seen it too, Jem. Oh, Mummy, Mummy, I seen it too.'

Education through entertainment, that was how he conceived of it. From the very start he set his sights on television's mass audience. For a year he practised at the kitchen table, performing only to his brothers, his sister, and, when the novelty wore off for them, his mother. He refashioned the papier maché heads, modelling chins and noses. (Rab's nose was a near-perfect globe.) He replaced Jem's red beret with a diminutive duncher, though not so diminutive that Jem could stop the peak falling over his eyes, and stuck shoe-brush bristles under Rab's hooter until the moustache covered his mouth entirely. The insides of the gloves he padded with foam rubber, less for Jem than for Rab, and the outsides he dressed in tan overalls.

Rab and Jem had been friends since they were born. (Later Stanley would make a pair of smaller puppets, Wee Rab and Wee Jem, which he sometimes introduced into the act, one with an orange juice moustache, the other with a satin bonnet flopping over his face.) Stanley invented addresses for them two doors apart off North Queen Street. In the house in-between lived Maisie McClure, fair but formidable, with whom they were both secretly in love.

Rab liked to take charge. He and Jem would be standing around on the corner of the street, wondering what to do with themselves and Rab would tap his hand on his forehead. Now, let me think, he'd say. I *know* ...

It wasn't that Jem never came up with ideas, Jem in fact was full of them. Rab, though, gave them short shrift, at least until he could convince himself that they were really his ideas all along.

Rab and Jem spent a good deal of time on the street corner. They never were able to hold on to a job for long.

'Last one in, first one out, that's all I ever seem to hear,' Jem complained.

In one early routine the two were deck hands on a cargo ship and had just been told they were going to be paid off when the ship docked in Belfast. Twenty miles off the County Down coast, the ship started to take on water. There was only one lifeboat and only two places left in it. Rab and Jem ran along the deck, the captain off-stage shouting after them: 'Come back! One of those places is mine.'

Rab and Jem looked at each other then slid down the ropes out of sight.

'You know the rule,' Rab shouted as they disappeared. 'Last one in, first one out.'

At the end of the twelve months, Stanley walked the city with cards for newsagents' windows. He placed a small ad in the paper.

Introducing 'RAB and JEM', Belfast's BIGGEST little comics. Puppetry at its best! LOW RATES. Book now, family FUN GUARANTEED!

His first engagement was an under-sevens Sunday school party. He had made a sort of lectern for the puppets to perform on with a floor-length black skirt behind which he kneeled on a velour cushion swiped from the settee at home. He did ten minutes. The children listened in silence for the first five. Stanley was starting to sweat, then one boy yelled, 'Jem, he's a big bully. Hit him a smack!'

The other children laughed at his daring. Rab's moustache twitched with indignation, his eyes darting here and there seeking out the boy who had maligned him. The children laughed more. A girl shouted at him, 'You are so a bully.'

Jem had snuck up behind Rab and now he gave him a dunt in the back knocking him flat on his big round nose. Rab bounced straight back up, Jem put his hands to his cap and fled. It sounded to Stanley, on the other side of the curtain, as though all the children were calling out at once: '*Run, Jem, run!*'

'Unusual,' said one of the Sunday school teachers afterwards, handing Stanley his fee.

'Very,' said a second, a bake on him that looked like a smile would break it.

That was fine by Stanley, he wasn't doing his show for Sunday school teachers.

Three months passed before he got another date, a works' Christmas party on the Albertbridge Road. He did the lifeboat routine which he'd just finished working on, he did the railway porters, where Rab and Jem load Lord and Lady Lucre's luggage for a weekend in the country: twenty suitcases and trunks Heather had made out of cigarette boxes and tea cartons. He did fifteen minutes and when the audience wouldn't stop clapping he did five minutes more. The parents were laughing as hard as the kids.

He was off then. For the next few years there was barely a weekend went by without at least one engagement. He splashed out ten pounds on a fifth-hand Ford Popular and added 'No Distance Too Far' to his small ad. His mother still worried about his social life. He assured her he was happy as he was yet a while.

'Just don't get stuck,' she said. 'Believe me, you don't want to end up on your own.'

There were two or three girlfriends during this time, but none whose idea of a fun Saturday night was driving home along dark country roads from a Tufty Club in Clogher, with a lectern and a pair of glove puppets occupying the entire back seat. The last one had given him the shove after Stanley told her he had to work Valentine's night.

'Look me up if you ever figure out something more worthwhile to do with your hands,' she said.

Stanley, for his part, never once doubted how worthwhile Rab and Jem were. The money wasn't the thing, rarely in all the years of parties and dos did he make more than a few quid above costs. It was what he was able to say in his little act that was important. (He had one routine about ecumenics. He had one about the B.U.M. for which he made extra puppets: Rab with a white moustache, Jem with a walking stick, still waiting.) And more important than anything else was that he should get to say it on television.

He decided to give himself a year – he would be twenty-five by the end of it – and go semi-pro. For some time past he had been getting neighbours knocking on the door at nights asking would he come and have a look at sets that had gone on the blink. He could still do a bit of that on the side.

After only a month he took first prize in a big talent night in Craigavon and was featured in one of the new local Home Service shows. Even though no one listening would have known if he hadn't, he had the lectern set up in the radio studio and did his routine kneeling on his mother's cushion.

Later that week he had a phone installed in the house and waited for it to ring. He picked it up ten times an hour to check it was working. He sent his sister out to the call box down the street and had her phone him.

'I told you there was nothing wrong with it,' she said when he answered.

He carried on mending neighbours' TVs and performing at children's parties. Money was getting tight, but he couldn't bring himself to raise his fee. Besides he was still hopeful of a break. He won another competition and the prize was two nights on the bill at Butlin's, Mosney, when it reopened at Easter. His mother suggested he try to get on to *Opportunity Knocks*. Heather was to be his proposer and together they wrote a letter to Hughie Green. A fortnight later a reply arrived with details of the auditions in London. It had never occurred to Stanley that there would be auditions. The way it looked on television someone wrote in proposing you and the next thing Hughie Green was asking them who they had brought along for the viewers this evening. The letter pointed out that the auditions were very competitive. Glove puppets, in their experience, tended not to do well. It didn't matter, Stanley couldn't have afforded the trip over to England anyway.

Easter and Butlin's seemed an eternity away. He was lying on his bed one December afternoon, in the room he still shared with the twins, reading the *Belfast Telegraph*. The Christmas panto had opened for booking in the Grand Opera House. *Aladdin*: 'Full West End London Company, including Peters and Dell, Audrey Man, Dennis Clancy, Charles Mylne, Claire Wilson, with Belfast's own Tom Raymond as Wishee-Washee'. Stanley read an interview with the guest director, Larry Bowen. Thrilled to be in Belfast, thrilled to be in the Grand Opera House, thrilled to be returning to live theatre, taking time out from producing the popular children's variety programme …

Stanley bent the paper and looked across the room to the chest of drawers on top of which lay Rab and Jem, their heads lolling one against the other.

'*Crackerjack!*' he said.

'Crackerjack!' Rab and Jem said back, in sequence, naturally.

Aladdin was booked solid until the Tuesday of its second week, but on the Tuesday of the second week Stanley was in his seat in the front stalls half an hour before curtain up. A family of four boys, all in school blazers, took their places on his left, a man and woman and their early-teenage daughter on his right. The girl sat low in her seat, chewing on a lock of hair.

'We never miss a year,' the father confided in Stanley. 'You can't beat a good pantomime.'

The lights went down and his daughter sighed.

With good reason, as it turned out. All in all it was a pretty feeble show. The jokes were so crusty no amount of scraping would have dislodged them from the bottom of the barrel. The girl's father laughed that much he got the hiccups. The two youngest boys on Stanley's other side nipped each other's bare legs until their mother cuffed them, whereafter the only time they left off looking sulkily bored was to exchange glances of mingled accusation and threat: *You're dead when I get you home, wee lad.*

The panto wore on, old gags and crucified songs. Tom Raymond wasn't the only thing on stage that was wishee-washee.

Stanley left the theatre a happy man.

He wrote to Larry Bowen, styling himself an admirer of 'your excellent television work' who had attended last evening's performance of *Aladdin* and found it (would he lie or tell the truth?) immensely enjoyable. (The truth would keep until he had a foot in the door.) He was in the children's entertainment business himself, a glove-puppet act, which critics had been kind enough to say had the potential for broad popular appeal. Perhaps if he and Mr Bowen could meet …?

He refused to contemplate the possibility that Larry Bowen wouldn't reply, but when the phone rang the very next afternoon and a woman, identifying herself only as Mr Bowen's assistant, asked him could he drop by the Opera House that Saturday morning coming, even Stanley was surprised.

Larry Bowen was something of a surprise too. Stanley, who had been expecting a much older man, would have put him at no more than thirty, though his hair was greying above the ears and in the little goatee beard which he had a habit of stroking when not talking.

A brisk young woman – Stanley supposed she was the assistant he had spoken to on Thursday, though she made no reference to that conversation – had met him at the stage door and led him down a corridor and up a flight of stairs at the top of which Larry Bowen was waiting with what seemed an entirely genuine smile on his lips.

'You must be Stanley. How nice of you to come.'

The woman departed without a word and Larry held a door for Stanley to pass through into a windowless room containing a dozen or so filing cabinets, two folding chairs and a small table. Stanley couldn't decide whether he was in an over-full office or a store which just happened to have a couple of seats.

'We *shouldn't* be disturbed in here, but you know what theatre is.'

'Of course,' lied Stanley.

They sat and for a moment neither said anything more. Stanley had brought a small case with him, which he centred on his lap. Larry Bowen locked his hands behind his head, crossing his legs and wagging one foot gently in the air. Stanley was no expert, but the shoe moving in front of him looked handmade and expensive.

'Yes,' said Larry at last, as though in answer to a question Stanley couldn't remember asking. 'I think it's important – when I'm out of London ... I like to keep abreast of what you are all up to.'

Stanley did not find that 'you' in the least bit patronising. On the contrary, he was rather pleased to be included in Larry's implied community of entertainers.

'I've had quite a year,' he said and Larry Bowen nodded. 'And Christmas, of course, is non-stop.'

'I'm sure.'

'And then I've a short season coming up this Easter in Butlin's.'

'Butlin's?' Larry Bowen's foot wagged the harder.

'Mosney,' Stanley said. 'Near Dublin.' Then, worried that the word season, even qualified, might have been going a bit far, added, 'It is very short.'

'But still,' Larry said encouragingly.

'Well, yes, that's the way I look at it.'

They were silent again, then both spoke the same word at the same time: 'So?'

They laughed. Stanley tapped the top of the suitcase with an index finger.

'Would you like me to ...?'

'Please.'

Stanley snapped the catches open, Larry pushed his chair back against the wall and leaned forward, elbows on knees, fingertips in beard. Behind the upright lid, Stanley slid his hands into the red and blue puppets. Rab adjusted Jem's cap, Jem ruffled Rab's moustache, they nodded their approval to each other and were just about to pop up and introduce themselves to Mr Larry Bowen of *Crackerjack!* fame when there was a knock at the door and the young woman returned to whisper in Larry's ear.

'Oh, dear,' Larry said. He stood up. 'I'm awfully sorry, but we appear to have a bit of an emergency all of a sudden. Widow Twankey, throat infection.'

He extended his hand to Stanley who, being unable to extricate his own from Rab in time, was reduced to gesturing with his elbows.

Larry's hand became a cocked gun.

'Tell you what, if you make the arrangement with Janet here, I'll come and catch a performance soon.'

And with that he was gone. Stanley finally shucked off the puppets and closed the suitcase. Janet was flipping through the pages of a large leather-bound diary, frowning.

'It isn't going to be easy, you know.'

For the first time since he had written to Larry Bowen, Stanley experienced a distinct sinking feeling.

Janet was right, it wasn't easy. Larry was due back in London the following Monday and wouldn't be returning to Belfast until the end of the first week in January. Stanley had no bookings for a fortnight after that. He suggested he simply call in at the theatre again, but Janet was adamant.

'Mr Bowen wants to see a performance.'

At Stanley's suggestion she pencilled in 7.15 pm on Monday 23rd. She paused, waiting for the venue.

'Let's see,' Stanley said. 'It's towards the top of the Ormeau – e, a, u – Road, on the left-hand side, there's a church and then a little further on there's like a path …'

Janet tutted.

'All I need is the name.'

'Well that's just it,' said Stanley. 'I'm not sure if there is a name as such.'

'Oh, for heaven's sake, the number then.'

They had been walking while they talked and had arrived again at the stage door.

'If you just write *Scout hut*,' Stanley said and left before he would read the contempt in her eyes.

A couple of days into the New Year, he wrote to Larry Bowen again. The Scout hut engagement, he explained, was a long-standing obligation, he hoped he could always find the time to accommodate such worthy causes. Larry replied as soon as he got back. Perfectly understood, couldn't agree more. He even proposed they meet for a drink – did Stanley know the bar in the International Hotel? – the afternoon of the show so that Stanley could tell him a little more about the act.

In fact they spent an agreeable half-hour (Larry was a little late, understandably) talking about almost everything but Rab and Jem. Larry did say, though, that he had been speaking, unofficially you understand, at dinner, to a colleague in

152

Light Entertainment and they were both of a mind that there were openings for fresh young talent in the glove-puppet line.

He touched Stanley's sleeve as he rose to return to the Opera House.

'Don't worry about this evening, I'll just slip into the back of the room. I *am* looking forward to it very much.'

Despite these reassuring words, Stanley had to struggle to quell the nerves three hours later as he went through his final preparations in the kitchen at the rear of the Scout hut, listening to the excited chatter of the Cubs out front. He had not been entirely untruthful when he told Larry this was a long-standing obligation, for he had played here once before and had been asked back. Appreciative audience, he remembered (Stanley kept a record of all his engagements), but no pushover. He told himself a touch of nerves was no bad thing, stopped you becoming complacent.

The Scout master rapped on the kitchen door.

'Ready?'

'Ready,' said Stanley and then the lights were switched out and he had fifteen seconds to crawl into position behind the lectern's black drape. The forward lights came back on. Stanley stretched his left hand above his head.

'Hiya, Jem,' a Cub Scout called and for the next twenty-six minutes the hut was a tumult of shouts and laughter.

He couldn't recall a better show. The boys clapped and whistled and stamped their feet in the darkness which brought it to a close. The Scout master came back to the kitchen to congratulate him. He offered Stanley a cup of tea. Stanley declined. A friend of his was probably waiting to have a word.

'Tall man, wee beard?' the master asked.

'That's him.'

'He left.'

Stanley wondered could there have been two such men in the hall; decided not.

'Are you sure he's gone?'

'I let him out myself,' the Scout master said. 'Halfway through.'

It was nothing to get worked up over. Leaving halfway through wasn't in itself a bad sign. Larry Bowen was a busy man – he had a show of his own to think about, for goodness sake; thirteen minutes might have been enough to convince him and he did say he would be as unobtrusive as possible. It *had* been a good performance, the first half if anything stronger than the second. No, there was no need at all to worry. Stanley even managed to sleep late the next morning. Philip and Paul were both at work, Heather, a nurse now, was on nights and was already in bed. His mother was out doing the things his mother did to put in her day since she'd gone on the sick two years before with her back: shopping, dropping in on friends.

Stanley lifted the lid of the porridge pot on the back ring of the stove and found someone had already set it to soak in Fairy Liquid. The bubbles had retreated to the sides, sliming the surface of the water. A solid circle of porridge, worked loose from the bottom of the pot, lolled in oily suspension, reminding Stanley of the jars in the science block at school with their bleached, arrested foetuses. He replaced the lid.

The family's assortment of cups, saucers and plates had dripped almost dry on the rack on the draining board. Floral patterns, blue and yellow checks, an abstract design of coffee tables and lamps. He ate a bowl of All Bran standing with his back to the kitchen sink. A women's magazine lay folded open at the horoscopes page on Heather's chair. Stanley briefly contemplated consulting his own stars, but decided that even reading them in jest lent too much credibility.

He tried to invest the moment with a sense of ending. All these fixtures and furnishings would change. It would be the first thing he did, after he had moved out himself of course. The phone bill was overdue and he had given his mother the fee from last night's show leaving himself more or less skint. That too seemed appropriate. He imagined, years from now, reminiscing: *I'd barely enough in my pocket that morning for ten Park Drive.*

It was mid-afternoon before the doubts began to nag. His mother had been home and gone out again. Heather came down to the front room and sat on the settee, the hem of her nightie tucked under her feet.

'I thought you were away to London,' she said.

'Yeah, well I won't be taking you along to write my scripts.'

Heather made a face – *sorry I spoke* – and pulled another magazine from under the cushion. Stanley stared at the telephone, squat and black and silent.

'Do you think …?' he began and then saw his sister's raised eyebrows. 'Never mind.'

He fetched his coat and walked to the shop for his ten Park Drive, but instead of returning home he carried on into town. The matinée had just come down in the Opera House. When he asked at the stage door, however, he was told that Mr Bowen was unavailable. Could he have a word with Janet, then? But, no, Janet had taken the afternoon off. Stanley left a note. He would be in the bar of the International Hotel if Larry had a moment free.

Walking away from the theatre he remembered he hadn't a penny to buy a drink.

He tried to make himself inconspicuous, though not so inconspicuous that Larry Bowen would have an excuse for having missed him, and remained, dry, in the bar for as long as he could bear the glare of the belligerent-looking black-browed barman. The second time he called at the theatre he was informed that Mr Bowen had left for the day.

The evening sky was the colour of mud. When at last he reached home, Stanley had been walking through sleet for a quarter of an hour, so that even Heather's note on the pad by the phone failed to take away the chill he felt:

Harry Bowen rang. (Clever Heather.) *Sorry 'bout today. Tomorrow OK? Same time, same place.*

'How do I put this?' Larry Bowen said.

He had arrived in the Blue Bar twenty minutes late, not as long as Stanley had been preparing himself to have to wait, but long enough to erode what little confidence he had been able to salvage from yesterday afternoon. The interview, having started badly, got worse. Stanley thought Larry found this highly amusing on some level, as though they had been talking at cross-purposes all along and were able now to see the funny side.

'Your act is very, ah ... Well, they're *Belfast* puppets.'

Stanley took a drink so as not to say anything too rash.

'But I thought I explained that to you.'

Now Larry Bowen really did laugh.

'Oh, yes, you said. At least, I knew they were Irish. It's just I was expecting ... oh, you know.'

'No,' said Stanley, too miserable to make this any easier. 'I don't.'

'Green suits – the little red beards?'

'Leprechauns?'

'*Yes,*' said Larry. 'Sort of.' Then hopefully: 'Leprechauns are instantly recognisable.'

Stanley let his gaze rove round the Blue Bar where very un-leprechaun-like Belfast men drank and chatted and smoked cigarettes.

'You do see what I'm saying?'

'I think so.'

Larry Bowen seemed to take heart from this.

'It's all a matter of what the public will accept.'

156

'Like Liverpool?' Stanley was thinking Doddie's fucking Diddie Men.

'Ah, well, now, Liverpool's a little different. Liverpool we've – people in the rest of England, I mean – we've grown accustomed to it. And then, of course, some of your material ...'

'I'm coming up with new stuff all the time.'

Larry Bowen blinked away the interruption and made a mallet of his fist to drive the point home.

'All that business about class ...' His voice tailed off, found volume again. 'These are children we're dealing with.'

'It's the world,' said Stanley simply.

'To you, maybe.'

Stanley was telling himself there was always Easter and Butlin's. He was telling himself *Crackerjack!* wasn't the only programme on TV. He was telling himself just about anything that would stop him wanting to hit Larry Bowen or burst into tears.

'Another drink?' Larry asked by way of conciliation.

Stanley shook his head. A minute passed. The *Blue Peter* hornpipe ran its jaunty course in the background.

'Well, then.' Larry stood. 'I am sorry I can't be of more help.'

Stanley took his offered hand. What else was he to do?

'If ever you do have an idea you think might be more in our line ...'

'Of course,' said Stanley.

'Good luck, then.'

Two legal-types stepped apart to let him pass. He checked a moment and turned back.

'The leprechauns, you know, would have a definite appeal. Just a thought.'

Walking home, however, Stanley had a better thought. Rab and Jem would *disguise themselves* as leprechauns to try and get work in England. They would be useless of course, terrible accents, beards coming unstuck. The worse they were the funnier it would be, a complete send-up of all the stereotypes, ending

157

perhaps – yes, why not? – with their own. I mean, who wore a flat cap these days in Belfast?

He wrote the routine that night, laughing aloud several times, and next morning borrowed money from Heather to take it into town to be typed. He left the envelope with the doorman at the Opera House with instructions to deliver it into Larry Bowen's hands. Saturday was the final night of the pantomime. The day after, Larry was leaving town for good. Stanley enclosed a handwritten note with the typed pages, requesting one last meeting in the International Hotel.

*

Janet it was who had come, black polo-necked, into the Blue Bar that morning of the fire with word that Larry Bowen was too tied up to get away. But Stanley by now was desperate. He would come round to the Opera House himself. (Janet didn't think that was a good idea.) He would return to the bar later. He would wait until closing time if need be.

Janet shrugged.

'So, wait,' she said.

I wish I could tell you I got Stanley's story straight from his own mouth. I wish I could tell you a lot of things I can't. Like that I didn't think Larry Bowen might have had a point; that Stanley's act didn't sound to me too like the worst load of crap.

15

Jamesie said he had never in all his days working in the International seen anything like it. He had feared the worst when he walked in the door of the Portaferry Room and every head turned towards him, for all the world, he said, as though they were looking for help. Seeing he was just a barman the heads turned away again. And that was when he heard the accordion. It was over on the far side of the room, the Donegall Square side. The drapes were not quite meeting in the middle and the light from the elongated streetlamp – so close you could nearly have leaned out the window and touched it – shone through and for a moment all that Jamesie could make out was this light and the accordion moving as though of its own volition. He had to squint to pin down the accordion player, starting with the fingers and working in. The head was wrinkled and entirely hairless. ('You couldn't go that bald,' Jamesie said, 'you'd have to have been that way from birth.') It bobbed fitfully above the bellows like a balloon left over from a long-ago party. The noise came to an abrupt end. The applause was on the discouraging side of polite.

'"Thank you," your man says in this squeaky wee voice. "That was the Tune the Old Cow Died Of," – well he might as well have – "And now I'm going to play you some old bollocks of a jig and I'd like to see you all up on your feet." And off he went again. Nobody moved but me,' said Jamesie. 'I fucking legged it over to the bar before someone snapped and grabbed the hold of me to dance.'

The bar in the Portaferry Room consisted of trestle tables, pushed together to form three sides of a rectangle and draped with white cloths. Flea Johnston (Flea? Don't ask me, even his wife called him that), who normally worked in the Cocktail Bar, was stood behind here, arms folded across his chest, staring blankly. Jamesie waved a hand before Flea's eyes. He said he still couldn't be sure the start Flea gave was put on.

'Wasn't there supposed to be a wedding here?' Jamesie asked him as the accordion shrieked and wheezed. 'Did the bride not turn up or what?'

Flea nodded towards an unhappy-looking young woman in a plain pale turquoise dress clashing calamitously with the wallpaper's magenta flowers.

('She wasn't bad, herself, like,' Jamesie said. 'I mean I'd've given her one.' Coming from Jamesie, this did little to distinguish her from the broad mass of women between the ages of sixteen and sixty in Belfast.)

The groom – 'A fucking glipe,' according to Jamesie – sat beside her patting her hand, possibly in sympathy, possibly in time to the music.

'That there's the minister,' Flea said.

'Who?' Jamesie was still eyeing up the bride.

'With the accordion.'

'Ah, fuck off.'

'I'm telling you.'

And sure enough when Jamesie looked a second time he saw that the neck beneath the shrivelled head was ringed by a shiny dog collar.

'Apparently he has an LP out.'

'Name of Jesus,' said Jamesie.

'I think that one was already taken.'

The racket went from bad to worse to woeful. The groom's father and mother came out on to the yawning space before the minister and walked around it a couple of times. Two women, handbags hanging like breeze blocks from the crooks of their arms, got up and followed them. As they passed Jamesie, he heard one of them counting to the other under her breath.

'One-two-three, one-two-three.'

'That's the way!' the minister shouted, launching into yet another tune. He was enjoying himself. 'Let's see you all out there.'

The two couples sat down. The groom pulled lightly on the bride's hand. She drew it away, sharp. Everyone else was looking at the carpet between their undancing feet. Not a single person came near the bar.

'He has them terrified,' Flea said.

'So what did you need me here for?'

'I'm sorry. The Swinging Vicar went out for a while. I thought he was finished. *They* thought he was finished. For about a quarter of an hour I never stopped. It was mental. Actually, it was great.'

Jamesie stirred with the point of an index finger the paltry collection of coins in the glass ashtray Flea had been using for tips.

'Somebody's going to have to do something,' he said.

Flea Johnston swore blind that Jamesie really did do what he told me he did next.

'I thought, fuck this for a lark, so the next time your man comes to the end of a tune I saunters over.'

'Jamesie, you didn't?'

'Fucking right I did. Saunters over and has a wee word in his ear.'

It was Tuesday before I got a proper chance to talk to Flea.

'It's true,' he said. 'I could hardly believe myself he was going to go through with it. You know Jamesie, most of the time, all mouth. I was half expecting him to swerve out of the way at

161

the last minute and start picking up glasses, but he didn't, he bent down and began whispering. The whole room was staring, they could see the minister frowning, and then Jamesie straightened up and the minister shook his head and leaned forward towards the microphone and says, "I've had a bit of an unusual request."'

'I said it was for the happy couple, for luck,' Jamesie told me. 'I said it was a sort of tradition in the International. He said it was the first he'd heard of it. I told him he could suit himself but that was the way it had always been and by that stage I think he was scared of not believing me, so he just made the announcement and handed me the microphone.'

Jamesie sang. He said he did, Flea said he did.

'I asked the Rev. did he know "Love Me Tender". I hummed him a bit. I didn't let on it was Elvis, for fear he'd take a buckle in his eye.'

'Were you not scundered?' I asked. Jamesie twisted his mouth. 'Ach …'

'He was fucking amazing,' Flea told me on Tuesday. 'I would never say it to his face, but he was. "Love Me Tender", "Crying", "Your Cheating Heart."'

'Nobody shouted at me to stop after the first one,' Jamesie said, 'so I thought I might as well carry on. I forgot the words a couple of times, like, but I just went la-la-la until I got on to the ones I knew again. I don't know why people make such a big deal of these pop stars, it's a piece of piss, really.'

The minister, it seems, joined in gamely, even if he never was one hundred per cent convinced he ought to be letting this happen.

'A bit ropy on "Your Cheating Heart",' Jamesie said. 'But, give him his dues, he made a pretty good fist of it. Even called the guests up to dance again.'

Jamesie had by now adopted his normal stance behind the counter of the Blue Bar, right foot a little to the fore of the left, head drawn back and inclined to one side, observing the fawn flow of Guinness into an angled pint glass. I realised that behind the bar or behind a microphone, it was all one to Jamesie. I realised that I hoped one day somebody would tell him he was in fact some sort of star.

'And did they dance?'

'Dance? Fuck! Those people wouldn't have got out of their seats if it had been Elvis himself standing up there in front of them.'

When he had finished his third song he replaced the microphone on its stand and shook the minister's hand.

'They're all yours, Reverend,' he said. 'And good luck to you.'

Jamesie rested the glass on the grid above the slops tray. The last Guinness in turned halfway down and started for the top again.

'I'm telling you,' he said. 'I've never in all my days here seen the like of it.'

Vi, Chester's wife and chief tormentor, was at the bar next to Stanley. The two had evidently been chatting a while for when at last I got round to serving her, Vi was urging Stanley to have something as well.

'I won't, thanks,' Stanley said.

'Nonsense.'

'No, really, I won't.'

'Don't listen to him,' Vi told me. 'Get him whatever it was he just had and I'll have two rum and black and a Power's.'

Stanley gave a weak smile of assent. I worried that he wouldn't last the night, but there was nothing I could say, I went and poured the drinks. Jamesie was peering over at the TV. Adam Adamant, the time-slipped sleuth, running down an alleyway with some girl in a miniskirt holding on to his hand. No prizes for guessing which one Jamesie was interested in. The bases of the shorts glasses clacked as I picked them up. Jamesie turned.

'Danny Boy ...' He motioned me to come back, still glancing over his shoulder at the television.

'In a minute,' I said.

Vi had her hand on Stanley's sleeve. She was laughing so hard her head was practically resting on the bar.

'Oh, wait till I tell Myrtle,' she said into the wood. Her head flicked back and I glimpsed the pink plate of her dentures. 'To think of the times I patted your bare bum!'

I stared at Stanley, too startled for a moment to set down the drinks, or even to disguise my surprise. His expression said he could explain, but Vi beat him to it.

'There I was wondering where I knew this fella from, and here didn't I used to chum with his mammy during the war.'

I had managed to let go the glasses. Stanley lifted his pint and swallowed as though it was more than the drink he hoped would disappear. Vi blinked back her laughter leaving a softness in her eyes.

'My own were all well up by then and Brenda, this one's mammy, would call me in sometimes to let me change him, for you'd miss that, you know, when they're grown. Such a lovely wee article.'

The softness seemed about to turn to tears, but instead of crying she set off laughing again.

'Such a lovely wee bum. Oh, son,' she said, stroking Stanley's arm. 'Wait till I tell Myrtle.'

When she had gone I detained myself at that end of the bar a while longer, wiping the counter, stacking empties. I huffed and I puffed a lot. I'm pretty certain Stanley twigged I was play-acting the wronged woman. I coaxed a smile out of him anyway.

'Old neighbours!'

'I'm saying nothing.'

I turned on my heel. I thought it was just possible I was starting to make some headway with Stanley.

Jamesie was in the middle of a big order.

'Don't go away,' he said as I passed.

'Dead likely.'

On the other side of him I took a wrinkled ten-bob note for four bottles of stout. Hugh was holding a glass, three-quarters full, under the Carling spout, flicking the tap up and down with his index finger. The lager trickled out, all pressure gone. Under cover of the counter he agitated the beer already in the glass until he had dribbled and swirled his way to a reasonably convincing pint.

'Jamesie, Danny, next one free,' he said moving to the till. 'We need a new keg of Black Label there.'

I had just been handed an order on a scrap of envelope by a man who appeared flummoxed by his own shorthand. People drink all sorts, of course, but I couldn't remember ever being asked for a Jameson and tonic before.

'No, see that's a g,' I said when I'd had a few moments to study the scrap: 'g and t.'

'I wondered,' he said.

'How many bottles of Tennents?' I asked.

'How many does it say?'

I read: '"Ten. botts."'

He looked at me disbelieving.

'It wouldn't be anything like ten.'

'I know,' I said. 'The Ten. is the Tennents. I'm asking how many.'

'Two,' he said, then counted on his fingers. 'Three. Hold on, what all else is there on that?'

I was preparing to recite the entire list when I felt Jamesie's breath close to my ear.

'She's gone.'

Of course I knew at once who he meant and the question Jamesie must have read sketched on my face was how I had let her slip from my mind so quickly and completely.

'Your girlfriend. I've been trying to tell you.'

I stared uselessly at the place below the television where Ingrid had been. She couldn't have left by the street door, of that at least I was certain, which meant she was, in all likelihood, still in the hotel. Jamesie eased the scrawled order from my hand.

'Barrel needs changing,' he said. I nodded slightly, then understanding, emphatically.

'Hugh!' I called and pointed towards the hallway and the store beyond. Hugh gave me the thumbs up.

'Right, then,' Jamesie said, squinting at the torn envelope. 'Ten bottles of what?'

Ingrid wasn't with Ted Connolly either. I had checked out the Cocktail Bar on the pretence of asking Len did he need anything from the store. Clive White was there, though, with Fitz and Councillor Noades, Fitz's favourite Armanda cigars plugging their chuffed gubs.

I changed the barrel as fast as I was able, faster in the end than was advisable. My trousers when I had finished were damp on both thighs from spilled lager and I had managed to tweak something in my neck trailing the old keg out of the road.

Stuff this, I thought. Why should I care if she wants to make a fool of herself?

I believe I was being rhetorical, so the answer, from whatever recess of my mind it sprang, was as unexpected as it was unwelcome: Just because.

I don't know what Ingrid had against it, 'just because' worked for me every time.

I wiped the front of my trousers with a folded apron and struck out once more in search of her.

The Master, who was master, above all things, of timing, was coming down the Long Corridor from the cloak deposit as I arrived at the top of the stairs. 'Ah,' I almost said. 'Danny,' he did say. 'Just the man I want.'

Over his shoulder I saw two waiters duck into separate doorways. I recalled reading once that whenever the Queen visits a place the toilets are painted in advance and wondering did she think that toilets always smelled of fresh emulsion; similarly I wondered now whether the International, to the Master, wasn't at times a curiously under-staffed hotel. He pursed his lips, making a steeple of his index fingers in the crease of his chin.

'I've been meaning to have a word.'

This could only be about one thing: *he had steamed open the Vances's letter before passing it on to Len Gray.*

'It's been a bit hectic today,' I said, stalling.

The Master bid good evening to a guest with his arm in a plaster cast before returning his attention to me.

'Hectic? Yes, yes. That was partly what I wanted to talk to you about. I've been watching you,' he said. I felt a sudden hot itch where my hip pocket came in contact with my buttock. 'You're very *enthusiastic*.'

I could hardly deny that.

'I enjoy my work,' I said, though with less conviction than I might have wished, for I had become aware of a commotion down the corridor where a huddle of young women and girls had gathered outside the Damask Room, all talking at once. I detected in their excitement the delicious horror of scandal:

'Did you see her face?'

'I near *died*.'

Well that's that, I was thinking, you're too late, and then the group nudged one another into silence and parted and a redhead, red-faced from weeping, scurried from the function room to the toilets, one hand twisted up her back holding together a busted zip.

'Two pounds of apples in a one-pound bag,' one young woman said and the rest of the group laughed behind their hands.

'As long as you don't let anyone take advantage of you.'

The Master, having monitored this little drama with his ears alone, was talking to me again. He lowered his voice.

'Guests can be very demanding. Being in a hotel is always a special occasion for them. They forget, some of them, that this is our job and that like all jobs it has its limits.'

I was not only certain then that he had opened the Vances's envelope but that the letter I had burned unread contained the precise and intricate details of what Bob and Natalie and I had got up to together in room 304. And yet he was smiling. I smiled back, at a loss to know what I was expected to say. He seemed to be happy with just the smile.

'Good,' he said. Sometimes I think we had the Master all wrong.

He and I had somehow in the course of our conversation become turned around, so that now when we parted the Master started down the corridor towards the Damask Room, as though that was where he had all along been headed. I had no alternative but to move in the opposite direction and not wanting to give the impression that I had walked upstairs only to go back down again (the Master, we said, kept his hair short at the back so as not to block the rear view) I decided to carry on up to the lobby.

Cecil was kneeling outside the porter's room rubbing at a burn mark with his thumb. The fickleness of fame, one minute you're in every home in Strabane, the next you're picking somebody else's fag butts off the floor. I said hello, Cecil carried on rubbing.

'See people,' he said. 'Hallions the lot of them.'

The Master popped his head in the door of the Damask Room. The rest of his body followed by degrees. There was no need for me to pretend any longer, I was going back to work.

Another thirty seconds and I would have missed her, coming round the corner from the lobby, tailing a man who was as broad as he was tall and sported the red carnation of the McAdam party, a flower of her own now pinned to the lapel of her soot-speckled jacket.

She froze when she saw me. Cecil, seeing her feet come to such an unexpected halt, looked up from the floor, glancing from her to me.

'It's OK,' I told him and at that moment Ingrid turned and ran.

'Is that woman a guest?'

Cecil was using the wall to help himself up. The world at large could mock him all it liked with its antics after dark, but once any part of it strayed over the doorstep of the International it was Cecil's business.

'It's OK,' I said again, pushing back the air between us with my hands, making in fast reverse for the lobby. 'I'll tell you later.'

In the entrance lobby a taxi driver, zipped tight into a Paddy Hopkirk rally coat, tossed his car keys from hand to hand, waiting for his fare. *Taxi for Moore?* Two children, short boy, gangly girl, chased each other in a figure of eight before the reception desk. An elderly couple teetered arm-in-arm from the dining room towards the lounge. No sign here of recent disturbance. A bell dinged announcing the lift's departure for the upper floors.

I clicked my fingers in reply.

Whatever else about the International, the lift wasn't what you would call lightning fast. I took the stairs and was waiting for it when it arrived at the second floor. Ingrid was alone inside.

'You've got to stop this,' I said.

She raised her camera and for an instant I lost her in the flash. I blinked. She hadn't moved.

'I'm serious,' I said. 'You'll get me the sack.'

'Did I ask you to follow me?'

She stepped out into the landing smoothing her skirt, rumpled from running.

'Exactly,' she said.

I tried another tack.

'You shouldn't be here. The night porter finds you, or the manager, they'll throw you out.'

'I don't think so,' Ingrid said.

She brushed past me across the landing to inspect a painting hanging on a narrow wall between bedroom doors. Fields, clouds, a ruined castle: landscape by numbers. The hotel was coming down with them.

A woman giggled in one of the bedrooms.

'Do you like art, Danny?' Ingrid asked, as though we were two people with an hour to kill in the Ulster Museum. My blood boiled.

'You're acting like a fucking header, do you know that?'

Even before she turned to face me, I could tell from the contraction of her shoulders that my words had wounded. Good. I told myself I really was past caring.

'And you're –' she started but couldn't finish.

Oh, fuck, who was I kidding.

'I'm sorry,' I said. 'You had me worried, that's all.'

'Am I supposed to be grateful?'

The lift doors closed at my back. There didn't appear to be a whole lot more to say. I stood looking at Ingrid's shoes (I don't know where Ingrid was looking), listening to the lift make its way to the ground floor. It paused there only briefly before ascending again. Somehow I knew it was coming for us. Somehow I knew it was Cecil inside.

'We've got to go,' I said, and steered Ingrid by the elbow. 'Now.'

All the floors in the International were split-level, the lift letting out on to the upper landing, where the larger bedrooms were to be found. Stairs ran down either side of the shaft to the lower landing, with a second staircase on the right-hand side leading to the floor above.

Going higher up was hardly an option for Ingrid and me. I knew my movies well enough, I didn't want to end the night, to say nothing of my life, slipping on roof tiles, dangling by my fingertips from a creaking gutter.

We took the nearest flight of stairs, two at a time, to the lower lobby from where we might comfortably have made good our escape to the ground floor had our way not been blocked by a fella and girl jammed against the banister, kissing.

Wait, did I say kissing? They were eating the faces off each other.

'Easy on there,' Ingrid whispered.

I could only guess from the flowered band in the girl's hair, the volume of her skirt and petticoats, that she was a bridesmaid and that she and her man had wrestled each other out of the Strangford Room at the far end of the corridor. I had seen or heard nothing of the day's reception there. The Strangford, in the International, was a state apart. Food was brought in by a lift direct from the kitchens and its bar staff guarded their eminence jealously. (The Strangford was a favourite spot for business conventions, you can imagine the tips.) For all I knew they were immune to the flu up there.

The bridesmaid's fingers pressed the buttons of her beau's spine. Her skirt rustled and rose an inch or two. He emitted a grunt which lengthened into a groan.

'Bloody hell,' Ingrid said aloud.

'Danny?' Cecil called from the upper landing. 'Is that you down there?'

The bridesmaid opened her eyes, or that eye at least which was visible over the man's shoulder. She may have attempted to say something but she had one tongue too many in her mouth. She grunted; he groaned some more. I waved as Ingrid and I scooted past. I'd had an idea.

By the time Cecil arrived on the lower landing, we were at the top of the stairs back up to the lift.

'Bright boy,' Ingrid said.

'Amn't I?' I said, and at that moment the lift doors shut and the lift began its descent without us.

'In the name of God!' Cecil had spotted the kissing couple.

'What are you gawking at, you dirty old shite?' The kissing couple had spotted Cecil, and the man, I think it's fair to say, was not best pleased at the interruption.

'Watch you your mouth,' Cecil said. 'I'm the night porter.'

'You're a fucking pervert, that's what you are.'

The red light lit up behind the G on the panel above the lift door, stayed there five or ten seconds, then went out.

'Leave him alone, Brendan,' the bridesmaid was saying. 'Come on back to the party. Come on.'

'Come on,' I urged the lift. It stopped on the first floor. '*Come on.*'

'I'll put a complaint in about this.'

'*You'll* put a complaint in?'

Brendan and Cecil were still having a go at each other, but from a distance now as the bridesmaid continued to coax Brendan back to the Strangford Room.

'You think I'm kidding?'

'You think *I* am?'

'He's not worth it, Brendan.'

It was music to my ears while it lasted; while it lasted Cecil would not be hunting for Ingrid and me.

The lift left the first floor, headed in our direction. I closed my eyes, clasping my hands in a theatrical show of gratitude at our imminent deliverance and it was in this temporary blind state that I knocked into the chrome waste bin by the lift door.

'Danny!' Cecil and Ingrid both shouted.

I caught the bin before it hit the ground. The lift arrived in the same instant that the bedroom door facing it was opened. Anne, the bride from the Damask Room, stood in the doorway, changed now into her going-away dress, though she was going nowhere until tomorrow, a diamante earring dangling from her left hand.

'What's all the noise?'

I hoped she wouldn't recognise me. Some hope.

'Hello,' she said. She screwed up one gold-shadowed eye as she jabbed the earring home. 'Fancy meeting you up here.'

'Yes,' I said. 'Fancy.'

Behind me, Ingrid whimpered, too quietly, thankfully, for anyone but me to hear. This close to the woman who had married the man she used to love she was as panicked as I was.

The lift bell sounded, the doors slid back, releasing a guff of cigar smoke from which emerged Fitz and Councillor Noades. Fitz hailed me with a hand whose thumb was hooked in the collar tab of a camel-hair overcoat. Somewhere in the bridal suite Joe shouted, 'Anne, I can't find my blue tie. Anne?'

'You wee skitter,' Cecil spluttered from close to the top of the stairs and then his voice went up an octave. 'Fitz!'

'Anne?'

Anne's brow kinked as Ingrid backed into the empty lift compartment, trailing me by the sleeve.

Fitz had his room key out. Cecil had one foot on the landing.

'Cecil!' said Fitz. 'The very man. What's all this I've been hearing about you being on the TV?'

Ingrid dragged me the final yard. I hit the button for the ground floor just as the door behind Anne opened wider and Joe appeared, his shirt collar standing stiffly about his ears.

'Anne?' he said and looked with her at me and the lift door closing.

Ingrid was pressed tight against the wall.

'Do you think he could have seen me?' she whispered.

'No.'

'Oh, thank God. Thank God, thank God, thank *God*.'

She cuffed my wrist with thumb and forefinger and placed my hand on her chest.

'Feel my heart.'

I felt warmth, a sloping tension, the faintest of flutters in the hollow of my palm. She took my hand away.

'I thought I was going to explode,' she said.

The lift jolted. For one awful moment I thought it had stopped. I imagined Joe and Anne, Cecil, Fitz and the councillor hauling on the ropes, inching us back to the second floor. I glanced at Ingrid. She wasn't breathing. Then there was another jolt and the lift was dropping smoothly again.

We were still laughing when we came to rest in the entrance lobby.

'Tell me that didn't happen,' Ingrid said.

'That didn't happen.'

'Oh, good,' she said. 'But thanks anyway.'

If I had known she was going to kiss me I would have prepared myself to remember it. Her lips were gone almost before mine had a chance to register they were even there, before I had a chance to respond. I wanted to ask her whether this hadn't happened either, but I didn't and it did. I know it did.

And yet stepping out into the lobby it was quite possible to imagine that Ingrid had succeeded in willing her fiction into fact. The taxi driver jingled his keys, the two children ran in their figure of eight, exactly as they had when I last saw them. The elderly couple had still not made it to the lounge.

'Time I wasn't here,' I said.

'Me too,' said Ingrid.

She asked the taxi driver was he free. He looked her up and down.

'I only wish I was,' he said sadly.

I gathered up empties from a table as I rounded the corner into the Blue Bar. Jamesie raised an inquisitive eyebrow.

My only reply was to whisper as I passed, 'If Cecil asks, I never left.'

Jamesie winked. Hugh was at the till.

'Carling's on,' I said.

'Good lad. Serve that man there.'

*

I had been back in the bar less than a minute when Stanley went out. He waited until he caught my eye then gestured vaguely to the half-drunk pint sitting on the counter. Fresh air. He looked like he could do with it. No matter what the weather outside, by this stage of a Saturday night the bar was a hothouse, so that staff and customers alike began to resemble some evolutionary off-shoot sustained by a gaseous mix of alcohol and tobacco. Some were better adapted to this atmosphere than others.

Sure enough, Cecil came looking for me. Jamesie intercepted him at the serving hatch.

'I'd love to talk to you,' he said, 'but I'm up to my eyes. Sorry, sport.'

That sport was a nice touch, it had worked before with Cecil, but he wasn't going to be deflected tonight. There was something going on, he said, and he wanted to get to the bottom of it. Jamesie abandoned the bonhomie, told Cecil he was dreaming. If Cecil had any wit, he'd have left it there. Instead he tried to push past Jamesie to me and got no further than Hugh.

'All right, what's the problem?'

'Your barmen,' Cecil said. 'Running about the hotel after women.' (Cecil pronounced it 'weemin'.)

'I hardly think so,' Hugh said.

'And I'm telling you,' said Cecil. 'Didn't I see it with my own eyes?'

Hugh had had about all he could take for one night of people interfering with his bar. He beckoned Cecil closer. Hugh was not a man to whom strong language came readily, but when it came it came with a conviction that was heartfelt.

'Cecil,' Hugh said. 'Unless you actually want my toe up your hole, you'll fuck off out of here and leave my boys alone.'

And Cecil did, fucked right off and didn't come near us the rest of the night.

Customers had begun buying drinks two at a time. We were on the countdown to last orders and the reasoning was that by getting a couple in now they would beat the rush, though you knew you would see the same people back at the bar a minute after you called Time, looking for just one more. I was in the middle of an order for more or less a full keg of Guinness when Barney Keenan presented his just-washed face on the other side of the counter.

'Did you not get enough of this place earlier?' I asked him.

A fair number of the staff did come in to drink in the Blue Bar when they were off-duty; Barney though wasn't normally one of them. He still had on his woolly hat and scarf, but beneath his coat I glimpsed what looked suspiciously like a new shirt and tie.

'You going somewhere?'

'Oh,' Barney said, drumming his fingers. 'You know.'

Well that was clear, then.

Jamesie lifted Stanley's glass from the bar.

'This dead?'

'No, he's coming back,' I said, realising as I did that Stanley had now been gone for some time. 'At least I think he is.'

Jamesie replaced the glass heavily.

'How's Marian?' he said, a greeting, not a question.

Christ, I thought, they're all in tonight. Marian's custom, like Barney's, fell well short of habitual. She had drawn up a seat at a table in the centre of the room and was tugging her arms free of her coat sleeves. She was wearing what my mother would have described approvingly as 'a nice frock' – dainty floral motif, lace at the collar and cuffs – and her hair had obviously been in curlers not too long since. I mean it as no disrespect to Marian, though, when I say that my mother would probably not have approved of the peculiar cast she gave to this decorous get-up, like a movie star version of a frump, at once unconvincing and sexy. She placed her coat and mock-croc bag on the seat next to hers to signal it was kept.

Hugh was taking Barney's order. A pint and a Bristol Cream on the rocks. (We'd had a run on these over Christmas after they were featured in an ad in the *Ulster Tatler*.) I added the two drinks and the two seats and belatedly got the two of them together.

'God, Barney,' I said. 'You kept that quiet.'

And Barney sighed.

'Isn't she lovely?'

Lovely didn't come close.

'Absolutely,' I agreed.

Jamesie had his back to me.

'That cheeky bastard,' he said.

'Who?'

'Smelly Arse. Lonely Pint. He's just come in the door with your bird.'

16

Perfect. Just perfect.

Second Cousin Clive could not have been happier.

There was nothing like getting even for raising the spirits. Experience had taught him that where revenge was concerned you had to be prepared to play the long game. Where most things in life were concerned, come to think of it. Business, drinking ... Especially drinking.

Clive knew his limit and stayed within it. Councillor Noades on the other hand was reaching for his steps like a man half-tore just now as he followed Fitz out of the Cocktail Bar. Fitz himself had seemed OK, but it was harder to tell with him. The night before, in the Royal Avenue hotel, he was perfectly lucid and coherent, then the moment he walked out into the midnight air for the taxi his legs went from under him.

Boy, was he hammered: had to go and lie down in the spare room a while when they got back to Clive's. Bobbie, the girl Fitz had taken the biggest shine to, had gone in to check on him and hadn't come out again for over an hour. Clive had tried to pump her for the dirt after Fitz left. How come she'd taken so long? Had anything happened? *What was he like?* But Bobbie had fended off all his questions. It was none of Clive's business. Fitz had been an absolute gentleman. What sort of a girl did Clive think she was?

Clive knew exactly what sort of girl Bobbie was, that's why he'd phoned her.

Angela, Clive's girl, said she thought Fitz was sweet. He had been thrown against her at one point in the taxi and had immediately apologised. No pawing or anything, though he was right up against her boob, and with it being such a squeeze in the back there, it was nearly harder not to. Bobbie was right, an absolute gent.

Yeah, yeah, yeah.

As soon as the girls had gone, sometime after four, Clive went into the spare room and pulled back the bedclothes. And sure enough there it was, a little to the right of centre, greying now against the pink sheets. *The* stain.

If you want to know the truth, he got a bit of a hard-on again imagining Bobbie coaxing Fitz's little load out of him.

Clive always imagined other men as having a *little* load to be coaxed out of them at such moments. He thought it, frankly, a sign of weakness or inadequacy to allow yourself to be enticed into the sort of set-up he had contrived for Fitz last night.

Noades was just as bad. That carry-on at dinner with the new waitress: a schoolgirl, practically. If only Clive had known, he could have saved Fitz five hundred pounds and just steered a couple of wee lassies in gymslips the councillor's way. Clive thought they were never going to get him out of that dining room.

Len, the bar manager, had been expecting them. Though the Cocktail Bar was hiving, as it always was at twenty past nine on a Saturday night, a table and three chairs had been kept aside for their arrival. As they were settling themselves, Len himself appeared with a bottle of Hine's Rare and Delicate Champagne Cognac which Fitz had rung down earlier in the evening to reserve. Cigars were handed round. Huge fuckers. Even now, twenty-odd minutes later, Clive's had barely burned beyond the first inch.

He rolled the end of the cigar over his tongue. He had to admit, Fitz knew how to entertain.

Fitz had had the bill for dinner charged to his room. It was no more than Clive would have expected, but still, the recollection of the unfussy way it was done made him think he had been a bit unfair to the fella over Bobbie. He was even prepared to concede that when he went down to Dublin, as some time soon he must, he would not want to insult Fitz by refusing to sleep with whatever young women he happened to introduce Clive to. (He made a mental note: *bring your own Frenchies*.)

Not that Fitz didn't have his faults, mind you. He'd put your head away sometimes, the way he went on. If Clive never in his life again heard that story about the grandparents meeting in the City Hall it would be too soon. It had been trundled out tonight upstairs with the coffee and the cheese. Noades managed to drag his eyes away from the waitress's arse for two minutes.

'And he stayed right here, in this hotel?' He must have been the only person left in Belfast who didn't already know it. Either that or he wasn't above a bit of scheming himself. Why spoil what promised to be a profitable friendship by saying, I'm sorry, but I think you've told me that before? 'Well, well. Isn't that amazing?'

'Hard to credit,' Clive said as Fitz piled in with his punchline.

'So you could say I owe my life to the Union!'

Noades dabbed his lips with a serviette, chuckling. Oh, yes, Clive thought, you know exactly what is at stake here.

Even if he hadn't made a point of checking out the councillor's background, Clive could have had a pretty good stab at it: father self-educated, working class and proud of it, more Red than Orange until the Home Rule crisis, joined Carson's Volunteers, signed the Solemn League and Covenant in his own blood, and spilled what remained of it four years later, six months before his son's birth, in a turnip field in Flanders; the councillor himself, even yet, sympathetic to the working man, but determined above all else to maintain what his father had given his life to secure.

Whatever that entailed. The world was changing and Northern Ireland was going to have to change with it. Anyone who pretended otherwise was a fool. The job of politicians like him was not to set their faces against the changes, but to manage them. The system here had been forged at a time when the state was young and under threat, from inside as well as out. Exclusion and suspicion were appropriate responses to interference and subversion. Of course once in a while a heavier hand than was desirable was employed (for make no mistake, there were some right old bigots in the Unionist Party). Of course there had been outrage, but one way and another the system had worked. Northern Ireland had survived and there was no reason why, with the application of a little common sense – and despite the cavillers and the troublemakers – it should not continue to thrive. It was all about money. Anyone could get up a meeting and pack the hall to the rafters, but when push came to shove money was what the voters cared about. Principles didn't put a television set in the corner, or aspirations a motor car outside the front door. This was the era of the practical man.

Clive would not have argued with that, any more, he was certain, than would have Fitz. Business and politics were the same the world over. The South, by all accounts, was just as pragmatic as here. (A mate of Clive's had had some dealings with a politician down there, Howie or Hoey or something, and said the only thing the man was missing was a stetson.) Clive doubted Fitz ever did tell the story of his grandfather and the Union in quite the same way back home. And why should he? Cut your coat, and all that.

He thought back to when he was fifteen, the hours he had spent in the cab of Titch's lorry, bumping around the B roads and C roads of Ulster, listening to Titch hold forth, to the accompaniment of 'genuine' crystal glasses ringing false in the rear, telling Clive that if he was as smart as he looked he would learn enough about human hopes and frailties in a single morning on the tailboard in Pomeroy to last him a lifetime, but that the best lesson he could ever learn was that a patter that worked in Pomeroy would be no use at all in Plumbridge. No two pitches were the same and the day you made the mistake of forgetting that would be the day you lost your edge and with it your immunity to failure.

A short time after they had come down to the Cocktail Bar, the councillor nodded to a party in evening dress across the room and excused himself to go and say hello. Clive watched until he was out of earshot before leaning in towards Fitz.

'Do you think he's going for this?'

'Oh, I'd say so,' Fitz said, stretching his legs under the table, signalling to Len for more brandy. Wouldn't you?'

'I'll be happier once I get this money out of my pocket and into his.'

Fitz ran a finger over the convex face of his watch.

'Ten minutes,' he said.

The brandy was served, the councillor returned and eased himself into his chair.

'Friends of yours?' Fitz asked.

'Loosely speaking. The man with the glasses?' The man with the glasses happened just then to be looking their way. Smiles were exchanged, eyes were hastily averted. 'Former councillor. We served together on a couple of committees.' He paused, puffing on his cigar. 'Nationalist.' Another puff. 'Nice fella. Came into City Hall an accountant, left it the director of a brickworks.'

The era of the practical man.

'A good head for business,' Fitz mused.

'You could say.'

The only word for how Noades did say this was overweening. Fitz was right, their moment was approaching.

A tall fair-haired man picked a path through the tables and chairs to the door of the bar, stood there a second or two pinching the bridge of his nose and frowning, then returned to his seat in the corner.

The councillor followed his every step.

'Isn't that your man … Whatyoumecallim?'

'Connolly,' said Clive.

Fitz was having difficulty identifying who they were talking about without staring.

'The footballer?'

'*Bap*,' said the councillor and smirked. 'You ask me, he's looking a wee bit …'

He sloshed his brandy around the glass by way of illustration. Clive willed a vision of dragging the smug little wanker up an alley and giving him a good digging. It was going to be a source of real satisfaction to him in years to come to remember that Councillor Trevor Noades had allowed himself to be bought like a dockside tart.

Clive's cigar had gone out. He relit it and tossed the used match into the ashtray. Instantly a sulky-faced kid whisked the ashtray away, only just missing Clive's ear, and replaced it with a clean one. Clive laid hold of the kid's skinny wrist as he withdrew it the second time.

'Have you no manners?'

'What?'

'Ever hear of "excuse me"?'

'Sorry,' the kid said. '*Excuse* me.'

He tried to take his arm back, but Clive held on tight.

'What's your name?'

'Stephen.' For all that his lips moved, the answer might have been delivered by a ventriloquist.

'Stephen? Does your mother know you're out?'

Stephen winced, bowed his head.

'My ma's dead.'

Clive loosened his grip.

'Aw, now, listen,' he said. 'I was only keeping you going. I didn't mean …'

The kid slipped his hold and skipped away, licking his finger and drawing a stripe down the air: *One–nil!*

Fitz and the councillor were trying their damnedest not to

laugh. Clive thought about it, then gave in to a snorter of his own. He waved Stephen over again, raising the palms of his hands to demonstrate his peaceful intentions. The boy approached, hesitated – Clive held his hands higher – then came on again.

'I walked into that,' Clive said, and took a half-crown from his jacket pocket. 'Here.'

Stephen worked the coin between his fingers.

'You mean keep it?'

'Keep it, spend it, do whatever you like with it.'

A boyish wonder surfaced through his earlier expression of bored cynicism.

'Thanks, mister.'

Clive took a sip of brandy. He told himself it was no loss of face to acknowledge when somebody had got one over on you. Besides, a little suggestion of gullibility sometimes played well in a situation like this. Noades for one could hardly have looked any more complacent than he did at that moment.

Clive focused on Fitz across the table. He tried to make his eyes say *now*. Fitz cleared his throat.

'I tell you what,' he said and stopped.

Clive cracked his knuckles and then, annoyed that he had let his impatience show, said the first thing that came into his head. Which was the right thing, as it turned out.

'Have you ever seen the rooms here, Trevor?'

'The rooms?'

Clive nodded.

'I can't say ... Not this long time, no.'

'They've them done out lovely,' Clive said. 'Haven't they, Fitz.'

'Oh, they have now.' Fitz finally caught on where this was leading. 'I've stayed in plenty of hotels in my time and I can tell you I've come across few better for the money.'

The councillor regarded them each in turn.

'Is that a fact?'

He pulled down a shirt cuff, aligning the link with the buttons of his suit sleeve. He recentred his tie-knot. By means of these adjustments he managed to compose his features into the picture of innocence.

'Maybe, if it's not too much trouble …?'

Fitz was already out of his seat.

'Not at all, not at all. Glad to.'

The councillor polished off his drink before getting up too.

'Clive?'

He was very sure of himself now. He was also swaying.

'I'll hold the fort here,' Clive said. 'You'll likely be wanting another drink when you're done.'

Fitz, Clive thought, was a touch pink about the temples and this pleased him, for he prided himself on never letting his own face betray his emotions. Another lesson Titch had drummed into him. Clive sent a silent blessing to whatever back road his old mentor was driving that night and commiserations to whatever town lay all unsuspecting at the end of it.

Clive waited until they were almost at the door before calling out.

'Fitz?'

Fitz nearly tripped over his own feet, such a start did he give turning. Jesus, man was a bag of nerves.

'Be a pal and take this coat up with you till I'm going,' Clive said. 'I don't want it getting all wrinkled here.'

Fitz returned to the table.

'Fuck,' he mouthed to Clive. It was short for *I'm a right bollocks, aren't I, going without that.*

Clive sat quite still for a minute or two after they had gone. It was done now. He could relax, enjoy the rest of the night. He thought about letting go altogether, getting very drunk. He thought about phoning Angela at the club she went to. And then, no, he decided, not Angela, Bobbie. Oh, definitely, that would be the thing to do. He would ask her, when he had picked her up in the taxi and taken her back to his place, he would ask her –

Righteous Brothers on the record player, her skirt and nylons over the arm of the chair – at the very point when she could not stop herself even if she wanted to, he would ask her: *Was that Dublin bastard as good as this?*

Was he? Was he?

His glass was empty. The other two could catch up. He raised a hand and Len brought the bottle. Clive fetched a pound from his wallet and folded it between the knuckles of his first and second fingers.

'No need,' Len said. 'Fitz is taking care of this.'

'I know.' Clive pointed with the note over his shoulder. 'I want you to get Ted Connolly whatever he's drinking. Just say it's from a fan. Or, wait, a Northern Ireland supporter. That's right, tell him to have one on a Northern Ireland supporter.'

The kid, Stephen, was mooching around. Clive bided his time till Len was back behind the bar.

'Son, come here a second, I want you.'

He trotted over, two-and-six times more enthusiastic than when Clive had last called him. Clive sat right back in his seat to get a proper look at him.

'What are you, fourteen, fifteen?'

Stephen, detecting an unpleasant something in Clive's tone, didn't say one way or the other. Clive shrugged.

'Well, whatever, just so as you know: you ever cheek me again, the day you turn old enough to fuck and marry I'll be round looking for you. Do you hear me?'

The kid attempted a sneer, but found it withered in Clive's unyielding glare.

'I'm telling you. I'll kick you from one end of that street out there to the other.'

The kid was gnawing on his lip. Clive held the stare an intimidating moment longer and then winked.

'One–all,' he said.

Fright and relief mingled wetly in the wee lad's eyes as he skulked away. Clive sucked his cigar. Slap it into him. The kid had to learn. The important thing was not that you were seen to do it, the important thing was that you did get even.

*

'Oh, that's just perfect,' I said.

Stanley and Ingrid had found seats at Liam and Rita Strong's table. The Achesons, or whatever you called them, were away on home. Rita shifted her and Liam's coats and shunted her husband ostentatiously with hip and thigh to make room for the new arrivals, as though to her had fallen the task of welcoming them into the true mute state of matrimony.

For badness I picked up Stanley's forgotten pint and launched it down the sink.

'Do you want me to bar him?' Jamesie said.

'Yeah, right,' I said. 'For what?'

Jamesie turned me by the collarbone and took me through the words in red on the laminated sign above the till: *The Management reserves the right to refuse service at any time.*

'You're not management,' I reminded him. Jamesie swatted the objection with a flick of his wrist.

'So, Hugh'll do it. Won't you, Hugh?'

'What's that?'

'Nothing,' I said.

'Well as long as it's nothing, of course I'll do it.'

Ingrid was wending her smudged pink way towards the bar. Jamesie stepped aside diplomatically, advising me less diplomatically, and almost without leaving me time to quell my look of horror, to give her a bit of a slap.

'Hello again,' Ingrid said.

'I thought you'd gone home.'

She registered my coolness, but seemed unable to account for it precisely.

'I'm not about to go back up there, if that's what you're thinking.'

I twitched my shoulders to show it was all one to me.

'What can I get you?'

'A tomato juice.'

'Just a tomato juice? Nothing for your friend?'

The bitter sound of that last word surprised even me. Ingrid gave a slight involuntary nod: *now I understand.*

'Tomato juice,' I said, and bent to get one. I shook the bottle as I reached for a wine glass. 'Ice?'

'Have you a problem?'

Yes, I have a problem, I wanted to say, but it's not what you think it is.

'Sorry,' I said, and showed her the water at the bottom of the bucket. 'We're all out of ice.'

Ingrid snapped open her purse – 'How much?' 'A shilling' – snapped it shut again.

'If you must know, though I don't know why you should, I was waiting on a taxi out the front when I saw him come staggering up the steps on to the footpath. He was all over the place. You couldn't leave anyone in that state. I tried to get him to go home – I was afraid of him stumbling out on to the road and getting himself killed – but he insisted on coming back in here. For the friendly service, obviously.'

The news had come on over in the corner. Pictures from Cape Kennedy. Ant ambulances, lights flashing, racing towards the mammoth upright incinerator of Apollo 1. I remembered the mannequin I had seen burning this morning in a window of Brand's department store and at last I felt a dreadful pity for the three would-be astronauts; for all of us, maybe, perched forever on the edge of what we can't control or understand.

'Anyway, between you and me,' said Ingrid, softer now, as though to make up for the friendly service jibe, 'I think he's had enough.'

'I know. He's been in and out of here almost from when we opened.'

The man beside Ingrid cleared his throat as she lifted her glass and left.

'Yes?' I said.

'I'm not interrupting, am I?' he said, Mister Sarcasm.

I rested an arm on a Guinness tap.

'That,' I said, jerking a thumb towards Ingrid's retreating back, 'is my sister and she's just had a very upsetting day.'

The man feigned a woman feigning concern.

'My heart's breaking.' Then, bully-boy gruff: 'More to the point, my glass is empty.'

'We couldn't have that,' I said with as much insincerity as I could muster.

He sucked saliva through his brown-stained teeth, scratched a sideburn you could have struck a dud match on.

'Could not indeed.'

Big Bad Belfastman. I saw his type every night of the week. You'd have thought there was a factory somewhere churning them out. (Grundig sounded about right.) I comforted myself that at least I wasn't one of those put-upon-looking Belfast women they made to go with them, lying in a bedroom somewhere waiting on him coming home wanting his Saturday night special.

I met Jamesie at the till.

'Did you sort her out?'

I didn't answer. Jamesie shook his head.

'There's no hope for you.'

I looked at the man waiting for his change at the bar, scratching his sandpaper sideburns. I looked at Jamesie. If you blurred your eyes they could nearly have been from the same batch.

'Whatever you say, Jamesie.'

Len Gray set Clive White up with another drink. It wasn't a brandy and Clive hadn't asked for it.

'What's this?'

'Laphroaig. It's what Ted Connolly's drinking. He wanted to get you something back.'

Clive White swivelled in his seat and raised his glass. Ted Connolly returned the gesture. They drank. Clive saw mist hovering ankle-high above a moor, a stag breaking cover: the power of advertising rather than a particular distillate of malted barley.

'Is he sitting on his own?' Clive asked Len, who answered under the guise of collecting dead ones from a neighbouring table.

'There was some woman earlier, but I don't know what happened to her.'

Clive turned again. Ted Connolly having Done the Decent Thing in buying him a drink back was already hunched forward, fingers forming a canopy over his eyes, thumbs wedged beneath his cheekbones, arresting the droop of his skull. It was not the pose of a man in search of company. And Clive White was not a man to force his company on anyone who preferred to be left alone to drink. Then again, it wasn't as if he was some bum stumbled in off the street looking for an autograph or an argument. He was a businessman, a fellow professional if you like, with pressures of his own from which to try and unwind.

'Ask Mr Connolly if he'd care to join me over here,' he told Len.

Noades's friend, the former councillor, and his party were getting ready to leave. The women wore fur of various species and hues. A flattened rodent head stared briefly and emptily over a shoulder at Clive and he found himself contemplating, as though it had only been invented that day, the word *stole*.

'That's the best whisky you'll ever drink. There isn't an Irish can touch it.'

Ted Connolly spoke past a cigarette angled into the corner of his mouth.

'Do you mind?' He tapped the back of the seat facing Clive. Clive half rose, Ted waved him back.

'It makes a nice change,' he said, sitting down. 'Me doing the asking.'

'I don't doubt it,' Clive said. 'That's what I said to Len, I said, "The offer's there, but it's entirely up to him," I said.'

You're repeating yourself, Clive. You're talking too fast. He took a deep breath. His pulse grew more sedate – *better* – then was off like the hammers again. It was impossible. Up close, Ted Connolly's face was like a map of fame itself. Every detail had about it a necessary quality, down to the red thumb marks either side of the crooked precipice of his footballer's nose.

'Half the time,' said Ted, 'all people want to do is look at you.'

Clive looked elsewhere. Ted Connolly swigged from his glass then, remembering himself, shot out an arm.

'Sorry. Ted Connolly,' he said, needlessly.

'Clive White,' said Clive and, pride swelling his heart, took Ted Connolly's hand.

At once his heart wizened and turned numb with dread. Ted Connolly had a wart at the base of his middle finger. It rose to meet Clive's skin in advance of Ted's palm and nuzzled up to him obscenely for the duration of the handshake. Which was protracted. Clive's mind flashed back to the verruca he had picked up at the Grove baths on his seventh birthday, turning a treat into the start of two years of treatment. (Verrucas *liked* Clive and kept coming back.) He was convinced he could feel wart spores already burrowing under his skin, attaching themselves to his dermis. Still Ted kept the handshake going. (Good God, the man was a public figure. Hadn't they a doctor or someone at these big football clubs who looked out for this sort of thing?) Now Clive recalled the infection he had contracted after he tried to remove one verruca with a compass. (Vim, he learned, was not a sterilising agent.) He remembered Ted's septic toe. He sneaked a look under the table.

Their feet were practically touching!

Move ... he commanded himself. *Stop staring,* but he could drag neither his leg nor his gaze away.

At least he'd wrested his hand back.

'How's the ... injury?' he asked, hoping the question would

justify his apparent fascination with Ted's shoe. 'Read about it in the papers. Sounds nasty.'

'It's not pleasant,' Ted admitted. His eyeballs bobbed as though on a tide of alcohol which had only by chance coincided with his open lids and which would carry them, two or three drinks from now, clean up into his brain pan. They performed a haphazard survey of the bar before arriving back at Clive again. 'Don't mind me saying, but sometimes it really gets me down.'

You can say what you like, thought Clive, it's your toe. Clive's right hand was deep in his trouser pocket, rooting around for a sixpenny bit. (It was a sixpenny bit you rubbed on warts, wasn't it?)

'I'm not bragging like, but I've been around – countries I couldn't even have found on the map a lot of years ago – and believe you me, I've seen some right holes.'

Clive wondered had he missed something, but grunted anyway, the acknowledgement of a man who had seen a bit himself and not been impressed.

'Different standards,' he said. Garlic, he was thinking. Sheep's eyes.

'In every one of them we got beat, hands down,' said Ted. Clive had *definitely* missed something. More than one thing maybe. 'It's tragic, I'm telling you.'

As a Windsor Park regular, Clive felt he ought to offer some defence, but in the circumstances that seemed a little absurd.

'Northern fucking Ireland.'

Clive sensed a pocket of silence at his back where before there had been easy conversation. If he couldn't actually tackle Ted head-on, he could at least try to shepherd him into less dangerous territory.

'I like the look of this young fella Clements,' he said.

Ted Connolly belched behind tight lips.

'... fucking ...' he breathed malodorously, 'not listening.'

'OK, we've had the odd bad patch,' Clive conceded. There was he remembered all too well, having sat through at least five of them, the small matter of eleven consecutive defeats at the turn of the decade.

Ash from Ted Connolly's cigarette peppered the copper tabletop as his hand scythed through Clive's concession.

'Away to the dogs. That's what I think, anyway.'

This wasn't quite the conversation Clive had fantasised telling his friends about. He dived in again while Ted Connolly took another swig of whisky.

'Maybe if we went back to the way it used to be: All Ireland.' Ted Connolly guffawed, Clive persevered. 'Like the rugby. Think about it: Big Pat, Tony Dunne, Shay Brennan, Giles, Bestie, your good self ...'

'Taxi for Moore?' Len shouted from behind the bar; Clive glanced round and Ted was boozily past him.

'I'll tell you a story, right? A mate of mine takes this girl over to Dublin last Easter. Lady-not-his-wife, you know what I'm saying. Anyway, he comes back to Sunderland and here he's to me, *God, Ted, you Irish*. That's what he says: *You Irish*, and he hands me this' – Ted looked for a moment as if he couldn't believe the word that suggested itself could possibly be the right one – '*paper*. Apparently they were in a pub, him and the girl-friend, Dame Street or somewhere, doesn't matter, the day of the – what's this you call it? Half centenary? Golden anniversary? – the Easter Rising anyway, the big parade that they had, and there are guys coming round selling papers. So my mate, you know, real easy-going, when in Dublin and so on and so forth, buys one and opens it and – fucking hell – he can't believe it, and this is the paper he hands to me. I can hardly believe it. Pages and pages of Easter messages from, I don't remember what all: the West Cork IRA, the Tipperary brigade, the something-else battalion.

'*What is this old cobblers?* my mate asks me. *The Great bloody War or what?*'

The pocket of silence behind Clive had filled with tuts and mutters. Ted jabbed a finger.

'Tell me this … Clive. Do these people ever stand back and think? Does it ever cross their minds how this all looks to loonies like Paisley, never mind my mate?

'*You Irish*, he says to me. *You're walking backwards, into the seventies.*'

Ted lit a new cigarette from the petering stub of the old, as deftly as tapping a ball from one foot to the other, without breaking stride.

'Take last summer. England has the World Cup. London's like … what am I saying, London? Even *Sunderland* – there's all these people, Chileans, Italians, *Koreans*, for God's sake – we were dropping fucking bombs on them when I was at school – and they're in and out of the bars, drinking with the locals, singing, swapping scarves. And what are they up to in bloody Belfast?'

Extinguishing streetlamps on the corner of Malvern Street and Ariel Street. Waiting in the self-inflicted darkness for four guys strayed into a bar on the 'wrong' side of town.

'Drink?' said Clive. He wasn't having any more of this, not so loud; not in here, for pity's sake. He brought his hand down hard on the tabletop. 'I said, *drink?*'

Ted Connolly, checked, pondered the dregs of his Scotch.

'It's a joke,' he mumbled. 'We're a joke.'

'I saw the Wales match last year,' Clive said. 'That hat-trick you scored?'

'Well, maybe Wales once in a while, obviously …'

'Mexico?' Clive went on, his confidence returning.

'*I* look like a joke.' Ted was beginning to run in circles. He passed a hand across his forehead. 'Over there, across the water, there's fellas now being asked to endorse boots and balls and all sorts. It's turning into a big business.

'And what do I get?'

'I don't know,' Clive said, thinking not Compound W, that's for sure. 'What do you get?'

Ted Connolly extended his index fingers and brought them,

slowly, shakily, to rest alongside his temples, as though that said it all.

You sad drunk bastard, said Clive, to himself. Ted's hands dropped to his lap.

'I'm thirty next birthday.'

Clive, who somewhere in the back of his mind knew this, was nevertheless startled. Ted Connolly looked worn out.

'That's an old man in football. If I'm lucky I have another two years before I'm sold off to Hartlepool or someone. Why shouldn't I make a few bob while I still can?'

Clive could not tell whether an answer was expected of him, but decided against giving one anyway. He made no attempt to disguise looking at his watch. Almost five to ten.

'*Match of the Day*'s on in a minute,' he said.

Ted Connolly shook his head, rousing himself.

'Never watch it,' he said. 'Too much like work.'

He heaved his bulk out of the seat.

'Jimmy Riddle.'

'Can I get you another while you're out?' Clive asked and was not disappointed when Ted said no, he was sure Clive's friends would soon be back and he had imposed himself for too long already. In fact, Clive wasn't expecting 'his friends' yet a while, but he recognised a get-out when he heard one. He kept his hand firmly in his trouser pocket.

'Good to see you back in Belfast anyway,' he said.

Ted Connolly appeared to mull this over. Either that or he'd something stuck in his teeth. His eyes wandered about the room again.

'You ever been to Tirana?' he said, though he must have known it was unlikely. 'Tirana's bad. Tirana's the worst.'

*

'*You think we look pretty good together.*'

Without warning, Jamesie had dropped into a pose, shoulders

rounded, arse pulled back, fingers splayed and forming a tunnel along which he sang to the mirror above the till.

'*You think my la-la-la-la-leather.*'

A timid-looking man who had just come round the corner into the Blue Bar was reaching across the front of his jacket and stayed the hand briefly over his heart. A woman, too like him to have been his wife, clutched his wrist. Together they had the haggard appearance of people who had experienced great and recent trauma.

'*Substitute me for him,*' Jamesie sang at random and left the rhyme hanging. He smoothed one black eyebrow. The traumatised man removed an exhausted yellow rose from his lapel and laid it limply in an ashtray. I thought the woman with him might cry.

'Refugees,' Hugh whispered, going to serve them.

'From the Portaferry Room,' Jamesie added to me. 'I recognise your woman's hat.'

The hat was navy fur-effect, soft, cylindrical and pitted here and there with dents which the woman seemed able to intuit but not pinpoint, touching the crown repeatedly and ineffectually with a white-gloved hand.

'God, but that minister has some stamina,' Jamesie said, not without sympathy for the victims. 'He must still be going.'

A minute later, another man and woman entered by the same door and exchanged guilty glances with the first couple.

'Fuck, there's more of them.'

'Maybe they dug a tunnel,' I said.

'What's the deal anyway with you Prods?' said Jamesie. 'Is it a mortal sin or what to do a runner on a vicar?'

Prods? The word caught me like a sharp stick under the ribs. No one in the International had ever made such direct mention of religion to me. I cast a sidelong look at Jamesie to see did he realise what he had just said. I took it, from the way he was crossing his eyes, trying to blow a speck of ash from the end of his nose, that he did not consider he had spoken at all out of turn.

'Jamesie, I'm not a Protestant.'

'Of course you're not. And I'm not a Catholic,' he said. 'What school did you go to?'

A florid-faced man at the bar spoke to his neighbour behind a hand tattooed with LOVE, upside down, as I looked at it, and back-to-front. I lowered my voice.

'What's it matter what school I went to? The nearest one.'

'All right, bad joke,' said Jamesie. 'Ignore me.'

But I wouldn't ignore him. I followed him down the bar.

'No, hold on a minute, you said "you Prods".'

Jamesie was trying not to hear me. I suppose I ought to have twigged then that he was annoyed with himself, but it wasn't something I saw every day. He turned, taking me by surprise, so that my nose practically collided with his Adam's apple.

'I said I was joking.'

Hugh was watching us now. He sensed trouble, but he was too far away and too tied up to intervene.

'I forgot, we're none of us anything,' Jamesie said. 'We're International barmen.'

The notion had never struck me as so heroic, nor so entirely hollow. The International was no protection to its four barmen drinking after hours in the Malvern Arms that Saturday night last June. If anything, the funny name old Nancy O'Connor had told me the hotel had acquired in certain places had weighed against them. The way I heard it, they were up at the counter chatting, waiting for their drinks to be served. A man came over, stood next to them. A bit of a scrapper by the looks of him, but friendly enough.

All right, lads, how's it going?

Not too bad thanks, not too bad.

Yous barmen yourselves, lads?

They had on them their white shirts and black dickey bows under their overcoats. They were hardly likely to be a barber-shop quartet.

Aye.

In the town?

Aye.

Don't tell me, let me guess …

The International.

Thought so. The International. Know it well. Enjoy your drinks, lads.

The man walked across to a table and spoke to his mates. Afterwards, one of his mates told the police what was said. What was said was, 'They are four IRA men.' (Friends of Jamesie's, the oldest twenty-seven, the youngest just sixteen.) 'They'll have to go.'

I took an order on the strength of a nod and a raised pint glass. Jamesie fell in silently at the tap beside me.

'I'm sorry,' I said out of the corner of my mouth. 'I didn't mean to go on.'

'That's the trouble with you Pr – …' Jamesie grinned. 'Us Belfast people. We never know when to stop.'

A busy bar is a place of noise, of individual voices all saying something vital all at once and all lost in the common clamour. I took comfort in the thought that what had passed between Jamesie and me had amounted to no more than a brief localised addition to the volume, a pulse of sound that drifted with the smoke towards the ceiling and there was diffused until not a coherent syllable of it remained.

The volume went up just then in another part of the room. A sound on the cusp of cheer and jeer. Ted Connolly had passed through on his way to the toilet.

'What was that all about with you and Jamesie?' Hugh wanted to know.

'We were just getting on each other's wick,' I said. 'It was nothing. Kissed and made up.'

'Glad to hear it. I couldn't be doing with sulks.'

Hugh drew his trademark H in the head of a pint and shouted out into the bar.

'Guinness here! Who ordered a Guinness? Going, going …'

A hand and a head with a cap on it emerged from between the bodies at the counter. 'Gone. Next?'

Jamesie called to me, asking had I seen the lime cordial.

'Shit,' I said. 'I just used the last. I meant to open a new one.'

'This is not the end of the world,' Jamesie said. It was one of Walter's phrases, smuggled out in cunning disguise from a film everyone but he had long since forgotten; I knew Jamesie used it now by way of a peace offering. I smiled; Hugh, despite himself, smiled; Jamesie grabbed a bottle of Rose's lime cordial from under the counter, flipped it in the air and caught it by the neck.

'Go on, admit it, yous'd be miserable without me.'

Ted Connolly double-checked his zip before letting go the toilet door and making his way back through the bar. Two voices detached themselves from the general.

'That must be the first thing you've got on target all year,' said the first, while the second from close by called:

'Give us a nod, Bap.'

Ted casually gave him and his friend the fingers instead.

'Missed, you stupid bastard.'

Hugh levered himself up on the counter, fingertips purpling. 'Hey, that's enough of that.'

But Ted, who seemed to have acquired a new resolve since I met him out in the back hallway, wasn't in the least perturbed.

'I get slabbers like that all the time,' he said. 'The only thing thicker than my skin is their fat skulls.'

Liam Strong was up for his last but one of the night.

'What does he care?' he said when Ted had gone. 'I wouldn't care either if I was on two hundred a week.'

Hugh was sceptical.

'Two hundred pound?'

And Liam said the words that clinched most arguments in the Blue Bar: 'It was in the paper.'

Hugh shook his head. 'Two hundred pound a week. That's amazing.'

'What's amazing to me,' said Jamesie, 'is that the fella's still able to stand after the amount he's had to drink.'

Personally I didn't think the feat so unusual. There was barely a working day that passed but I didn't witness some customer or other defy the laws of physics, chemistry and human biology in refusing to keel over. And as for the economics of it, well that was perhaps most fabulous of all. Belfast in its bars was a city of uniformly wealthy men: no round was too big, no acquaintance too slight, no night too long. Not that I was in much of a position to be judgemental, I made my living out of them after all.

Ingrid was back at the bar.

'He's changed his mind about the drink,' she said. 'A half. He says you'll know what it was.'

'If you're sure it's wise,' I said, knowing how ridiculous I sounded. I poured Stanley's lager and took Ingrid's money. She remained at the counter.

'He was telling me how good you'd been to him today.'

My pulse quickened at the thought that he had noticed my attention. *How good I'd been to him*; it was hard to know what that meant. I managed to sound off-hand.

'Well, he was sitting up at the counter, you know, I talked to him.'

Ingrid was pursing her lips to keep them from smiling.

'What?'

'Nothing. You just make me laugh,' she said.

'Thanks a million.'

'You're welcome.'

I waited for her to leave.

'Is that everything?'

'Unless you'd come to the flicks some night when you're not working?'

They were putting each other up to this, Stanley and her. Had to be. I tried to formulate a reply and came up with something vaguely vowellish.

'It was only meant to be a suggestion,' Ingrid said. 'Not a moral dilemma.'

This time I couldn't even manage the vowel thing. My mouth was dry. Ingrid was gone again.

'Your sister, sure thing,' said the Big Bad Man with the scratchy sideburns and circled thin air with his arm. 'Meet my friend the rabbit.'

'Do I laugh now,' I asked him, 'or will you give me a cue?'

I walked along the bar pulling empties to me with crooked fingers. When I had no more fingers free, I took the glasses to the sink, which was when I realised that at last there were more of them coming in than going out. The corner had been turned.

Match of the Day was starting.

Alerted by its brassy theme tune, Hugh yelled, so loudly he lifted up on his tiptoes: 'Last orders at the bar!'

17

Len Gray, as required by law, called last orders in the Cocktail
Bar and prepared himself for another couple of hours behind the
counter, reaching down last week's *Titbits* from a shelf above the
till and turning to the crossword. Someone else had already
started it. Six down: *A country in Central Africa.* Four letters.
PERU, the someone had written firmly in green biro and then,
more faintly, either side of the R (five letters, clue: *May I have
this* ... ?) D–INK. Len couldn't decide which he needed most, a
new hiding place for his magazine or smarter bar staff.

Clive White, meanwhile, laced his fingers behind his head, the
better to persuade himself he was completely at his ease. A
minute before, his wandering mind had stumbled into a night-
marish scenario in which Trevor Noades had been transmitting
every word spoken since he arrived tonight via a microphone
taped to his body (Clive read *Titbits* too); in which, at the very
moment the money changed hands, there was a knock at Fitz's
bedroom door (Fitz, as he went to answer it saying, 'But we
didn't order room service.'), and in which burly cops were
now sitting on the bed, on the chairs, on the dressing table, on
Fitz himself, waiting for Clive to lose his patience and come up
to the room.

It was pure nonsense, of course. Trevor Noades wouldn't have had the balls for it. Something could always go wrong, a trailing wire, a noise – what did they call it? *Feedback* – on the mike. A person could find themselves falling out of a hotel window fairly sharpish ...

Whoa, Danny! *Whoa!*

I know I said I'd take liberties telling this story, but maybe that's taking one liberty too many. Fitz was no killer, neither was my second cousin. I worry about some of the thoughts I have been putting into Clive's head, worry that the picture I am drawing is too partial. There had to be more to him than wheeling and dealing and women and ego.

I might have mentioned, for instance, that I visited his parents' house once – or parent's house, for there was only his father left by then – with Andy and Edna, my father and mother. I suppose I would have been about eight. Family visits, as I am sure I did say, were not altogether in Andy and Edna's line, but Clive's father, my not-strictly-uncle Gabriel, had recently been in the hospital: heart condition. We got a bus, the three of us, to Carlisle Circus and walked from there up the Crumlin Road. Edna went into a bakery below the courthouse and bought a Florence cake. I remember being delighted that the very next street we passed was Florence Place and amusing myself reconstructing a Belfast of Tatie Bread Ways and Gubstopper Entries.

Uncle Gabriel's house was the last of a terrace of six wedged between a flour mill and a coachbuilder's yard. Collectively they had the kinked appearance of overcrowded teeth.

An ancient dog – some make of bull terrier – lay curled up in the doorway. Its coat, which must have been white when new, was yellowing and lustreless, its ears and pointed muzzle in places hairless. My father clucked his tongue and the dog opened an eye half brown, half milky-blue.

'Sure, you're all right,' Andy said.

The dog half looked at him.

'Course you are.'

He scratched a threadbare ear and stepped over the heaving flank, rapping the hall door. I followed close behind him, hardly daring to look down, but while I was still astride the dog I heard the scrabble of claws on the tiles as it tried to raise itself. I felt its nose, rough, at the top of my knee-sock. I couldn't not look.

Its mouth was like an injury: an unhitched display of gums and livid tongue. I froze.

Uncle Gabriel called us in. My mother thumped me between the shoulder blades; the dog, unable to bear its own weight, lay down again, panting.

'It thinks you're our Clive,' Uncle Gabriel said. 'Poor oul' thing forgets they're neither of them pups any more.'

My mother had warned me that Uncle Gabriel's heart condition was caused by a problem with his thyroid gland. I think I had imagined a swollen throat. In fact, Uncle Gabriel filled the two-seater sofa, which with the radiogram and a leatherette pouffe made up the entire furniture of the front room. My father perched on the arm of the sofa beside him; my mother sat on the leatherette pouffe. I stood.

'How is Clive?' my father asked.

'Sure, I hardly see him at all.'

Edna tutted, too soon.

'He's in here and has the fire set for me before I'm down out of my bed in the mornings. Leaves me the paper and a note not to take the ashes out.'

A brass hearth-set, with handles in the shape of thistles, stood, polished, by the fireplace in which red coals were beginning to eat away at a crust of damp slack. Directly above the brush and pan, on the mantelpiece, was propped an oval picture frame containing a tinted photograph of a boy about the age I was that day, hands lying unnaturally loose on his lap, legs crossed at the ankles. For some reason he wore a slipper on his left foot.

'I hear him at night, the odd time, coming in and I shout down to him – "Who's that?" – and he shouts back to me – "It's only me, Daddy, don't be getting up." And that's about the height of it so far as talking goes, but I don't know where I'd be without him all the same. Honest I don't.'

The pouffe parped as Edna shifted from one buttock to the other. Parped again as she shifted back to prove that the sound was the inevitable by-product of Crimplene on leatherette. On the doorstep the dog drew a rasping breath. From where I was standing I had a clear view through the rest of the house, out the scullery window into the yard. A bicycle tyre clung to the sloped asbestos ribbing of the outhouse roof, a twisted length (an *ampersand*, I would have said if I'd known the word) of green hosepipe beside it. The guttering was weighed down at one side with moss and stones. A tea towel was tangled in two converging washing lines.

I looked from the yard to my uncle, to the tinted boy in the photograph wearing one shoe and one slipper, trying to connect them in some meaningful way.

I don't remember Uncle Gabriel dying, though he could not have lasted long after that visit. Clive was away on business the day his father's heart finally gave out. When my own father died, getting on for ninety, the year before last, and I was sorting through the biscuit tin in which he kept his papers, I found a letter, elegantly written in black fountain pen. Thank you for all your help … Thank you for asking about Sally (*Sally?*), but it wouldn't be fair to move her … Old and tired … Sad, but humane, like falling asleep. Thank you anyway. If ever there's anything I can do … Sincerely, 'Clive'.

That's exactly how he signed himself. 'Clive'. That's the point of this reminiscence – not the father, not the dog, the inverted commas. I want you to remember, before I bring him back in, that my second cousin was a man who signed his name as my father and mother signed theirs, the shy, old-fashioned way, in inverted commas. Whatever that tells you.

At ten or a quarter past ten that January Saturday night, and having left word with Len where Fitz and Noades were to find him, Clive dandered into the Blue Bar and ordered a pint off me. (Brandy was fine for business, but football called for beer.)

'Nice dinner?' I asked. He rolled his eyes.

'God, you can't scratch yourself in this town but somebody knows it.'

He was shamming, of course, and didn't care that I knew it. I was to understand that I could not begin to guess the half of what Clive White was at.

'You were only up the stairs,' I muttered, like it mattered what I said. Clive had already turned towards the television, not following the match so much as the faces of the people who were following it. A lot of the time he could not decide which he enjoyed more, the football or the barroom fans, shouting at games which had already been decided and whose outcome, even if they had been in the ground, they had not the slightest chance of influencing.

Or maybe I'm losing the run of myself again, for in no time at all Clive was hollering with the best of them: Go on, shoot yourself, shoot *yourself* ... Ah, fuck, *shoot* yourself. So engrossed was he, in fact, that he did not at first notice Councillor Noades come into the bar and look about him.

A goal was scored. Cheers and groans and loud appeals to the referee. The man with no neck next to Clive – his name, for we knew him well in the Blue Bar, was Gerard, pronounced Jurd – said something in what Clive thought might be Swedish, which was the language drink often seemed to use when it was talking through Jurd. Clive laughed regardless, because let's face it, most of what strangers said to you in a bar was designed to make you laugh. The man, encouraged (that was always the danger), carried on incomprehensibly. Clive carried on smiling, all the while searching out a spot he could slope off to at the first opportunity. He spotted Noades at last, though, strangely, he was now reluctant to move. He didn't want Noades, or Fitz, thinking he had been biting his nails waiting on them showing up. He waved a hand in a slow arc above his head: *over here, thicko.*

Twenty voices shouted *Penalty!* Clive whipped round to catch the replay – a clear dive – and when he turned back Noades was standing by his shoulder.

'I don't know what yous two fellas take me for,' Noades hissed. His lips were tight and flecked with spit. Clive's first thought was that five hundred pounds was not enough; his second was that he had not been wrong about the secret microphone.

'I haven't a clue what you're on about,' he said to the top button of Noades's waistcoat.

'Don't you start wasting my time, too.' This was a different Trevor Noades talking. 'And you can tell your friend, wherever he's got to, that I don't do business with amateurs.'

All thought of microphones fled Clive's head.

'What did you say?'

'Are you deaf? I said yous are behaving like a pair of amateurs.'

Clive could hear the thump of his own heart and supposed everyone else could hear it too. He felt curiously empty. Gas gurgled through the echoing streets of his intestine.

'No, no, you said, *wherever he's got to.*'

'Well, I've looked and he's not next door. The last I saw of him he was coming down to have a word with you. I've been sitting there in that bloody room of his for the last three-quarters of an hour listening to yon porter fella.'

And it was then that Clive realised, what you could probably have told him from the start, that he had suspected the wrong man.

'Oh,' he said, 'fuck.'

Clive made a move towards the door. Noades blocked the way.

'Where do you think you're off to?'

'Time, ladies and gentlemen, please!' Hugh shouted and Clive White, almost lazily as it looked to me from behind the counter, landed one on Trevor Noades's cheekbone.

The word spread to all four corners of the bar in an instant: fight. Where a moment before there had barely been room to flex a muscle, a ring opened up. People capped their drinks with their hands. The more enthusiastic stood on seats. I thought I saw a camera flash. Hugh and Jamesie were both out from behind the bar.

Clive had hauled Noades up by the tie and was screaming into his face. 'Why didn't you come and get me sooner?'

The councillor's body sagged at the knees.

'Get him off me, somebody. Police!'

'You want the police, do you? You want the police?' (I have seen a fair few bar fights in my time. So far as dialogue goes this was about par for the course.) 'I'll give you the fucking police.'

Clive flung the councillor aside – Noades, though he yelped, appeared to prefer this to being throttled, in fact if anything aided his own propulsion. Jamesie caught him before he hit the deck again.

'Quick, Hugh,' Clive said. 'I need your phone.'

'Wait a second, wait a second,' Hugh said, but Clive was already stomping towards me.

'Give me that phone there.'

'Danny,' Hugh said. 'Call Len.'

Clive summoned a stare from his darkest depths as I lifted the receiver from its cradle.

'Give me the phone.'

I did not know then, of course, about the thing with his name and the inverted commas. My second cousin at that moment seemed to me composed of unalloyed malevolence.

I closed my eyes and dialled the Cocktail Bar.

'Fuck!' Clive *head-butted* the counter. 'Are yous all stupid?'

He raced out of the bar towards the back hallway. Len answered the phone – 'Yes?' – but before I had a chance to speak I heard Clive's voice over the earpiece.

'Len, get that wee lad off the phone and call Hastings Street barracks. That fucker Fitz has robbed us all.'

'What's going on?' Len asked me.

'You know as much as I do,' I said, and Len hung up.

With Jamesie's help, Noades had managed to stand and recover enough breath to reassure himself he was not dying.

'Where is he?'

'Who?'

'Clive White.'

'Away phoning the police,' I said.

Noades shook his head. There was swelling, faintly opalescent, under his left eye where Clive's knuckles had connected.

'No.'

'What do you mean, no?' Jamesie said. 'It was you was girning for them.'

'You've got to stop him.'

Noades laid a hand on Jamesie's chest. This was not the best idea he would ever have, any more than was ordering Jamesie about. Jamesie pinched the hand's middle finger, like he was taking hold of a rat by its tail.

'You can do what you want, pal. I'm going back to my work.'

The spectators had begun to disperse. Noades retreated into them, making himself scarce.

A few people still stood on chairs, chatting over the heads to friends they'd missed earlier in the night. Hugh brought his hands together in a sharp clap.

'All right, everyone, would you start drinking up there?'

He came back in behind the bar.

'Give them a few minutes extra,' he whispered to me. 'Make up for the interruption.'

The phone rang. I was first to it.

Right, uh-huh, right.

'Hugh,' I said. 'That was Len. He wants you to take over next door a minute.'

And Hugh did something I never thought I'd live to see Hugh do. He bit a sliver off his thumbnail and spat it into the sink.

'Is somebody going to tell me what this is all about?' he said.

I don't know who did tell Hugh in the end, but the rest of us were not left long in the dark.

Barney had come over to check with Jamesie and me were we OK.

'Marian's away upstairs,' he said. She had taken it upon herself to tail Trevor Noades. 'If anyone can find out it's her.'

Marian returned a few minutes later at her familiar, graceful, asymmetric trot and indicated that not a word of what she had seen would pass her lips until someone supplied her with another Bristol Cream. We watched her drink. ('Sorry,' I told her. 'No rocks this time.') Waited.

'Are yous ready for this?' she asked finally.

Right, the hotel manager, the hotel *bar* manager, the receptionist, the businessman and the politician are arguing in the hotel lobby. (There had been another businessman, but he had disappeared; he was the reason the hotel manager, the hotel bar manager and so on were in the hotel lobby at half past ten on a Saturday night.) And then in walks the taxi driver ...

'Quit messing about, Marian,' we said.

'Who's messing? I'm telling you, that's what it was like.'

OK. Fitz had fucked off. Nicola had seen him go. Well, not seen him actually walk out the hotel door: she had been talking away to him at the desk and then she had to lean over to get the phone and when she straightened up again he wasn't there any more. Neither was the taxi driver who had been standing in the lobby for the past twenty minutes saying, in that hopeful singsong taxi drivers have, *Taxi for Moore? Taxi for Moore?*

The taxi driver who had just walked in the door again, in fact.

('See,' said Marian. 'I told you that's what it was like.')

The taxi driver had come back to give Nicola a pen. The pen was a gold Papermate. It had Nicola's name engraved on the shaft and a date which was the date of her eighteenth birthday. The man the driver had picked up earlier had pocketed the pen by mistake. He had sent the driver all the way back from Lisburn to return it.

Lisburn was where the man wanted to be dropped off. He went into the train station and came out with a suitcase, then he got into a private car and drove away. The suitcase had been taken to the station earlier in the day by another taxi driver from the same firm, a friend of the second driver's, as it happens. He collected it from a room on the second floor of the hotel. The two friends had talked about this when they met each other out the front of the depot earlier this evening as the first driver was going off and the second was coming on. They agreed it was a bit strange. Then the first driver said, 'Talking of strange ...'

He had been stopped at traffic lights this afternoon when a horse and carriage passed in front of him. Not any old rag-and-bone cart. This carriage was painted white and gold, you'd never seen the like of it. There were pink plumes attached to the harness on top of the horse's head. Strange right enough, said the second driver. And what about all those fires today? His wife had been up the town shopping at lunchtime and had come home carrying a sheet of pale yellow paper. A carbon copy, which gave him and her a good laugh, because it was practically turned to carbon in places. The paper was from the department store in Brand's Arcade. Menswear. It had on it the inside- and outside-leg measurements of a man with an address in Hannahstown. Seems he was having bother with the trousers of his suit. There was an additional comment in the shop assistant's hand: 'Well to the left'. The well was underlined three times. The driver's wife found the thing lying on the footpath in Hill Street, half a mile from the fire.

But where was he? Oh, yeah.

The taxi driver did not make the connection at first between the man he picked up this evening and the suitcase his friend had taken to Lisburn train station. A fare from the International was all he knew. Name of Moore. He did not know that the man he picked up was not called Moore. He had been told to be outside the hotel at half past nine. He had been told he should be prepared to wait, anything up to half an hour. This was not an unusual request with a hotel or restaurant pick-up. He would be paid for the waiting time. But he had got bored sitting in the car so he had come into the lobby. He liked hotel lobbies. You know: busy, busy. The man who said he was Mr Moore had passed him, going to the lift, shortly before he came down and got into the car, but he was talking to a man – this man here, with the shiner – and perhaps he didn't hear the driver say, *Taxi for Moore*?

('He had something in his room he wanted,' Noades blurted, then faltered, 'to show me,' and blushed.)

At some point the driver asked the receptionist to ring the downstairs bars in case Mr Moore was waiting there.

The first thing the man did when he came back down in the lift was sidle up to the driver and whisper in his ear.

'One minute,' he said. He made a kind of a joke of it. 'I'm Moore.'

The driver saw no good reason not to believe him. So, he drove him to Lisburn and it was only when he was pulling up in front of the station that he remembered what his friend had told him earlier about the suitcase.

No, he hadn't thought to take down the number plate of the car the man had driven off in. Listen, he had once had a hamster for a fare. Picked it up from the pet stores in Smithfield and dropped it off at the rear of a fish and chip shop on the Newtownards Road. They were in the hotel business, they didn't need him to tell them how peculiar people were.

He thought it might have been a Vauxhall. The car. Dark blue. Or dark green. Dark, anyway, and anyway it was dark and he was only going on what he could see in his rear-view mirror. He wouldn't even have seen that much if the guy Moore hadn't come running back after he got out of the taxi, waving his arms, and handed him the gold Papermate. The driver thought he had better hang on a minute or two longer to make sure there were no other little emergencies. He had been given an extra ten bob to take the pen straight back to the hotel in case the wee girl was looking for it.

('That's *my* ten bob,' Clive White said. The driver gave him a hard sideways stare.)

Nicola had been looking for the pen, though not frantically. She assumed it had rolled off the counter and on to the floor somewhere. The last time she could remember having it was when she was adding the final figures to Fitz's bill. He had asked her to start preparing the bill earlier in the evening. Something had come up, he said. He might have to leave first thing in the morning. Sooner, maybe.

Thinking about it now, mind you, she remembered that Fitz had been fiddling with the pen while he was standing waiting for his receipt.

He had paid his bill in full, tonight's dinner included. Cash. He had pulled a big bundle of notes from his coat pocket and counted out the exact amount. The bill, which Marian got a glimpse of, came to seventy-something pounds. Seventy-something, thirteen shillings and four-pence. Nicola didn't say whether or not Fitz had told her to keep the six-and-eight change.

'That's *my* money,' said Clive.

Clive had lent Fitz a sum of cash until the banks opened on Monday. The Master pointed out that it was only Saturday night. Fitz had not yet broken the terms of the loan. Besides, Fitz must have known he would have to pay his hotel bill, that was probably what he wanted the money for, wasn't it? The councillor, no longer blushing, blanched.

'He's a con man,' Clive insisted.

'He's a scrupulous one,' the Master said. 'He paid his bill.' (He paid his taxi fare too, the driver said. He even paid for the brandy, said Len.) 'You still have two days. Who's to say he won't pay you?'

Clive was staggering about, grabbing fistfuls of his own hair, ranting.

'I don't believe you people. I don't believe you.'

And then he started shouting for the police again.

'I swear,' said Marian, 'it was like something out of the Marx Brothers.'

We had towelling mats over the taps, but when Liam Strong moseyed up looking a wee half-un, Jamesie served him anyway. What use were rules if you couldn't bend them a little for a regular?

'And the best of it is,' Marian went on, 'in the middle of all this, there's these two poor fellas trying to register: came in late on the Liverpool boat. I'm sure they were wondering what sort of a madhouse they had walked into. The Master was smiling away for all he was worth, but you could tell he was ripping it.'

A man leaned over the far end of the counter asking for a pint.

'We're closed,' Jamesie said.

'But I just saw you serve somebody.'

'He'd been waiting,' Jamesie said, not caring that it was a patent lie. 'Danny Boy, give us a hand with the shutters.'

'So, are the police coming?' Barney wanted to know.

Marian shook her head.

'Your man Noades got Clive White out the front door eventually and talked to him a while and then came back in on his own. "Terrible mix-up," he says, or something like that: "I'm sure we'll manage to sort it out."'

Jamesie and I snibbed all but the central shutter, which we left a couple of feet short of the counter. Jamesie called for glasses, I took a bucket and a cloth and went out to empty the ashtrays. Stanley was putting on his overcoat sitting down. He had one arm stretched above his head, the other twisted round his back. Ingrid, in trying to help him, had got caught up in the tangle. Her hand appeared briefly out of one of the sleeves. I avoided going near them for as long as possible, torn between, 'It's time you were making a move,' and plain, 'Get out.' When at last I arrived at their table, however, I told them they didn't have to go just yet.

'You can still get a drink next door if you hang on. Say you're with me.'

Ingrid drew her head back out of range of Stanley's and made a discouraging face.

'Or you don't have to drink if you don't want to, just sit and have a Coke or something.'

This was pure selfishness on my part, even a Coke in Stanley's state might not have been wise; but I didn't want them to leave together. I didn't want them to leave without me.

'Well,' said Ingrid.

'*I* know,' said Stanley. 'Let's go dancing.'

Jamesie shouted: 'Can I have your glasses now, *puh*-lease!'

I took the ashtray from Ingrid and Stanley's table.

'Let me know what you decide,' I said, and tipped the ash and butts and torn beer mats into my bucket.

Hugh was back, talking to Barney and Marian.

'He's going to get himself arrested,' he was saying.

'Who is?' I asked, catching up.

'Clive White. He's running up and down the street like a raving lunatic: "Bloody bastard bugger ... !" Pardon my French.'

'Fitz is probably halfway to Dublin by now,' said Marian.

'Why doesn't Clive just go after him and get his money back?' Barney asked.

'That's the problem,' said Hugh. 'He already phoned the number Fitz gave when he checked in. It's a convent in Stoneybatter.'

'Rough,' said Barney.

'But,' Jamesie spoke for us all, 'funny, you have to admit.'

All the while the bar was emptying. The fella and white-stockinged girl I'd seen earlier, feeling each other up, kissed just inside the door. Jamesie whistled and cupped his hands over his mouth.

'Hey! Save that for later.'

Marian looked suddenly uncomfortable.

'I'm away up to the bog,' she said, though to see Barney's moony expression, it might have been the finest love poetry she had uttered.

Jamesie beckoned to him.

'Have you any doofers with you?'

'Any what?'

'Shut you up,' I said to Jamesie.

'Any what?' Barney asked again.

'Never mind him,' Hugh said. 'Just you make sure and look after that wee girl.'

Barney blinked, bewildered.

'I'm only kidding you on,' Jamesie said.

I started wiping tables. Hugh followed me out with the brush.

'Is he all right, do you think, your mate Barney?'

I didn't get at first what he meant. I told him Barney seemed fine.

'That's not what I'm asking.'

He paused, leaning on the brush, said goodnight to the two old boys from the Markets, who, as ever, had decided just in time to leave that they were firm friends after all. I waited for Hugh to continue, but all he said was that there were still tables needed cleaning.

'Come on ladies and gentlemen!' he shouted as he bent again to sweep. 'Start moving towards the doors.'

He stopped by Ingrid and Stanley's table. Ingrid said something and I saw Hugh look back at me and I nodded, whooping not seeming quite appropriate. A lit cigarette had been abandoned in an ashtray I had cleaned earlier and had burned down to a curved grey replica of itself which disintegrated when I nudged the table. The butt remained perched on the edge of the ashtray, like the foot I had been told always remained after spontaneous combustion. I didn't hear Hugh approach.

'Only, she took that business last summer very bad,' he said, pitching his voice low. He meant Marian, he meant the shootings. 'They used to go to parties a lot, her and some of the other girls and the fellas that worked down here. Now the papers are full of your man Burns and what have you, it brings it all back. And, of course, it was a Saturday night ...'

'Barney's fine,' I said again. 'It'll be OK.'

That was the sort of thing I did say in those days, incidentally. It would all be OK. A not unreasonable assumption and I wasn't alone in making it.

Oscar was leaving. He clapped Hugh and me on the back.

'See you next week,' Hugh said, and Oscar gave him the thumbs up.

Half a dozen men remained at the tables in front of the television, sitting very still and quiet, as though hoping we would somehow fail to notice them.

'Yous're going to have to make a move, lads,' Hugh told them and when they said there was only another couple minutes of the match left he said all right, but finish off your glasses and let's get them cleared.

I worked my way round to Ingrid and Stanley.

'You decided to stay, then?'

'Just for one,' said Ingrid.

'One's all I was thinking,' I said.

I went for a slash. The toilets were a state. Paper towels on the floor, in the sinks, even plastered to the wall. Fag ends clogged the urinal's strainer. The piss, backed-up, phosphoresced: fizzled, practically. I considered doing a bit to help out the cleaners, but I had neither the heart nor the stomach for it. I went into the cubicle, automatically reaching for the flush as I approached the toilet. My cock looked slit-eyed tired and mopey in my hand. I tried to jolly it up with thoughts of fingers not my own, but it wasn't buying them. One of my spots had got worse, I could feel it throbbing at the hinge of my jaw. My cock was right, nothing was going to happen tonight.

I waited for the cistern to fill, flushed again, and left the cubicle.

Stanley was at the wash-hand basins, splashing water on his face.

It is possible to be too handsome, if you ask me, to pass through and out the other side, to become, well, Stanley. Studying his drenched reflection in the toilets' mirror I wondered what it was I saw in him. He looked as though he had been ordered up from a catalogue of somebody else's dreams. (Conjure the face yourself. That was Stanley's.) He looked as though, when you finally got him home and unwrapped, he could only disappoint. And yet ...

'I think us two need to talk,' he said.

'Do we?'

I had to wash my hands, if only for something to do. He stood aside to let me at the taps. My forearm brushed his thigh as I scrubbed. Whether he didn't notice, or didn't mind, he didn't move. I scrubbed some more. He cleared his throat.

'I know what you're thinking,' he said.

This was not a bad start. I turned off the water. He was looking at my fingers. Soapy drips fell from them on to the toe of my shoe. He reached behind him and pulled down a wodge of paper towels.

'Thanks.'

I dried each finger separately and with care, remembering Natalie Vance outside the hotel this morning, the ten separate tugs on her emerald green gloves; banishing her finally.

'Always look after your hands,' Stanley said solemnly. 'Our hands are our livelihood.'

'Funny, that's what Hugh says, the older guy works with me.'

'The other one hates me.'

I wasn't going to make a liar of myself. I stuffed the used towels into the waste bin.

'You were going to tell me what I was thinking.'

He was looking at his own hands now.

'About me,' he said, distracted.

Again, this was encouraging, if slow.

'What about you?'

He held his hands in front of his face, turning them to show me front and back.

'Do you know what I do with these?'

'Something amazing, I'm guessing.'

'That's not what Larry Bowen thinks.'

'Larry Bowen knows nothing, whoever he is.'

Actually, I had a fair idea that Larry Bowen was the man I had seen Stanley with earlier in the week.

'Larry Bowen's with *Crackerjack!*'

'*Crackerjack!*?' This was getting too much. 'You don't say.'

'It's no joke, you know.'

Out in the bar Hugh was calling to Jamesie, asking where I was.

'Crapper,' Jamesie called back.

'I think I'm wanted,' I said and waited. 'Are you going to tell me, then?'

I was still keen to know what he thought I was thinking.

'What?'

'It doesn't matter.'

As I reached the door he called my name. I knew there was nothing for me to turn back for. I looked at him over my shoulder.

'She's not your girl, is she?'

'No,' I said. 'She's not.'

The *Match of the Day* credits were rolling, the same half dozen men sitting now in virtual darkness watching them, reluctant to let go of their Saturday night. Jamesie had taken advantage of my absence to try his luck with Ingrid, since I obviously didn't

219

seem to know how to handle her. Giving her some load of old guff, no doubt.

He pushed himself back from the wall with the elbow he had been leaning on.

'There you are. I thought you'd fallen in.'

'How's Stanley?' Ingrid asked.

'*Stanley?*' said Jamesie, looking at me.

'Don't start,' I said to him, and to Ingrid: 'He'll survive.'

Jamesie took himself off back behind the bar. Ingrid stood up beside me.

'It's men you go for, isn't it?' she murmured.

'Mostly.'

'I don't think Stanley knows what he wants.'

'What do you want?' I asked her.

She didn't hesitate for a second.

'Nothing too complicated.'

Except of course that's not what we said. We just looked at the toilet door, waiting till Stanley came out. Seeing us side by side, he made a low bow and stumbled forward a few steps, knocking into a chair. Ingrid heaved a sigh.

'I think we'd better leave after all.'

I couldn't offer a convincing argument against it.

'Will you be back in sometime?' I asked. I was hoping she might bring up going to the pictures again.

'You never know.' Then Ingrid slipped her arm around Stanley's waist. 'Come on, you, let these people get away home.'

Jamesie and I washed the glasses while Hugh counted out Monday's float and put the rest of the takings into bags. He carried the tray with the float in it and the bags through to Len and stayed in the Cocktail Bar while Len took the money up to the safe. Still Jamesie and I washed up. Pint glasses with handles, pint glasses without, half-pint glasses ditto, wine glasses, shorts glasses, highball glasses, dimpled glasses and plain. Each bore the prints of the fingers, thumbs and palms that had held them. I felt an almost parental affection, equal parts love and loss.

Barney and Marian said it was time they were making tracks. They were heading round to the Fiesta in Hamilton Street. Marian hadn't been there for months, though she had used to be friendly with one of the doormen and was sure they could get in free for the last hour. She turned to get her coat, but couldn't find it. She couldn't because Barney was holding it for her and there was a moment when she seemed to take this for some sort of wind-up and I thought she was going to stamp on his foot again. But then Barney smiled at her and the moment passed. She climbed down off her seat and allowed him to slip the coat over her arms and shoulders. Her thank you was quiet.

We had locked the street door. Hugh came in the other door as Barney and Marian were going out it, one step ahead of Rita Strong, two steps ahead of Liam, who turned, clicked his heels and gave us a valedictory salute – Comrades! – and then there were just the three of us once more in the Blue Bar.

'Thank God,' Hugh said.

He lifted three tumblers from the draining board and half filled each of them with Bell's.

'"Afore ye go",' he said. 'From Len.'

It didn't even matter that Len had probably specified Bell's because it was the cheapest brand we sold, the whisky was welcome and to be savoured. We stood for a time drinking, lost in our own thoughts. The television had been switched at some stage to Armpit Theatre, by Jamesie I didn't doubt. The sound was down, though it hardly mattered. The bedroom scenes were what most people watched it for. Tonight's play looked promising in the write-ups. Some rich guy seeing some woman he shouldn't have been; rich guy's wife plotting revenge; but we had tuned in too late for the sex and all we saw were the recriminations. Some days it seemed we couldn't even get it vicariously.

18

Clive White was slumped on the second-last stair when I came out into the hallway from the Blue Bar. His shoes and trouser bottoms were sopping wet and muddy splashes stretched in a perfect arc from his shins to his lapels. His camel-hair overcoat was somewhere between Belfast and Dublin. Without it he looked like your common-or-garden office drunk. He glowered at me from under heavy lids.

'I shouldn't even be speaking to you, after what you did in there,' he said.

'You put me in a difficult position,' I said and he humphed.

'Wee lad, I put you in the frigging job.'

He pulled a handkerchief from his breast pocket and wiped at the spatters on his trouser leg.

'I heard about Fitz,' I said. 'I'm sorry.'

'Don't worry.' He levelled a finger sheathed in soiled white linen. His initials were picked out in thread which a few moments ago had been scarlet and was now turned rust. 'I have mates all over, I'll find him.'

An hour or two before, I would have taken any threat of Clive White's very seriously, but he cut such a ludicrous figure out there on the stairs that I was prepared to credit Fitz with having considered the risk of his retribution and discounted it.

He attacked his trouser leg again.

'Do you want a cloth for that?' I said. 'You'll ruin your hanky.'

As my mother used to say, before the Unpleasantness anyway, I'd have made someone a lovely wife.

'Would you fucking give over?' Clive said and threw the hanky at me. 'I just lost five hundred pounds.'

From the top of the stairs came the sound of a throat that didn't need it being cleared. Clive jumped to his feet and I to something close to attention. The Master descended with his schoolteacher's measured tread. Behind him, and more uncertainly, came two men – brogues, flannels, tweed, brilliantine – who I assumed were the late arrivals off the Liverpool boat.

'Sean,' Clive White said, falsely bright, retrieving the hanky and stuffing it back into his pocket.

The Master conjured one of his less appealing smiles. Only the combination of Clive's longstanding custom and the presence of the two guests, it seemed to me, stopped him reaching for his belt.

'Danny,' he said. 'You're not going this minute, are you? Maybe you'd be so good as to show these gentlemen to a table.'

I led the gentlemen into the Cocktail Bar.

'Is it always like this?' one of them asked me when we were inside. He smelled like he'd bathed in Bay Rum.

'Not quite,' I said. 'You just caught us on a good night.'

The shutters were down in the Cocktail Bar too, but this was no more than a necessary fiction should the police stop by, which they had never been known to do, not on business, at any rate. There were maybe twenty people seated around the room, only a handful of them residents, the rest customers Len liked to refer to as being 'of the better sort'. Well, their clothes were more expensive, that's for sure. Not a few would still be here a couple of hours from now when even the Cocktail Bar ceased serving and drinks had to be ordered from the little dispense bar up in Cecil's office. Cecil, in fact, was probably the only member of staff who was sorry to see them go. At least there was talk while they were around, at least he was part of things.

'I hear you had a bit of a rough crossing,' I said to my charges, small talking, and then, getting no response: 'Are you here with work or what?'

The Bay Rum guy mentioned a meeting tomorrow in the hotel at which they were to speak. I remembered hearing about it earlier in the week and saying I might be able to come in for an hour or two to cover: 'Political,' Len had said. 'They'll likely be wanting a bar.'

'I hope yous get a good turnout,' I said. God knows there wasn't a big lot of competition in Belfast on a Sunday.

'You can never tell with these things,' the talkative one replied, 'what way they'll go.'

I took their order and went back out of the room and in the side door to the serving area. Hugh was behind the bar with Len. He had his overcoat and titfer on, but was still pulling pints.

'Tell this man to go,' Len said to me.

'Hugh,' I said. 'Go.'

'Go you.'

'He says he won't,' I told Len, and Len said there was no talking to some people.

I wrote down two brown ales and the number of the room they were to be charged to on a notepad next to the till. There was no sign of Len's nephew.

'Is the wee fella away?'

The wee fella was long gone. I asked Len how he'd got on.

'I think,' said Len, 'he'll be studying hard at the school books from now on to make sure he never has to come back here.'

A face framed by a neat chestnut wig appeared at the grille. It was the wig I recognised.

'Mr Doran.' One of the butter men from this afternoon.

He brought his face right up to the grille to get a closer look at me.

'It's Danny,' I said. 'From next door.'

He was delighted I had remembered. Guests usually were.

'Long old day for you,' he said.

'And for you.'

In fact, he looked as unnaturally well, for the time of night, as his hand-woven rug. I guessed he had not passed the hours since I'd last seen him in hotel bars.

I brought the brown ales through. A limp Clive White was now seated at a corner table. He looked like the subject of an especially lurid sermon. Which was perhaps the quality that attracted the kohl-eyed woman who had been sitting near, but not attached to, the party of farmers from north Antrim, in town for a tractor show, and who now slid sideways and asked Clive for a light. He handed her his Ronson, she handed him it back, and waited for him to start the conversation. Across the room, Ted Connolly sat with Doran's mate, Charlie, listening as Charlie talked, nodding his head, silent, acceding.

That was the Cocktail Bar after-hours. A mood of final ordering. I told myself it was no place for a young man of eighteen to be hanging around. I went and got my duffel coat.

No-neck Jurd was in the hallway, crooning to himself. There was always at least one customer got marooned between the Blue Bar closing and the Cocktail Bar refusing to serve him. It was quite often Jurd. In another ten minutes Cecil would find him and buck him out on to the street.

The tune of 'Goodnight Irene' struggled against the gloop of his vocal embellishments. Every other word appeared to start with a Q. He seemed unaware of my passing. As I reached the top of the stairs, though, he segued into 'Danny Boy'. The last refuge of the sentimental soak. I had heard much injury done to this song, not least by Nancy O'Connor, but Jurd sang it that night as though he meant to kill it off for good and all.

The din of departing wedding guests on the ground floor was a decided improvement.

With the happy couples gone to their confetti-filled beds above our heads or driving through the dark, tin cans trailing, to the Wicklow mountains, the guests lacked all direction. You'd have needed a sheepdog to get them out some nights. Men and women drifted hither and thither about the Long Corridor, making promises to meet up, call, drop the odd line. Teenage cousins, closing their minds to all they understood of theology and taboo, made dates. I pressed forward, sticking close to the wall, stopping only when I happened on the big-nosed wee man for whom I had earlier in the day carried a tray of drinks up to the Damask Room. He was standing by the cigarette machine, smiling and nodding to everyone who passed. Nearby a man who could only have been his son, judging by the nose and the wiry build, gave another man, in the red carnation of the bride's side, the sort of white-knuckle handshake-with-shoulder-grip combination that bordered on a threat, pulling the reluctant recipient close enough to see his tonsils as he talked into his face:

'Amn't I right? Amn't I right? Tell me I'm right!'

The old guy recognised me and gave a jaunty wave off his forehead.

'You look like you enjoyed yourself,' I said.

He sucked air through his pursed lips and held a hand to his heart as though to say any more enjoyment would have killed him.

'That's what it's all about, isn't it?' I said.

'Great people,' he said and the hand on his heart became his word of honour. 'Not a bit of side to a one of them.'

'You are, you're right,' said the man in the red carnation, and took a step back.

'Sure I'm right,' said the old man's son pulling him into the clinch again. 'Didn't I tell you I was right?'

'Excuse me there, ladies and gents!'

The band from the Damask Room were fighting their way towards the lobby. The double bass player clutched the instrument to his trunk for safekeeping and between glances out from

227

behind its black case did a fair imitation of the humanoid bottle in the Mackeson's stout ads.

'Excuse me!'

A path was cleared eventually for Thelma Beckett, bringing up the rear, to quick-step through, a music stand in one hand and a tangerine cocktail cigarette between the first and second fingers of the other. A fawn raincoat was belted rather than buttoned over her sequined dress, the collar flipped up so that the points met under her chin which she held high and proud. I wondered where she was telling herself she was leaving. Caesar's Palace, the Carnegie Hall – the music stand a bouquet. I imagined her in black-and-white in a room laced with New York smoke and sweat. I imagined unscrupulous managers, broken marriages, lovers dead too young.

She spotted me appraising her progress through the heads leaning in to say well done, love, and that was smashing, and she raised one eyebrow the barest degree, but enough to warn me not to judge or to mistake my fantasies for her own. She knew exactly where she was.

I watched out for Thelma Beckett after that, though I never again heard her sing. I noted the ballrooms and the clubs where she was appearing, neither bigger nor smaller than where she had been appearing that winter, and when, a few years later, the live circuit began to sound like a sick joke in Belfast and I read of her retirement at the age of thirty-five, I searched between the lines for the raised eyebrow that said I wanted to quit while I was still in the middle.

The Master came out of the Damask Room behind Lar and drew the doors to. I let Lar catch me up. He staggered the last few feet.

'Jesus, Danny Boy,' he said.

'Bad?'

'Bad?'

He patted a heavy pocket and winked.

'You did all right, then?'

'Fucking earned it, though. Come on round to the dining room and I'll sort out your share.'

'I was barely there,' I said, but Lar was already up the steps ahead of me, listing extravagantly to the tips' side.

In the lobby, a clergyman wearing a peaked motorcycle helmet and with a box strapped to his back had waylaid Thelma's guitarist. Perhaps to ask him how well the barman had sung at their function. I hurried on into the dining room.

The only light here now came from the still room, where, when the restaurant was open, tea and coffee was made and the waitresses collected their orders. In this less than half-light I made out the forms of a dozen or so of my workmates, scattered about tables already set for the morning's breakfast; smoking, talking or simply waiting.

'Is it true there's no lifts the night?' someone, I think it was Lynn, the head waitress, asked as I entered.

I told her I hadn't heard anything and another waitress, Betty, said they needn't expect her to walk with her legs.

'I'm sure the Master'll not see us stuck,' Lynn said, as though to reassure herself. 'Should he have to drive us himself.'

'Lord, I think I'd rather walk than sit beside him to Ballyhackamore,' said Betty.

'Danny Boy!'

Lar had found us a table and was counting money into his lap. He flicked his tongue off a taut bottom lip as I joined him.

'There's the guts of thirty bob here.'

'That's better than a kick in the head.'

He held out a pile of silver to me.

'Here.'

'That's too much.'

'It's ten bob.'

'It's too much.'

He squinted at me. Another night I'd have squinted at him refusing me. I shifted in my seat. Itchy bum again.

'I was only up with you an hour ...'

229

'The worst hour.'

'… and we had a good night downstairs.'

He thumbed a couple of coins into his other hand – 'Be serious,' I said – and then a couple more.

'Five,' he said, 'and that's my last word.'

I didn't argue.

'Have you a cigarette?'

I had three, we took one each. From the street came the noise of car doors slamming. A woman shouted, *Sammy, would you get over here now!* And a man who may have been Sammy shouted something that might have been anything.

'Ah, the sweet sounds of a Belfast night.' Lar dragged a chair round with his toe and put his feet up. 'Isn't this place great when you've money in your pocket?'

The dining room doors were flung open. Lar pulled his feet off the chair, everyone else sat up straight, and Jamesie strode in.

'Scared yous!'

Lynn said that face of his would scare anybody and Betty, who had bashed her knee on the underside of a table, told him if he'd another brain it'd be lonely. All this, needless to say, was music to Jamesie's ears. He was still grinning when he joined me and Lar.

'The Beast of the Blue Bar,' Lar hailed him.

'I do what I can,' Jamesie said.

'Where's all the nurses tonight?'

It seems I wasn't the only person Jamesie had regaled with his previous evening's escapades.

'Funny you should ask,' Jamesie said and took my last cigarette. 'Remember I was telling you about that Karen one last night?'

The tips of his index fingers became nipples dancing left and right in synchronicity.

'She phoned.'

'Your head.'

'I'm telling you.'

230

He withdrew a folded piece of paper from his jacket pocket. Lar snatched it from him and opened it. I recognised Nicola's handwriting.

'*Jamesie*,' Lar read, '*Karen called. Party at her place Dunluce Avenue. Ring top bell.*'

'Ding-dong!' Jamesie said. 'Look, no hands.'

If a hard-on was to have put on a bow tie and a smile, it would have passed for Jamesie's twin just then.

'Jamesie,' I said. 'When was the last time you went home?'

Jamesie decided this did not even merit a direct response.

'Lar, tell me he's joking.'

'When was the last time you had a wash?' I persisted.

This time he did address me.

'You're fucking serious.'

He seemed genuinely offended, not by the slur on his personal hygiene, but by my failure to rejoice in his good fortune.

'Wee lad, I'm going to get my *hole* tonight.'

Of course he was; for once his interpretation of the situation did not seem like wishful thinking. He was and I wasn't and some miserable part of me was miffed.

'Sorry,' I said and massaged my forehead. 'I'm not feeling good.'

'Not another one.' Lar lifted his seat back a foot from mine. 'It'll be self-service here next week if this keeps up.'

Priscilla Coote, sitting with her shoes off a couple of tables to our left, said wearily that if anyone had the flu they were welcome to come and breathe all over her.

'Poor lamb.' Jamesie touched my knee. He had not yet decided whether to forgive me. 'And there was me was going to invite you to the party and all.'

I could just picture it. Two hundred people to three armchairs and a busted sofa, a bath full of risk-your-life punch and a queue for the bedrooms down to the street. I really didn't think I could hack it tonight.

'Thanks, but I'd better get home.'

'Jesus, you must be sick,' Jamesie said.

'Young ones,' said Lar, who was twenty. 'They've no stamina. Can I come?'

As he and Jamesie were leaving, Priscilla called out to them to be careful. Priscilla always did. Jamesie promised her they would be. Jamesie always did, gently, without sarcasm. There were some things then in the International that you just did not joke about.

'See that you are,' said Priscilla.

Cecil popped his head into the dining room.

'You all waiting for lifts?'

'Oh, bum, have we missed Christmas?' Betty said, Cecil rose above it.

'The Master says another ten minutes.'

He closed the door, but returned, backwards and bent double, a moment or two later.

'What's that you have there?' Lynn asked, fatally.

'Did you not hear?' Cecil was carrying the tape recorder. 'I was on the news tonight.'

I was beginning to swelter in my duffel coat. I wondered whether I mightn't be coming down with something after all. I totted up with my fingers on my thigh and got sixteen hours that I had been on the go. I hadn't eaten a proper meal since breakfast. My legs felt like pipe-cleaners when I stood.

Cecil had the tape recorder up on a table and was calling for a bit of quiet.

'You're not away, are you?' he asked me. Either he was forgetting, in the reprise of his glory, our little game of chasies earlier, or he was still mindful of Hugh's warning. 'The Master'll not be long.'

'Can't hang about, Cecil, things to do.'

'At midnight?'

'I'm going to treat myself,' I said, thinking as I made it up that was exactly what I would do: feed a fever, starve a cold. 'I'm going round to Queen Street for a steak.'

A steak *and* a taxi. With what Lar had insisted on giving me, I had about eight or nine shillings in my front left trouser-pocket, and the Vances's fivers in my back right.

Well you didn't think I'd burned that too, did you? *It was more than a week's wages.*

I'd learn to live with myself, and as Lar would say, I'd fucking earned it.

Only a handful of room keys remained uncollected behind reception. The lobby was deserted, the lounge too, I thought, and then passing the door saw that there was one person still inside; a woman, her face averted from me, a magazine open in her lap. She licked a finger and thumb, lifted a page by the corner, held it perpendicular, and let its own weight carry it the rest of the way. Her hand dangled over the side of the chair. Then she raised it to her lips again, licked, and I tiptoed away. Not until I was out the front door did it occur to me that this was Mrs Williams, the woman whose husband was bad with his nerves, and who had been sitting in the exact same seat, while her children played jacks on the floor, when I arrived for work this morning. I remembered too the man I had seen, at lunchtime, semi-naked in the window overlooking the mews and from him my thoughts turned to the Czech minister in Nancy O'Connor's story. I glanced up at the top of the hotel and imagined how it would be to launch yourself into the air with only a flag for company. For some reason, in my mind's eye the flag was not a parachute, but worn like a superhero's cape, though it was every bit as useless.

I don't know where such thoughts came from. I had no intention that night of ever dying. I did not skip down the hotel steps, but placed my feet carefully, ransacking my brain in search of the rote-learned formulae for the forces that kept me simply moving forward, neither flying off into space, nor plunging beneath the earth's surface. My legs did not feel quite as weak. Perhaps the flu was only in my mind after all.

(Hypochondria? That's the one thing I've never had.)

I crossed the street to the back of the City Hall and peered through the gates. Somewhere in there people's broken toilets and blocked drains and leaking roofs awaited official consideration. Somewhere in there lay the plans for our B.U.M. Families were sleeping tonight in houses where no houses might be next year if the councillors who traipsed in and out of here and over the road to the International decided it. If men like my Second Cousin Clive decided it.

A Coke tin had been left on the kerb farther along where the wall of the building ended and the Garden of Remembrance began. I was enough of a boy to step down on to the road and aim a kick at it. A real toe-poke: *Connolly shoots* ... The can was fuller than I had expected, which helped. It sailed over the low hedge – I was amazed, I was proud – and splatted against the central column of the cenotaph. I legged it up the street, the way I had come, past the front of the hotel and round the other side of the City Hall into Donegall Square East. Three guys slouched against the railing of the Methodist church, eating chips. I slowed to a walk and tried to look like I wasn't looking. The three guys had no such reservations and openly stared as I passed by on the opposite footpath. I was close enough that I could smell the vinegar on their chips. I walked in that awkward way you do when three fellas are watching you for all the wrong reasons late on a Saturday night, like you've just recovered the use of your legs. (Which, in a sense, I had.) And then just when I was beginning to think I was in the clear one of them shouted:

'Fruit!'

I told myself they didn't mean anything by it. Fruit was what they would have shouted at any young man unfortunate enough to walk by on his own. This didn't stop my heart from launching itself against my ribcage.

'He's not denying it. Bum boy!'

The only way back to the International, without passing them, was right round the City Hall and they could easily head me off by running round the other side. I made it to the corner, where the Square opened on to Chichester Street. Two cars approached at speed and were past me before I could raise a hand. They left a long echo. In the road before the Water Office, an island of weak green light signalled a human presence in the underground toilets but in the circumstances this did not strike me as a clever place to seek refuge. I took a couple of shaky steps off the footpath, towards Robinson & Cleaver's, and then for the second time in a minute I bolted.

They were coming after me, I was certain of it. My right foot smacked the wet tarmac so hard it sent a pain shooting up my shin. I felt I would fall and only then, when I thought they were about to pile on top of me, did I look back. The three guys were dandering in the opposite direction. I couldn't hear them, but I convinced myself I could see their shoulders heaving with laughter. I slipped up the side of the department store, ready to run again should they so much as glance back, and when I was satisfied they really were far enough away, yelled until my lungs were empty: 'Pack of wankers!'

Well, it made me feel better.

'Charming,' said a woman crossing the street with her husband and holding more tightly to his arm; and then from behind me another woman spoke: 'Danny?'

Ingrid Titterington stood, like a washed-out Vivien Leigh, before the blackened front of Brand's Arcade.

'What's all the shouting about?'

'Wankers with chips,' I mumbled, walking out to meet her.

Hundreds-and-thousands of glass glittered on the pavement. A spar of charred wood, missed by the street sweepers, lay in the gutter at the foot of the kerb. The air held the damp bonfire reek of Twelfth of July mornings. It had novelty then in January.

'I'm glad you came,' Ingrid said.

Like we'd planned this.

'It seemed the right thing to do,' I said. She smiled and pushed the hair out of her eyes. Her hand was filthy. The whole left side of her suit was filthy.

She turned and walked towards the arcade. The ropes which had been slung across the entrance were tramped down, a triangular danger sign on its back beneath them, like a welcome mat. I became aware of someone breathing heavily, drunkenly, within.

'Are you trying to get yourselves killed?' I said.

I didn't like to think what else they could have been trying to do in there together for the last hour and whatever.

'It's not a bit dangerous.'

'I have to get something to eat,' I said, but Ingrid was holding out her hand for me to take.

'Come on, I dare you.'

Dare me? What age did she think I was.

'Double dare you.'

'This is so stupid.'

I took her hand.

Stanley was hunkering about ten yards in, before the boarded door of a pen shop, his face buried in his hands.

'Look who I found,' Ingrid said.

A narrow gap opened between Stanley's middle fingers; closed again.

'My life's a mess,' he moaned.

'Catch yourself on,' said Ingrid. I got the impression that she had heard this complaint once or twice already. I admit to feeling instantly less glum. Stanley apologised, then carried on as morosely as before.

'What am I going to do?'

Ingrid had wandered further into the interior. I couldn't judge the tone of her reply.

'You'll do the same as the rest of us,' she said. 'Grow up.'

A thin black ooze escaped from a crack in a tile high up to Stanley's left. Water was dripping in the ceiling cavity directly overhead. I couldn't close the sound out, nor shake the sensation that the drip had worked its way inside my coat. I shivered, even as I began to feel hot again. A few minutes was all I could stand of it.

'I really do have to get something to eat,' I said when Ingrid had returned, dirtier than ever, from her exploration.

'OK. But you have to do one thing before you leave.'

'What's that?'

She held up the camera.

'To finish off the day,' she said.

Out on the street again, Ingrid took a photograph of me and Stanley, then Stanley took one of Ingrid and me, then I took one of the two of them and, when I wound on, the film was out.

Ingrid left the prints at reception for me the following week. I wasn't at work. I really had come down with the flu by then.

I have those photographs before me now and Ingrid, whether she meant it or not, was right: I look at them and I see three people barely adult, so that I wonder that between us we were able to muster all the trials and the heartaches of that day. I wonder too whether I couldn't have saved myself the angst over the Vances's money, it wasn't my services they were paying for, but my silence. I was a bloody child. *They could have been arrested.* Well, three decades for a tenner, Bob and Natalie, that's not a bad deal.

I have other photographs which Ingrid gave me, museum pieces now, the sort of things the rebuilt bars of Belfast would kill to have on their retro walls.

The city in these photographs is another place entirely, the mere passage of years cannot account for the sense of rupture.

19

By the time I had returned from sick leave, Stanley had left Belfast and I never saw him again. That spring, Ingrid told me she'd had a letter. The weekend in Mosney had gone well, he had been booked on the strength of it for a summer week in the Butlin's in Skegness. He was still hoping to break into television.

'Poor Stanley,' Ingrid said, 'breaking in's the only way he's likely to get there.'

Perhaps he did make it in the end. I don't know, I have never been much of a one for television, apart from the wrestling.

Ingrid it was who told me all that I have written here about him. She seemed to have picked up a lot in a short time.

She was a Blue Bar regular for a while, sitting at the counter two or three evenings a week, reading a newspaper or a book, attracting the attention of more than one man transformed in his own eyes, by two or three pints, into Tom Jones.

'How can I tell you?' she would say to these men, 'how *un*interested I am?'

'How can I tell you you're barred?' said Jamesie, to those who were slow on the uptake.

And then one night she stopped by to tell me she would not be in for a few weeks and that was the last I heard of her too.

Some part of me suspected that she had gone off to join Stanley in England, but a couple of summers later Hugh returned from his holidays in Enniskillen and said he had seen her come out of an office in the town and drive off in a flash new Rover. I asked him was he sure it was Ingrid. He told me he had crossed the road and it was her name on the door of the office. Titterington, wasn't that it? There was a child in the car, he said, a girl and beautiful.

I often meant to go to Enniskillen, but somehow I never got around to it. Hugh went every year and, six weeks after quitting the International, died there, or just outside, driving past an army foot patrol on the dark road to Boho. Accidental discharge, army headquarters said and that, as it so often was with the army, was that. Liam Strong was bereft, and then a few months later was dead himself. He and Rita both, killed breaking the habit of a married lifetime when a satchel full of gelignite was thrown into the restaurant they had gone to for dinner one Saturday evening early in 1972. That same year, Oscar had a bag put over his head in an entry behind a drinking club and was shot for informing. Oscar. Jamesie lost almost the entire male line of his family to Loyalist assassins and Republican feuds. His hair turned white. (Women like the distinguished look, he tells me.) My own brother was shot in the thigh in mistake for another man and bled to death. Oh, it just goes on and on, I shouldn't get started.

Ted Connolly played for Sunderland for two more years before being transferred to Workington. He carried on as the voice of the Dairy Pride cow for several years after that. Kids here whose *parents* barely remember the hat-trick of headers against Wales still butt the air in perfect time when chanting the slogan, 'You'll never put another butter on your *bap*!'

Fitz turned out to be neither Fitz nor Moore. He was arrested and charged under the name of Thomas Kavanagh, in Galway, for selling guns to a Garda Siochana he believed to be a Provisional. Which was lucky for him in a way, had the Garda really been a Provisional, Fitz-Kavanagh might have wound up, like so many others, missing to this day, in an unmarked grave: *There were no guns.*

Rumours continued to circulate about Clive White's doings for much of the seventies. According to one, he cut some deal with a local British Army commander – and who knows what other kinds of commander – and made a packet using his lorries to move rubble from bomb sites out to the north foreshore of Belfast Lough. Explosions to order, was the suggestion. Insurance companies and all sorts were said to be involved. Who knows? Anything's possible.

Last I heard, Clive had married and was importing Italian leather furniture. I'm sure someone has thought to look down the sides of the chairs as they come through customs.

Councillor Trevor Noades became Trevor Noades MEP, no scandal that I am aware of ever attached to his name, and with the aid of European money we got a B.U.M. of sorts eventually. Contractors on the Westlink, as they ended up calling it, were paid a foot at a time, so many individuals and organisations wanted them dead, for so many different reasons. It is hard to ascribe civic-mindedness to people who were blasting the fuck out of their own city, but there would appear to have been something of that in the paramilitary threats.

The arterial route that was to have been the new Shankill Road failed to materialise, but the developers made a mess of the road anyway. Malvern Street is altered beyond all recognition. You'd have to ask the people living there whether it has changed for the better.

And the Bishop of Ripon never did make it to Belfast. The Tuesday after the fire in Brand's Arcade, his visit was called off. One of the organisers said now was not the right time. He was asked when the time would be right.

He thought long and hard before replying.

'Not for a good many years,' he said.

For a good many years, in fact, Belfast disgraced itself. There is no other word. And no justification, least of all the beautiful ideals of tolerance and equality on which the Civil Rights Association was founded in the International Hotel in January 1967. But, like I said, I shouldn't get started.

*

Some years ago I was attending the funeral of Priscilla Coote, funerals having become a sort of habit with me then, when I met Paula, now a stoutly pretty woman of forty. She was living in Sligo, she said, and was up north visiting her mother when she read the death notice in the paper. ('Suddenly, at home,' I am, in an odd way, happy to report.) Priscilla Coote; it wasn't a name you were likely to forget. She called me Jamesie by mistake and blushed when I corrected her. No one else from the International showed, so Paula and I sat together at the back of the church. Paula said it was funny, she didn't suppose if she'd been living in Belfast she'd have come either. She hadn't known the woman all that well. It was just being at home again and seeing the death notice like that.

'I'm afraid,' she said, 'I came as much to see who else would be here.'

We walked a bit with the mourners behind the hearse, but didn't go out to the graveyard. When the cortege dispersed to the cars we drove to a bar by the university. We talked, the way you do, about the old days and who was where and when we last saw everyone. The times being what they were, it was all a bit grim. To lighten the mood, I asked Paula did she remember when she started at the hotel; her uniform, the way it sat on her, like it had been cut out of a Cornflakes' box. That was the week of the Civil Rights meeting. Paula looked blank. The week, I said, that Brand's Arcade went on fire. Paula said she had no memory of a fire, no real memory even of Brand's Arcade. She was fifteen and had only just arrived in Belfast, everything was a mystery to her.

Two things did stick in her mind from those first few days: her absolute terror of cocking up and being sent home to the country in disgrace, and the man who went berserk one morning and had to be carted away in a straitjacket.

'He'd written all over his face and chest with lipstick. Devil symbols, somebody told me.' She smiled at the recollection of her naivety. 'I think he'd, you know, dirtied himself.'

We stayed in the bar the rest of the afternoon, watching the customers come and go.

'Are you still …?' She pulled an invisible pint and I grimaced into the one I was drinking: no. She asked me how long I'd stayed in the International and I told her, till the very end.

'I'm sorry,' she said, 'I've been away a long time.'

'God, Paula,' I said, 'if you were to try to keep up with all the things that have happened here … It's like a whole new city now, sometimes I hardly know it myself.'

She nodded at this with great sincerity and I realised we were both a bit tipsy.

'Was it a …' She looked out the window. In a first floor office across the street a man was talking on the telephone, tossing a pencil and shooting his hand out to catch it. 'You know.'

'A bomb? Nothing so dramatic. We went the way most things did, not with a bang but a whimper. Business those last few years?' I held my nose.

'Sad all the same,' Paula said.

'At least they didn't knock it down. The City Council took it over for extra offices.'

This amused Paula, as I had hoped it might.

'The way I remember it,' she said, 'some of those councillors spent more time in our hotel than they did in the City Hall.'

'I could tell you stories.'

'Couldn't we all,' she said and looked at me slyly.

We had one more drink for old times' sake.

Paula wrote her address on a cigarette box and of course I lost it before I was halfway home. If she managed to hang on to mine she never used it. Like I really thought she was going to.

It was dark when we left the bar. I decided to pick the car up in the morning and walked with her into the city centre for a taxi. We said goodbye at the fortress front of Fon-a-Cab. Paula apologised again for getting my name wrong earlier.

'Danny Boy. I don't know how I could have forgotten it.'

'It's only been twenty-odd years.'

'The Master!' she said suddenly, as though delighted to have retrieved another name.

'Yes,' I said. 'The Master.'

She raised a finger, hesitated a moment then jabbed the air between us.

'There was another night, it could even have been the very first one, I was sitting in the dining room late on, waiting for a lift. I heard someone crying somewhere off the lobby. I was like ...' She mimicked a shudder and ended up by pulling her coat tighter. 'It kept on going and I'm sitting there on my own and in the end I did that thing you see people do in films and you swear blind you'd never do yourself, I went to the door to see who it was was doing the crying. It was coming from the lounge.'

'Williams,' I said, remembering the family name of the man who had been straitjacketed. 'His wife always sat over there.'

'No,' said Paula.

She narrowed her eyes, the better to peer into the past.

'What did you call ... ? The receptionist – the one with the ... ah – got hitched, you remember, to – what's this you call him?'

'Marian,' I said.

That's her. She was hunched up in one of those big chairs they had in there, sobbing her heart out and the Master was sitting on the arm of the chair, stroking her hair. And I thought, well, you can imagine, but when I said this the next day to one of the older women – God, I think it might have been ... it was, it was Priscilla – I told Priscilla what I had seen the next day, like it was some kind of naughty secret, like she would find it a big laugh, and she got all cross on me and said I wasn't to repeat it to anyone else. She told me I was too young to know what I was talking about. Something awful had happened, before I started there. A boy had been killed. She scared me half to death, she was that annoyed. I never did mention any of it again.'

A pizza-delivery scooter pulled up at the kerb. The rider wore yellow rainproofs and ox-blood Dr Marten's. He produced a tissue from a shoulder pocket and wiped his mirrors, then rode back into the traffic.

'It was years before I found out the whole story,' Paula said. 'I don't suppose it matters, but I wish I'd known sooner, so that I could have said something. Marian was really, really crying that night.'

*

On Thursday 13th October 1994, in Fernhill House in the Glencairn area of west Belfast, a group of men representing the Combined Loyalist Military Command announced a ceasefire, effective from midnight, echoing the ceasefire called six weeks before by the Provisional IRA and bringing to an end what people here were in the habit of referring to, even long afterwards, as 'the last twenty-five years of violence'. A quarter of a century, it was a neat figure, giving the impression that a sensible, even preordained period of history was coming to a close.

The announcement was made by a stocky man in his early sixties, dressed in a shirt and tie and wearing strong-lensed reading glasses. He held a pipe in his left hand and when not called upon to speak busied himself with the pipe-smoker's arcane rituals.

Bar a single, dimly remembered newspaper photograph, this was the first time I had ever set eyes on Gusty Spence.

It was difficult, watching these proceedings on television, to comprehend how much of an influence this dapper, gentle-sounding man's actions had had on my life, on all our lives.

More than twenty-eight years had passed since the UVF released its statement, signed 'Captain William Johnston', declaring war on the IRA. The first act in their war had taken place on 7th May 1966 when a petrol bomb was thrown at a Catholic-owned bar off the Shankill Road. At, not into. The petrol bomb hit a neighbouring house. Matilda Gould, the elderly woman who lived there with her son, was badly burned. She took several weeks to die.

Towards the end of May, John Scullion was killed as he walked home, late and alone, off the Springfield Road. So unused to violent death had Belfast become by that stage of the 1960s that police at first thought John Scullion had been stabbed. Only when his body was exhumed, in the light of subsequent events, was the cause of his fatal stomach wound found to be a bullet.

The men who killed him had been looking for another man to shoot that night, a man alleged to be in the IRA. He had been named by James Burns, Rocky to his friends, who had done time in the Crumlin Road and claimed to have met a lot of IRA men there. Before too long Burns was back inside, sentenced to nine years for the unlawful and malicious possession of a revolver and ammunition in the Canmore Street home of an eighteen-year-old Catholic man early in the morning of 25th June. A couple of days before he was gaoled, three other men, associates of Burns, were given life terms for the murder of Peter Ward, on Malvern Street, twenty-four hours after the incident in Canmore Street. Among those men was Gusty Spence. During the trial the confession of one of his co-accused was read out in court identifying Spence as Captain William Johnston. Spence denied he was Johnston, just as he has always denied being the man who fired the shots that killed Peter Ward.

At the end of his short prepared speech that morning in

Glencairn, Gusty Spence engaged the cameras and spoke of the abject and true remorse of the Loyalist terror groups on whose behalf he was speaking.

It took me a while, but I believed him.

*

Peter Ward was a good barman. He was earning eight pounds eight shillings at the time of his death, twenty-five shillings above the union rate.

I can't tell you much else about him, except that those who knew him thought the world of him. He is, I realise, an absence in this story. I wish it were not so, but guns do that, create holes which no amount of words can fill.

We're powerful people for remembering here, I hope that's one thing we don't forget.

Author's Note

The International Hotel closed in 1975. The staff and guests portrayed in this novel are invented; however, the names of certain people already in the public domain have been left unchanged. These include Peter Ward, murdered by the UVF in June 1966.

**BOOK
ENDS**

opinions
interviews
and more

About
Glenn Patterson

Glenn Patterson began his first novel, *Burning Your Own*, while studying at the University of East Anglia, where he was taught by Malcolm Bradbury and Angela Carter. In 1989 he was appointed writer in the community for Lisburn and Craigavon by the Arts Council of Northern Ireland and started work on his second novel, *Fat Lad*, which was published in 1992. A year later he went to University College Cork as writer in residence, and the year after that became writer in residence at Queen's University Belfast.

Black Night at Big Thunder Mountain was published in 1995 and was followed in 1999 by *The International*. His fifth novel, *Number 5*, appeared in 2003, his sixth, *That Which Was*, in 2004. A collection of his journalism was published in 2006 under the title *Lapsed Protestant*. His most recent novel is *The Third Party* (2007), set in Hiroshima. A first full-length work of non-fiction, *Once Upon a Hill*, will be published in autumn 2008.

Glenn's television work includes documentaries for BBC, RTÉ, Channel 4 and Granada. He teaches creative writing at the Seamus Heaney Centre for Poetry in Queen's University Belfast and is a member of Aosdána.

Glenn Patterson on writing
The International

Shortly after my third novel, *Black Night At Big Thunder Mountain*, was published I got a job presenting an arts review programme on RTÉ. This was autumn 1995. For six months, through to Easter the following year, I didn't write a word of fiction: the longest I had gone without writing in more than a decade. Actually, maybe the longest I had gone without writing since I was five. (When I was in P1 I would be taken around the P2s and P3s to read out my 'wee stories' as a lesson to the older children. This didn't make a writer of me, but it did make a runner: I spent my break-times dodging P2s and 3s intent on teaching me a lesson of their own.) I told myself when I started at RTÉ

> And almost at once ... I could see the book, or the vague outline of the book, I would write.

the change would do me good and that I would come back to writing refreshed. By the end of six months, though, all I was was panicked. And of course the more I panicked the less chance there was of me ever writing anything again. The very sight of my desk made me feel ill. It was easier, frankly, to leave the door closed between it and me. Easier, but no more productive. Eventually I set myself a task: stay on the same side of the door as the desk from breakfast to lunchtime. It would help if I could find something more than cigarettes to entertain me. An idea, say...

After an idea-free hour and a half, verging on despair,
I picked up Jonathan Bardon's *Belfast:
An Illustrated History*. I can't remember why exactly I
turned to the index, or why more specifically I was looking
under 'Hotels and public houses', but I do
remember vividly my eyes being arrested,
as they swept down the page, by the
reference to 'International H. 278'.

Flipping back to the page in question I
read, 'It was in the International Hotel, in
Donegall Square South, that the Northern
Ireland Civil Rights Association [NICRA]
was formed in 1967.'

And almost at once – it had never
happened to me like this before – I could see the book, or
the vague outline of the book, I would write. The title was
obvious. The title was half the attraction. I loved the
optimistic, outward-looking note it struck; and I couldn't
help but reflect on the contrast with the bleak, inward-
looking decades that Northern Ireland was pitched into so
soon after the NICRA meeting.

It wasn't as if I had never heard of the International
Hotel before: one of my brothers had worked in the City
Hall in the early seventies and had gone across to the hotel
from time to time for after-work drinks. (He had told us
how some of the politicians we saw arguing night after
night on TV regularly stood together at the counter,
drinking, having a laugh.) Later, when the hotel closed and
City Hall took it over for extra office space, the basement
bar was his canteen.

And then I knew that Peter Ward had been working in
the International on the night he was murdered by the UVF
on the Shankill Road in June 1966.

> The title
> was half the
> attraction.
> I loved the
> optimistic,
> outward-
> looking note
> it struck

By lunchtime on that first day the outline had become a bit clearer. My novel would cover the months between Peter Ward's murder and that first Civil Rights meeting. I was even fairly certain I had my central character – a barman – although I did not know then that he would also be my narrator. I had shied away from first-person narrators up till then, a question of confidence, or simply concentration: the first person demands the maximum consistency of voice.

A few days later I went to the Linen Hall Library and ordered up back copies of the local papers to see what they had made of the NICRA meeting in 1967. The answer was, scarcely nothing. I was intrigued by the gap between how events were viewed with hindsight and how they were experienced in the moment of their unfolding. Back home again I played around in this gap, literally messed about on the page, trying out sentences, and eventually the opening line came, with the voice – the whole tone of the novel – coded in it: 'If I had known history was to be written that Sunday in the International Hotel I might have made an effort to get out of bed before teatime.'

Still the question remains: why then? Like I said, I had known about the International and events associated with it for years. The 'hindsight' angle undoubtedly helped, but I didn't have that on the first morning. The Provisional IRA had broken its ceasefire a few months before I started to write (broken? had blown it to pieces at Canary Wharf, killing two newsagents in the process) so I don't think either it was a case of my saying 'here we are at the end, let's go back to

> I was intrigued by the gap between how events were viewed with hindsight and how they were experienced in the moment of their unfolding.

where this was all supposed to have started'. The timing, though, undoubtedly played a part, as it always does when a writer selects a subject or a setting from the past. Twelve months before, or twelve months after, I could have read down the index of Jonathan Bardon's *Belfast* and never have stopped at all at the International.

One afternoon before Christmas 1995, in the middle of my RTÉ run, I called at the offices of DBA Television on Belfast's Lower Crescent, a short walk from Botanic Station. The DB in DBA was David Barker, a close friend; the A was for Associates, who in those days consisted pretty much of Carlo Gébler and Robert McLiam Wilson. The four of us had been developing an idea for a documentary on punishment beatings, 'Baseball in Irish History', a play on James Connolly's *Labour in Irish History*, the joke being that in Belfast in recent years there had been as much true socialism practised as baseball. Maybe that's why I called at DBA that day. Maybe I just stopped in for coffee on my way home from Dublin. Whatever the reason, I was there at four o'clock when the IRA shot and killed Paul Devine in Claremont Street, about five hundred yards away.

> The novel as a form would not exist if characters, human beings, could be summed up and dispensed with in a few words.

Drug dealer, the IRA said, as though even if the allegation could have been proven beyond reasonable doubt (I believe the convention in most democracies is 'by a jury of one's peers'), that would have justified murdering a man.

The leader of the UVF gang who killed Peter Ward in June 1966 had pronounced him and his friends 'IRA men', adding, 'they will have to go'.

The novel as a form would not exist if characters, human beings, could be summed up and dispensed with in a few words. It thrives on complexity and contradiction.

I think that was the connection I made, however subconsciously, the first morning I spent thinking about *The International*: in the near three decades between the murders of Peter Ward and Paul Devine the challenge for us all here – writers and non-writers – had remained essentially the same, to refuse the reductive sentences (the death sentences) and to throw open the doors on life. Not unlike a bar, or a hotel, come to that.

255

Anne Enright on reading
The International

The drunks were shouting it in the street. Well it was one drunk, but she was certainly shouting. She was pointing at Glenn Patterson, saying, 'This man. This man. This man wrote the best book about the Troubles ever written.' I said I believed her. She shouted it again.

I know people are supposed to shout drunkenly about books in Ireland, but the fact is that this is the only time I have ever witnessed such a thing. It happened outside the student union building opposite Queen's University in Belfast and it made me feel all old fashioned.

> *The International* insists that Belfast existed before the Troubles.

I hadn't actually read the book at the time, though I had looked around it, in a funny way. I stood for a while in Glenn's study, on a visit one afternoon – a dark, spare, functional space, with an architect's drawing on the wall. The drawing was a floor plan of the International Hotel and it covered the space where his eyes would rest when he was not looking at the keyboard. And there it is in the writing, in the descriptions of people moving along corridors, going in to back rooms, disappearing around corners – as if the narrative secret was also three dimensional, and its resolution a question of choreography as much as one of plot. It is as though the book itself wants to occupy a physical space.

Glenn smuggled the plans of the hotel out of City Hall

under his clothes. He walked out under the ULSTER SAYS NO banner that was hung over the main entrance – at a guess in a sharp pair of Chelsea boots and some skinny cut jeans – and he walked down the steps. He was like some argument from popular culture. A little piece of the modern world. An ironic counter-terrorist who was taking a corner of Belfast back from the people who had locked it up in bigotry and noise.

> Writers can make caricatures out of people, but it is society that makes characters

This was the heist, then, as the book is a heist. It was a repatriation, a liberation, an act of irony and innocence. *The International* insists that Belfast existed before the Troubles and that it was owned by the people who walked its streets before those streets were taken from them. It says that there are different ways to describe people's lives – different maps, if you like – and those maps can be stolen. And so the man who describes himself as gay becomes a Catholic gay, or a Protestant gay, but only if he is wants his knees capped for deviant sexual behaviour. Because Belfast in the seventies was too busy blowing itself up in a patriarchal fashion – and sex was, famously, when people had their tea in Ballymena. So it is another heist to make your narrator gay – and easily, naturally gay; like a wildflower growing from the cracks in concrete; gay without anguish or blame. It is another insistence on things being what they are.

The action of the book takes place over the course of one evening in the hotel, where the narrator, Danny, is a barman. It is set just before the outbreak of the Troubles, when no one knew what was about to hit them. This novel is steeped in Danny's regret, not just for the town that was lost to violence, but also for his own lost romantic opportunities.

Innocence is a difficult quality to capture in prose.

The International, as a bar and as a book, serves innocence in the form of drink. This is a redemptive, dangerous sort of substance; the kind of innocence it produces is far from safe. Drink is the writer's friend, because of the things it shows and undoes in people, but there are no tearful, slurred revelations in *The International*; instead, there is a slow stripping of the scene to its drunken essentials. Drink reduces the crowd to anecdote, and connection. It twists character and turns people into unexpected cartoons of themselves. Danny is a watcher. He is sober. He is gay. He has a ready and helpless heart.

The International is rich with the pleasures of personality. 'The thing about that guy is . . .' The punters and the barmen share the same wit; barbed and forgiving at the same time. 'Flea Johnston', 'no-neck Jurd', these are the names of people who, if they drink steadily for another ten years will become 'characters'. Writers can make caricatures out of people, but it is society that makes characters – and this is another clue to the importance of the book. A culture which treasures personality is also a watchful one; it is a consensus culture. *The International* captures this group sensibility before it turned nasty. It captures the personality, not just of this or that individual, but also of a distinctive place and time.

'History is an angel being blown, backwards, into the future' said Walter Benjamin. We cannot see what is ahead of us. *The International* works strangely on our ideas of causality and guilt. Belfast is the angel, and the bomb is what blasts her away from us, her face full of longing for what might have been. By returning to the moment before the blast, this novel insists that things might have been

> **The International is an act of courage. It is the best book about the Troubles ever written.**

otherwise. It gives the city its humanity back. It is the kind of book a girl has to shout about in drink. *The International* is an act of courage. It is the best book about the Troubles ever written.

also by
Glenn Patterson

Burning Your Own

'Remarkably assured . . . Patterson's novel,
needless to say, is neither afraid nor prejudiced,
but courageously magnanimous.'

GUARDIAN

'A passionately engaged portrayal
of a troubled boy and city'

OBSERVER

ISBN 978-0-85640-810-6

£6.99

www.blackstaffpress.com

also by
Glenn Patterson

Fat Lad

'A triumph. Maybe the finest novel written out
of Ulster in twenty-five years.'
SCOTLAND ON SUNDAY

'Humane, wise, funny, absolutely contemporary. It is
exhilarating to see such a novel stretching moment by
moment, alive to what language brings.'
GUARDIAN

ISBN 978-0-85640-811-3

£6.99

www.blackstaffpress.com